Bonanza™ 6

THE TRAIL TO TIMBERLINE

STEPHEN CALDER

G.K. Hall & Co.
Thorndike, Maine

Published in 1996 by arrangement with Bantam Books,
a division of Bantam Doubleday Dell Publishing Group, Inc.

G.K. Hall Large Print Western Collection.

The text of this Large Print edition is unabridged.
Other aspects of the book may vary from the original edition.

Set in 16 pt. Century Schoolbook by Minnie B. Raven.

Printed in the United States on permanent paper.

Library of Congress Cataloging in Publication Data

Calder, Stephen.
    The trail to Timberline / Stephen Calder.
        p.   cm. — (Bonanza ; 6)
    ISBN 0-7838-1828-9 (lg. print : hc)
    1. Large type books. I. Title. II. Series: Calder, Stephen.
Bonanza ; 6.
[PS3553.A39493T73   1996]
813'.54—dc20   96-19297

For Frank and Sara Ann,
who shared Harriet with me

BONANZA
The Trail to Timberline

Ben Cartwright — He knew the joy of having three sons and the pain of having lost three wives. Now he wondered if he would live to see grandchildren, as he rode against a murderous band of outlaws waiting at Timberline Pass. . . .

Little Joe Cartwright — High-spirited and reckless, he was about to have his first taste of responsibility for a small part of the vast Ponderosa empire. Neither Little Joe nor his father knew that the Cartwrights' California logging camp would prove to be a death trap. . . .

Sara Ann Coffee — The granddaughter of Sheriff Roy Coffee, she had already lost her mother and father to the three Wharton brothers. Now the outlaws were coming back again, and this time they'd use Sara Ann as bait in a deadly trap. . . .

Lem Wharton — He'd waited twelve long years to avenge his father's death. Masterminding a daring jailbreak, he led his brothers to the Comstock Lode to find Ben Cartwright and Roy Coffee — and kill them. . . .

Nat Greer — He called himself the "bull of the woods" and ran the Cartwright logging camp with an iron fist. But Little Joe quickly discovered that Greer wasn't just cruel, he was up to something more sinister. . . .

Roe Derus — As rugged as the West itself, the outspoken bullwhacker let Little Joe know from the beginning that all was not well at the Ponderosa camp — and just how much danger Little Joe was in. . . .

CHAPTER 1

The prison guard yawned as he shuffled from unlit cell to unlit cell, the darkness broken only by patches of murky yellow light seeping from coal oil lamps at each end of the caged hallway. In the crook of his left arm the guard cradled a ten-gauge sawed-off shotgun like a sleeping baby. The footfall of his hard-heeled brogans echoed off the cold stone walls like a distant drumbeat, and the cells hissed with the sounds of sleeping men, six to a cell. A few men snorted or snored, but these were usually new inmates, men who still had some fat on their bones. The guard, after years on the graveyard shift, had long ago observed that while fat men snored the most and the loudest, no man stayed fat on the gruel served up in the Nevada State Prison. And the men in this sector were the skinniest of all, having been imprisoned the longest because they were the worst — murderers, rapists, and men without conscience or hope. They would spend the rest of their lives within the prison's stone walls, their only escape being the daily trips to the quarry, where they slaved and sweated to hew blocks of fine-grained sandstone from the earth's hardness. These were prisoners who talked of good food, bad women, and the mistakes they made — not in committing crimes, but in getting caught.

The guard, a stocky man whose muscles had atrophied to mush over the years, walked the same route he had every night for the past seven years, maintaining the same schedule he had his first night as a prison guard. The prisoners called him "Quick" because he was slow of mind and body. While other guards avoided night duty, Quick requested it. The night watch required less work than other shifts, when prisoners had to be released from their cells for meals or work detail or visitors. Quick, with his inclination toward laziness, could come up with no reason to do more when he could get by with doing less, especially when the pay came out the same.

Though guards were instructed to carry a lantern on rounds, Quick had disobeyed that rule for so long that he no longer worried about getting caught by the warden. The warden never checked on him during his rounds. Why waste coal oil when the lamps at each end of the cell block were all he ever needed to get his bearings? And, too, why waste energy toting a lantern when he could get by just as well without it? He carried matches in his pocket and he could always light one of the darkened lamps. He pretty much had it all figured out.

All except the bubbling noise.

It pricked his ears and grew louder as he neared the end of the hallway. His fingers turned suddenly clammy around the shotgun. He could not explain what he had never heard before. Was it a trick? He stopped in front of a cell, trying to pinpoint the noise, then advanced to the next human cage, his hand patting the shortened barrel of the shotgun. Finally, he reached the babbling cell. He cursed. What he could hear, he could not see in the dark recesses of the cell. The light from the coal-oil lamp at the end of the hall puddled at his feet but did not seep into the cell's deep darkness. The gurgling continued.

Quick eased closer to the iron bars, careful to stay more than an arm's length from the cell that housed the Wharton brothers, a trio of men so malicious that no other prisoners were forced to share a cell with them. Quick cleared his throat, then called into the darkness. "What's going on in there?"

Only the bubbling answered him.

The Whartons were vicious men, sentenced to life for killing a young couple a dozen years ago in Virginia City. Quick cocked the twin Belgian hammers of his double-barreled shotgun. "What's going on in there? Somebody answer me."

Silence was followed by a mumbled response.

"What?" Quick shouted. He twisted his ear

to the cell, his fingers quivering on the shotgun as he leaned toward the iron bars. "What is it?"

"It's Lem," came a voice Quick recognized as Vern Wharton's. "He can't take any more."

The gurgling continued.

"Any more what?" Quick shouted, his voice rising, like his nerves.

"Prison," Vern calmly said. "He's drowning himself."

A laugh of skepticism hung in Quick's throat. He knew he should move on, but what if this were true? He'd never had an incident like this, not in seven years of guard duty. "Drowning how?"

"In the water bucket, damn you," Vern called back. "Leave him alone."

"My God, man, he's your brother. Do something," Quick pleaded, fearing this would blemish his tolerable record as a guard.

"Can't," Vern answered back, unruffled as ever. "I bet Willis my breakfast that Lem won't succeed."

Then the gurgling faded. Then all was silent except for Quick's excited breath.

His pulse racing like his muddled mind, Quick retreated from the cell door to the lamp a dozen paces away. Hurriedly, he lifted it from its wall mount and ran it back to the Wharton cell. Willis and Vern Wharton, both lounging lazily on their bunks, shaded their eyes from the sudden brightness outside their barred door. Quick was terrified at what he saw on the floor.

In a puddle of water, Lem Wharton was doubled over, his head sunk in the water bucket. Silent and limp, Lem Wharton knelt over the bucket, his arms flaccid. Quick, his mind slogging through the confusion, glanced back and forth between the two Whartons on the bunks and the one on the floor.

"Guess you win, Willis," growled Vern. "I didn't figure he'd keep his head in there long enough to drown."

Willis grinned. "Lem always liked me better than you, Vern, but damn, he didn't need to go and kill himself just to prove it. What are we having for breakfast, Quick?" Both brothers laughed.

"Move him," ordered Quick as he stepped closer to the cell door.

"Handling dead people ain't our job, Quick," Willis growled.

"Even if he was kin," Vern added.

"Stand back and don't move," Quick commanded. He lowered the lamp to the floor, where its jaundiced light could seep into the cell. Pulling the key ring from his belt, he fumbled for the correct key, then slid it into the lock, which released its iron grip as he turned. The door creaked open. Quick leveled the shotgun, then stepped inside.

From parallel bunks on opposite sides of the narrow cell, Vern and Willis Wharton watched

13

but never lifted a muscle.

Quick stepped to Lem and toed at his socked feet. Lem's form made no movement.

"He's dead," Willis offered.

"Damn him," Vern interjected, "for costing me breakfast."

Quick swung the shotgun from Vern to Willis, but neither man moved. Cautiously, Quick stepped beside Lem's limp form and squatted.

He saw a quiver in Lem's chest, but too late. He had been tricked.

Lem Wharton jerked his head out of the bucket and lunged for the startled guard, who stumbled backward into Vern's bunk. Willis bolted from his bed and grabbed the shotgun just as the guard pulled the trigger. Willis screamed as the twin hammers snapped shut on the web of flesh between his thumb and forefinger, saving Lem from a blast of shot into the gut.

Vern grabbed the guard's arms from behind while Willis ripped the sawed-off shotgun from his hands. The guard screamed for an instant when Lem kicked him in the groin. Grabbing the water bucket by the handle, Lem swung it for the guard's head, smashing the thick wooden container into his jaw and nose. The guard went limp in Vern's arms, then slid to the ground, Lem towering over him. Willis raised the shotgun and smashed the gun stock into the guard's head. Venting

14

the pent-up furies of a dozen years behind bars, Willis battered Quick until his head was a bloody pulp.

Finally, Lem grabbed his raging brother. "Save your strength, Willis, until we're out of here," he commanded, tossing the gory bucket into the corner, then grabbing the guard's key ring. His cold eyes stared at his two younger brothers. "We've waited twelve years to avenge Pa's death, and nothing'll stop us now."

Vern nodded. "I'm ready to kill the sons of bitches."

"We won't get them from in here," Lem answered. He grabbed the shotgun from Willis's sore hand. "Once we're outside, nothing'll keep us from killing Roy Coffee and Ben Cartwright."

The odor of cheap cigars mingled with the aroma of overpriced liquor in the Delta Saloon. The spindly hands of the clock above the ornate and mirrored back bar showed the time to be half past the hour. Outside the double doors, C Street teemed with miners who had just completed the day shift in the silver mines that catacombed the earth beneath Virginia City. The battered piano against the side wall tinkled a merry tune at the touch of a musician wearing a derby, a starched shirt and starched smile. Individually and in clumps the miners answered the piano's siren call, pushing their way inside the Delta, where accommodating women hawked conversation, drinks, dancing, and more.

As the miners discussed their shift or the latest stock prices on the fifty-plus mines scattered throughout Storey County, the noise grew. The louder the human din, the harder the piano player pounded the keys, until each tune more closely resembled the rumbling racket of a stamp mill than music.

At a back table, Hoss Cartwright emptied his third mug of cold beer, then pulled his hefty right forearm across his lips. "That sure hit the spot, Little Joe."

His younger brother nodded absently, which was not an uncommon reaction for Little Joe, especially when women and excitement were around. Before him Little Joe watched the changing canvas of humanity as closely as a gambler watches cards. Occasionally he would grin at one of the women circling the crowded saloon like rouged scavengers. Little Joe was in his element, and saw fit to ignore his older brother, Hoss, who fidgeted to go.

A big man, Hoss Cartwright grew quickly tired of the crowd that pressed toward him and the adjacent tables. Each passing miner seemed to jostle him, trespassing on his space. A man Hoss's size — six feet, four inches tall, and 240 pounds the last time he weighed himself — appreciated space because he re-

16

quired so much of it. The world got crowded a lot quicker for Hoss than it did for Little Joe, the runt of the Cartwright family at 160 pounds and not quite five-foot-ten.

"What do you say we go on, Little Joe?" Hoss suggested. "Things are getting so crowded you couldn't cuss a cat without getting fur in your teeth."

Little Joe snapped out of his trance for a moment and offered that same impish smile that the ladies always found so charming and that Hoss found so infuriating. "Go on, Hoss, I figure on having me a little fun for a while. I deserve it, working as hard as I did to drive those cattle to Virginia City. And that's after breaking horses yesterday. I didn't see you breaking any. Of course, you'd break them or crack their spine if you just sat on one. No, Hoss, you go on without me."

"I'm not leaving you here, not with five hundred dollars in your pockets." Hoss sighed, then lifted his empty mug in the air, waving it over his head until a red-haired woman with a few more empties in her hand sauntered his way.

Stopping at the table, the barmaid leaned over and gave Hoss a glimpse down her silk dress. She winked at him. "What'll it be, fella?"

Hoss looked away from her, feeling suddenly warm. "Another cold beer, the colder the better," he sputtered.

Little Joe stared at her, licking his grinning lips.

She took in Little Joe's leering brown eyes, then turned and winked again at Hoss. "Is your son old enough to have a beer, fella?"

Little Joe's smile melted like grease on a hot griddle.

Hoss laughed, and pounded the table with his fist. "Sure, ma'am, go ahead and let junior have a drink."

Little Joe cocked his head at the woman and lowered his hand from the table to his britches pocket. Slowly, he turned it palm up over the table. As he spread his fingers, he exposed a roll of greenbacks. "Junior here can buy his own beer, and plenty of beer to boot."

"Little Joe," Hoss sputtered, "put that away." Hoss glanced hurriedly about and saw several men staring at the wad of money.

The woman, who years ago had learned the short life of big money and big talk, gave her head a sorrowful toss. "The money always stays, junior, but the pockets change. I like men who can keep it in their pocket for a while."

The dimple on Little Joe's chin deepened at her words and the sparkle was snuffed in his brown eyes. "I can hang on to it," Little Joe answered as the woman turned away and retreated toward the bar. "You ever hear of the Cartwrights? I'm Little Joe Cartwright and my family's got money, lots of money." His voice rose with each word, until the men at the surrounding tables heard him over the din of activity and celebration in the Delta Saloon.

Hoss grabbed Little Joe's arm as his younger brother started to stand. Hoss figured it was the beer more than Little Joe that was talking. Little Joe hadn't had that many, but he hadn't eaten any lunch after the two of them had herded fifty head of Ponderosa cattle into Virginia City to sell to the meat markets. While Little Joe had collected the money from the butchers, Hoss had found himself a good meal.

Little Joe settled into his seat and tucked the money back in his britches pocket, sitting sullenly until the red-haired woman returned with the two beers.

"Two bits," she said, sticking out her hand.

Little Joe moved to get his money roll, but Hoss grabbed his hand. "I'll pay," he said. He fished two coins from his britches and pressed them into her hand. "Keep the difference."

"Thanks, big fella, but I'd get junior out of here before too long, if I was you."

Hoss nodded, his lips tight. He figured they could finish their beers, then leave. Hoss gulped down his beer, but Little Joe dallied over the mug. When Hoss finished his, he slammed the mug down on the liquor-stained table and motioned for Little Joe to drink up. As Hoss glanced up from his younger brother, he saw standing over the table a slender man with a vulture's eyes beneath a fine silk derby. The man carried a jigger of whiskey in one hand and a chair in the other.

"Mind if I join you fine gentlemen? The name's Cartwright, isn't it?" Before Hoss could refuse, the man had seated himself beside Little Joe. Placing his drink on the table, he introduced himself. "Blake Tipps is the name," he said. He reached across the table and shook Hoss's tentative hand, then Little Joe's. "I couldn't help but see your roll of money, young man, and hear your soliloquy on your riches."

"My what?" Little Joe asked, his brow furrowed.

"Your soliloquy," Tipps replied, "your eloquent speech on the riches of the Cartwright family."

Hoss grabbed Little Joe's arm. "We need to get out of here, Little Joe. We're supposed to meet Pa for supper."

Little Joe jerked his arm from Hoss's grip and grinned at Tipps. "I want to hear what he has to say, Hoss."

"Thank you, sir," Tipps replied, ignoring Hoss's presence. "Since you are a wealthy man, I know you're always looking for ways to increase your wealth."

Little Joe cocked his head and nodded. "That's how we stay rich, it sure is."

"Well, sir, Mr. Cartwright — I can call you Mr. Cartwright, can't I? — I've a simple proposition for you, if you're interested in increasing that money roll of yours by a hundred dollars."

Little Joe thrust his chin forward. "I'm interested."

"It's all very simple," Tipps said as he pushed his jigger of whiskey to the middle of the table. "I'll bet you that I can empty that glass of whiskey," he removed his hat from his head and dropped it over the jigger, "without lifting my derby."

Little Joe jerked his head from Tipps to the derby to Hoss. He licked his lips as his hand slid from the table to his pocket. "You bet you can drink that whiskey glass without lifting your hat?"

"Yes, sir, Mr. Cartwright," Tipps said as a crowd of miners circled the table, "it's that simple."

"It's a trick, Little Joe," Hoss said. "It has to be."

"It's a bet," his younger brother said, ignoring the interruption, extracting his money roll and peeling off bills as confidently as if he were shucking corn.

Tipps smiled, and his thin lips accentuated his predatory eyes. "Let's ask someone to hold the money until we're done."

"Agreed," Little Joe replied, spotting the red-haired barmaid in the circle of people around the table. "She'll do," he said.

When Tipps nodded, the barmaid stepped forward and palmed the bet money, shaking her head as she looked at Little Joe.

Tipps stood slowly from his chair, spread

his arms and waved them toward the crowd. "Step back," he demanded, "I need plenty of room and silence." The crowd began to hiss for silence, and other patrons across the room quieted. Finally the piano died in the middle of a lively tune.

The crowd retreated a step. Suddenly, Tipps dropped to his knees as if a trapdoor had been sprung beneath him. Instantly, he disappeared under the table. In the saloon's sudden silence he could be heard. "Glub, glub, glub."

Then just as quickly as he had disappeared, he stood up, wiping his lips with the back of his hand. "Good whiskey," he sighed.

Little Joe laughed. "You expect me to believe you drank that whiskey?"

Tipps grimaced. "Perhaps you should check for yourself."

Without thinking, Little Joe lifted the hat. He smiled at the full jigger of whiskey until Tipps leaned over the table, grabbed it, and downed it with a gulp.

"You lose," Tipps taunted.

"What?" Little Joe cried.

"I said I could empty the glass without lifting the derby. The glass is empty and I never touched the hat." Tipps folded his arms across his chest.

Around the table men and women laughed.

"You cheated," Little Joe said in desperation and embarrassment. "You cheated."

The barmaid handed the stakes to Tipps.

"The money stays," she said to Little Joe, "just the pockets change."

"Thank you, ma'am," Tipps said sarcastically, then turned to Little Joe. "And thank you, sir."

Little Joe glared at Tipps, then turned to Hoss.

"Dad-blame-it, Little Joe, I tried to get you out of here." Hoss shrugged. "You can explain it to Pa."

"He's a cheat," Little Joe exclaimed.

"And you're a rich fool," answered Tipps, picking up his overturned hat.

Little Joe lunged for Tipps, grabbed for his lapels, but a flint-faced miner intercepted him. Tipps scurried from the table, and the crowd parted to give him an escape route. Little Joe's anger flared at the retreating swindler and he flailed his fists at the miner. The miner screamed in pain as Little Joe's fist plunged first into his jaw, then solidly into his nose, which blossomed red with blood. Stumbling backward, the miner lost his grip on Little Joe just as another miner ran up and swung at Little Joe, striking him full across the cheek.

Little Joe fell hard to the floor, then scrambled to his knees, but the next miner kicked his heavy boot at Little Joe's shoulder. Little Joe dodged the man's foot, then dove headlong into his stomach, knocking the miner into a chair that collapsed beneath the two of them.

Three more miners rushed Little Joe. Their fists thudded against his body, knocking him to the ground amid the scurrying feet of the men and women trying to get out of range of the melee.

Hoss watched a moment, knowing all along that Little Joe's cupidity was responsible for the brawl. Unable to stand by and watch his brother take a beating, Hoss waded into the miners, pulling two off of Little Joe and tossing them aside like dolls. They landed on tables that splintered beneath them. Little Joe grabbed a chair leg and swung it wildly at the growing circle of miners around him. One feinted for Little Joe, who caught him on the arm with the club, sending the miner screaming for the door. Another dove for Little Joe's legs and was met by a boot to the jaw. Then another attacked from behind, clipping Little Joe across the back of his head with his fist. Still another charged from the side and knocked Little Joe off balance. Little Joe managed to stay on his feet, but the circle of miners was closing around him like a pack of wolves around a wounded dog.

Hoss screamed in anger, then charged the circle, and miners tumbled before him like stalks of wheat before a scythe. With his tremendous strength, he tossed miners away from Little Joe. The tumult and anger grew as more men had their drinks spilled or peace disturbed. Within moments a general brawl had broken out throughout the Delta Saloon. Men who just moments before had been sharing drinks together began to attack one another. Women and those men with weaker constitutions poured out of the Delta onto C Street, giving the alarm. Other men, either with a natural inclination for fighting or with a courage heightened by liquor, joined the battle, grunting, grasping, grappling with each other.

"Where's Tipps?" Little Joe shouted, cocking the chair leg to swing at an approaching form until he realized he was about to strike Hoss.

"It's time to get out of here, Little Joe," Hoss implored. "Now!"

"Not until I find that runt Tipps," Little Joe cried, then swung his club for a miner angling toward him.

Little Joe cocked his club to unload on another man when the explosion of a gunshot echoed through the room.

"The fun's over," came the voice of Sheriff Roy Coffee. The tumult died instantly, as if the smell of gunpowder had curative power over each man's aggression.

Men stood up, rubbing their chins, touching blackened and tender eyes, gasping for breath.

"That's better," Coffee said, reholstering his revolver. "Now who started this?"

Everyone turned and stared at Little Joe and Hoss. A bartender in a clean, starched apron stepped up to the sheriff and pointed at the brothers. "They started it," he said.

Hoss grimaced. It was useless to argue with everyone in the saloon, though that didn't stop Little Joe from putting up a protest.

"I was swindled, Roy," Little Joe pleaded, "and was just trying to make things right."

The bartender abandoned the sheriff and walked around the room, nodding to himself as he assessed the broken chairs and tables and the shattered glassware. The bartender spoke to Coffee as if this were a frequent conversation between them. "I'd say $375 will cover it all," the bartender announced.

"I can pay it," Little Joe said.

"You will, Little Joe, but first you've got a lot of explaining to do."

"Sure thing, Roy," Little Joe said, starting to offer his excuses.

"Not now, Little Joe, but at the jail. You and Hoss are under arrest."

CHAPTER 2

With hands on hips Ben Cartwright waited impatiently in the lobby of the International Hotel. He shook his head and paced back and forth between the elegantly apportioned furnishings. His three sons were to have met him at six o'clock for dinner. Adam had been there as scheduled, for he was ever punctual. But Hoss and Little Joe had yet to show themselves. Had he not seen them earlier, driving fifty head of Ponderosa beef into Virginia City for sale, he might have feared some type of problem on the drive. After waiting ten minutes for his brothers, Adam had volunteered to find them. He had left precisely twenty minutes ago, Ben noted as he shut the cover of his key-wind gold pocket watch.

Adam spent so much time in Virginia City these days, tending to his duties as superintendent of the Cartwrights' Bristlecone Mine, that it was difficult for Ben to get his sons together for a meal. In fact, Adam was gone so much from the Ponderosa that his suite upstairs in the hotel was more his home than the ranch house. Because of varied responsibilities with mining, ranching, and logging, this was the first chance the four

Cartwrights had had to dine leisurely together since the Bristlecone had struck its share of the lode that had become known throughout the West as the "Big Bonanza."

This was Little Joe's doing; Ben knew it as well as a man knows his sons. Adam was always punctual. Hoss was always dependable, as his Swedish mother, Inger Borgstrom, had been, give or take five minutes here and there. But Little Joe, he was something else. Maybe it was his mother's hot French blood, or maybe it was just the forgetfulness of his age. At nineteen, Little Joe figured he was grown. Ben sometimes had his doubts. Through all of his fifty-eight years, Ben had been blessed many times with success and fortune, the find in the Bristlecone being only the latest stroke of good luck, but for all his riches, none added more wealth to his life than his three sons.

Straight as a Ponderosa pine, Ben strode from the lobby to the gentlemen's reading room, where the day's San Francisco newspapers and the important East Coast newspapers from yesterday were neatly arranged on a table. Tugging the lapels on his wool coat, Ben picked up the *San Francisco Chronicle* and seated himself in an overstuffed velvet chair to study the stock prices of the Bristlecone's competing mines. The speculation in Virginia City mining stocks had fueled much of San Francisco's wealth since the 1860s. As long as the vast deposits of silver held out, Virginia City would remain the most important city between St. Louis and San Francisco. Overall, mine stocks were up, a good sign that the public still had confidence in the mines. Scanning the page, Ben found news that lumber prices were going up yet again, reaffirming his decision to acquire from the federal government a timber lease west of Lake Tahoe in the Sierra Nevadas.

Mining required forests of timber for fuel and for shoring up the unpredictable rock, which gave up great wealth and great danger in equal doses. For miles around Virginia City, the mountains had been denuded, first of trees and later of even the stumps and roots, which were used for Virginia City firewood.

By the strength of his determination and his love of the Ponderosa, Ben had not succumbed to the pressure or the money to sell Ponderosa timber for burial beneath Virginia City's sloping streets. He was proud of holding on to the Ponderosa with its timber intact, except for insignificant ranch and mining uses. Looking up from the columns of gray print as Adam walked into the room, Ben folded the paper and tossed it to the reading table.

"Pa," Adam called, an odd smile upon his face.

Ben stood up regally from his chair, eyed

Adam, then craned his neck to see if Hoss and Little Joe had remained behind in the lobby. He saw neither. "Did you find them?"

"Not exactly," Adam replied. "Let's take a table in the dining room before I explain."

"They are okay?"

Adam nodded sheepishly. "In a manner of speaking."

Father and son marched out of the reading room side by side, walked through the lobby and up a short flight of broad, carpeted steps to the dining room, with its twenty-foot ceiling and its elegantly carved wooden sidebar by the entrance.

A waiter in coat and tie seated them and left menus after they requested a brandy apiece.

"I ran into Sheriff Coffee, Pa, and we'll be dining alone tonight."

Ben shook his head. "What did Little Joe get into this time?"

Adam delayed his response as the waiter brought their brandies and took their orders. Ben requested baked trout, and Adam roast lamb with mint sauce.

"Seems they got in a brawl that tore up the Delta Saloon."

Ben sipped at his brandy, savoring its velvety taste. "Little Joe started it, I suppose."

Adam nodded. "He lost a hundred dollars on a sucker bet and tried to whip the man. A few miners got involved before Hoss jumped in to help out. Everybody went wild until Roy broke it up. No serious injuries except to Little Joe's pride. Roy said the damage was about $375."

Ben stared silently beyond Adam while he contemplated the situation. "What can I do to get that boy's attention, Adam? He's smart enough to do more than just work the stock or break horses. I don't think he'd be satisfied working livestock the rest of his life, but I can't see giving him more responsibility with Cartwright Enterprises until he proves himself."

Adam stroked his chin. "I've been thinking, Pa, maybe he isn't responsible because we haven't given him much responsibility. Maybe you ought to reconsider what you have him doing."

"Any suggestions?"

Adam nodded. "The timber operations across Tahoe."

Ben propped his elbows on the table and kneaded his hands as he pondered the suggestion. "The timber operation is too important to the Ponderosa to leave in unsteady hands."

"That's my point, Pa, to show we trust him for important duties, not just working cattle and busting horses."

"Perhaps, Adam, but he'll just see it as my way of banishing him into the wilderness where he can't get into trouble."

Adam finished his brandy as the waiter placed their dinner before them. "He's smart enough to figure it out, if he'll just think about it. Anyway, I've serious concerns about the logging operations. It's never operated efficiently, at least not by my books, but I don't know logging and don't have time to learn, not with the Bristlecone consuming so much of my time. He doesn't have to know that. Just let him go in, supervise and make his own assessment."

Ben took his fork and speared the baked trout, which crumbled from tenderness upon the plate. "Maybe you're right, Adam."

Adam sliced into the pinkness of roast lamb cooked to perfection. "It's worth a try, Pa."

At the rattle of the front door, Sheriff Roy Coffee looked up from his desk and smiled. In walked his granddaughter, Sara Ann Coffee, carrying a basket with his supper inside. Even without food, Sara Ann at seventeen could bring a smile to any man's face. Her eyes sparkled like dew in the early morning light, and her smile was as pure as spring water. She moved gracefully into the office, her auburn hair as bouncy as her temperament. There was never a time Coffee saw her that pride didn't well in his chest beneath his badge.

Had he not worn that badge, Coffee knew his son and daughter-in-law might have lived to raise her themselves. He hadn't done badly, raising her, but they would have done better. He remembered that terrible night a dozen years ago. Had he not been sheriff, Coffee would never have killed Clifford Wharton in a shoot-out at Timberline Pass. Had Wharton lived, his three avenging sons might never have ambushed Coffee's home that night. Coffee survived and so did his wife, at least for a couple of weeks, before dying of a broken heart, but his only son had died instantly in the hail of gunfire. Coffee's daughter-in-law had run to protect her husband, taking a chest wound that proved fatal three days later. One generation of Coffee's family had been wiped out, with only little Sara Ann left to carry the family into the next generation.

Sara Ann had forgotten that terrible night, but Roy Coffee never could and never would. He had tracked down the Wharton boys, had captured them with a posse's help, and had sent them to prison for life, even though his every fiber had wanted to kill them with his bare hands for the terrible thing they had done to his son and the mother of his grand-daughter.

"Evening, Grandpa," Sara Ann said, placing the basket on the desk in front of Coffee. "I brought you fried chicken, creamed potatoes, and apple cobbler."

Coffee smiled gently. He could take for supper what the prisoners ate, but Sara Ann insisted on fixing his meal each evening and delivering it to him. She rarely missed his supper, except on those occasions when she was called upon by an intrigued young man or when winter blizzards made it too treacherous to be out. "Smells delicious."

"Sure does," came a voice from the nearest jail cell.

Sara Ann glanced up from her grandfather to the cell and lifted her hand to her mouth, hiding her surprise and the ensuing smile as she studied Hoss, his hands on the iron bars of the cell door. Behind him, propped up on a bunk, was Little Joe, with a sly smile upon his face.

"What are you in for, Hoss, stealing cookies, or was it somebody's pie?" Sara Ann giggled.

"Disturbing the peace," Hoss replied sheepishly, "but I'm not in for good." With that, he pushed on the cell door, which swung open with a groan.

"Hoss," Roy Coffee said, glancing over his shoulder. "I told you to keep that door shut, lest someone walk in and think I'm not treating you two the same as any other fellows that start a brawl and tear up a saloon."

"Sure thing, Roy," Hoss replied. He stepped outside the cell, grabbed the bar and pulled the door back. It clanged loudly shut and Hoss grimaced, knowing he had closed it too hard. Hoss looked at Sara Ann, his eyes wide as those of a boy who had seen a puppy he would like to take home. "Roy's already fed us, but it didn't taste near as good as yours smells."

"And there wasn't as much of it, was there, Hoss?" the sheriff taunted in jest as he pulled the red-checked cloth from atop the basket and extracted a plate of fried chicken and creamed potatoes. Coffee looked back over his shoulder again in time to see Hoss lick his lips.

Coffee figured Hoss hankered to court Sara Ann but couldn't quite get up the nerve. Part of it may have been the age difference, Hoss being eleven years her senior. Another part of it was the size, him a big man at six-four, and her barely five-two. And Sara Ann loved to dance, while Hoss was as clumsy as an avalanche on the dance floor. After the death of her parents, Hoss had taken to Sara Ann like a child to a wounded bird. He seldom came to town from the Ponderosa without bringing her a bouquet of mountain flowers or a trinket he had carved. Sara Ann might find a man smarter or richer for a husband, but she would never find one with a better heart.

The sheriff attacked a breast of fried chicken as Sara Ann marched to the potbellied stove and poured her grandfather a cup of coffee. She carried the tin cup gracefully to her grandfather's desk and placed it beside him, then snatched a chicken leg from his plate. Coffee raised his arm to protest, until she lifted it to her lips. She smiled at her grandfather, and his protest caught in his throat. When he glanced back down at his plate, Sara Ann scampered across the room to the cell and offered the chicken to Hoss. "No feeding the animals, Sara Ann," Coffee said, laughing between bites.

"Obliged," Hoss said just before biting into the drumstick. As he chewed, he smiled. "Good, real good," he mumbled.

"What about me?" Little Joe called, rising from the bunk and tossing his hat on the wool blanket. "What're you going to give me, Sara Ann?" He smiled widely, as confident of his charm as he was that the sun would rise in the east tomorrow.

"A little advice." She giggled. "Don't get Hoss in any more trouble."

"Me?" Little Joe shrugged. "Hoss was as much at fault as me."

"No, sir, Little Joe," Sara Ann replied. Her words pointed at him like her finger. "I know it's mischief, not meanness, but you can raise five dollars worth of hell faster than any man in these parts."

"Sara Ann," her grandfather chided, "that's not proper language for a young lady."

"Yes, sir, and I apologize for such talk, Little Joe," Sara Ann answered.

Sheriff Coffee smiled to himself, delighted that his granddaughter could read Little Joe like a book. Little Joe's charm worked on a lot of women, but Sara Ann was an exception.

Coffee was as proud of that as he was of her initiative, not to mention her cooking.

"Apology accepted," Little Joe answered with a grin, but Sara Ann folded her arms across her chest and stared sternly at him. His smile disappearing quicker than the chicken in Hoss's hand, Little Joe slid back to the bunk and pulled his hat over his eyes.

Sara Ann offered Hoss a teasing smile. "If you're still here tomorrow night, Hoss, I'll bring you a plate of supper."

Coffee pointed his fork at his granddaughter. "They'll be gone shortly, Sara Ann. Adam said he would bring Ben over after dinner. Ben'll deal with the boys then."

The jail cell clattered as Little Joe jumped out of the bunk and shouldered Hoss away from the door, which creaked open.

"Keep the door shut, boys," Coffee said over his shoulder. "We want to keep appearances up."

Little Joe closed the cell door softly. "What did you tell Adam, Roy?"

"About the same thing you told me, Little Joe," Coffee replied between bites. "I figure Ben'll want to hear it from you about the damages at the Delta and the bet you lost."

Little Joe retreated from the cell door to the bunk. "Roy, would you lock the cell before Pa gets here?" He collapsed on the bunk and pulled the wool blanket up to his chest.

"Maybe when I finish my apple cobbler,

Little Joe," answered Coffee as Sara Ann exchanged his plate, clean except for chicken bones, for a dish of apple cobbler from the basket. The aroma of baked apples spiced with cinnamon and sugar floated gently through the room.

"Smells mighty fine, Sara Ann, mighty fine," said Hoss.

"Tastes fine too, Hoss," said Coffee. A spot of cobbler sat on his lip before he dabbed it away with the red-checked napkin. As he finished his cobbler, the office door swung open.

"Uh-oh," said Little Joe, pulling the wool blanket over his head as his father and Adam entered.

"Evening, Roy, Sara Ann," said Ben Cartwright. His voice was polite but tinted with anger as he tipped his hat and stared beyond them to the jail cell.

Adam nodded and removed his hat as well, his lips quivering with a slight grin at his brothers' misfortune.

Hoss withered under his father's glare and shrugged his regrets. Ben cleared his throat, then called to the cell. "Joseph."

The brown woolen blanket wiggled and slid slowly down from Little Joe's head, revealing worried eyes and a grimace. "Howdy, Pa," he said meekly as he sat up. Rather than sit motionless and wilt under his father's eyes, he stood, then bent over the bunk, brushing the wrinkles out of the blanket.

Sara Ann giggled. This drew a wink from Adam, but a stern look from her grandfather.

"What did your mischief cost, Joseph?"

Little Joe took a deep breath, then let it out with resignation. "About $375 for damage and one hundred on the bet," he said softly.

"I didn't hear, Joseph," Ben said.

"Some $475, Pa," Little Joe repeated.

Ben stood stolid as a rock, his feet wide apart in the seaman's stance he had picked up from his years on the rolling decks of clipper ships. "What did you get for the cattle?"

"I got five hundred, Pa," Little Joe said meekly. "I guess the money changed pockets on me."

"Yes, sir, Joseph, it did, but you know what I want you to do with the twenty-five dollars you've still got?"

"No, sir," Little Joe replied, stepping humbly to the cell's iron bars, his hands as limp as his frown.

Ben Cartwright studied Little Joe, then nodded. "Spend that money on some work clothes, because you're gonna be working hard for a while. And while you're at it, get a haircut."

Little Joe gave a slight smile and ran the fingers of his right hand through his curly brown hair.

"You look like a riverboat gambler with your

hair like that, Joseph, so have it cut short. It's gonna be a while before you get back to town for another visit to the barbershop."

Little Joe's faint smile dissolved. "Pa, it wasn't my fault. A guy just bet me he could —"

Ben held up his hand. "Don't try my patience, Joseph."

"And what about Hoss?" Little Joe countered. "He fought too!"

"Joseph, a drowning man can take another man down with him."

"Yes, sir," Little Joe said, his head drooping. It was hard to defend or explain as stupid an act as that bet.

Ben crossed his arms over his chest. "You're going to be working in California for a while."

Hoss needled Little Joe. "I bet it ain't San Francisco either."

Ben cleared his throat. "Hoss," he said, and needed to say no more to his middle son.

Hoss nodded. "Yes, sir."

Sara Ann moved beside her grandfather, quietly picking up the bowl and utensils and placing them gently in the basket. She leaned over and kissed her grandfather on the cheek. "I'll be leaving," she whispered.

Roy Coffee nodded. "Fine supper." He patted her hand as she picked up the basket.

Before she stepped away from the desk, everyone in the office stopped at the sound of boots clopping like a stampede on the plank walk outside. Coffee pushed himself up from his desk, his hand falling instinctively to his sidearm. Everyone froze at the hurried knock a moment before the door swung open. In marched one of the young runners used by the telegraph office.

A tousle-haired kid with a gap between his front teeth and wide blue eyes sputtered for breath. "Telegram, Sheriff." He shoved a paper to Coffee, who grabbed a pencil from his desk and signed the receipt. The runner handed Roy the yellow envelope and waited a moment for a tip that wasn't forthcoming, then turned and disappeared outside, leaving the door open behind him.

"I best be getting home," Sara Ann said, marching for the door. "Good night, all."

Coffee nodded absently as he ripped open the end of the envelope. His eyes widened and he seemed to pale. The telegraph quivered in his suddenly unsteady hand.

"Just a minute, Sara Ann," Coffee said, then turned to the jail cell.

"Hoss," he said, "would you mind escorting Sara Ann home and waiting with her until I close up here?"

"Glad to, Roy," Hoss said. He pushed the cell door open and left Little Joe behind.

Roy squatted behind his desk and opened a drawer. When he arose, he held Hoss's holstered revolver and gun belt. "Take this with you now, why don't you?"

"Sure, Roy," Hoss replied, his brow furrowed with confusion.

"Anything the matter, Roy?" asked Ben Cartwright, stepping to the sheriff's desk.

Coffee shook his head curtly.

Hoss strapped on his revolver as he stepped beside Sara Ann, dwarfing her. "Anything else, Roy?" When the sheriff shook his head, Hoss motioned for Sara Ann to precede him out the door. Hoss, so pleased to be out of jail, shut the door with too much exuberance, rattling the glass panes.

Once the footsteps of Hoss and Sara Ann grew silent, Roy Coffee slumped into his hard-back swivel chair. He tossed the telegram toward Ben. "The Wharton brothers escaped from prison early this morning."

Ben grabbed the yellow paper and read the message, whistling when he finished.

"Who are the Wharton brothers?" Little Joe asked from the cell.

"The men who killed Sara Ann's parents," Ben said.

For a moment Roy Coffee seemed to stare beyond Ben, beyond the office walls, into the past.

Ben offered the telegraph to Adam, who read it and dropped it back on the desk.

"I guess you know what this means, Roy?" Ben said.

"Yes, sir, Ben, they vowed to kill us after the verdict came back guilty! You and I are going to have to watch our backs until they're recaptured."

"Or killed," Ben said.

"Or killed," Coffee repeated.

CHAPTER 3

The spring mountain air was thin and brisk, prickly against the skin and invigorating to the lungs as Hoss escorted Sara Ann Coffee toward the modest house she shared with her grandfather. In the coolness, each breath turned to a vapor that seemed to glow in what little light the darkness squeezed out of the stars. The darkened street was splotched with dim light, a golden halo that circled a gas lamp at the end of the block, and rectangles of hazy light that puddled at the foot of curtained windows in the buildings Hoss passed. Beyond the muddied, murky glow, in the deepest recesses of the darkness, lurked something sinister, Hoss knew. It was made all the more evil by Hoss's ignorance of what the danger might be. Imagined dangers rode a man harder than known perils. Whatever the hazard, Hoss knew it was real, because Sheriff Roy Coffee was not a man to scare easily. He had been a sheriff too long, had faced danger too often and had seen death too closely to panic at the imagined, but Hoss had watched him open the telegram. He'd seen fear in Coffee's eyes, a quiver in his lips and then a tightness in his jaw. His demeanor, his usual

44

stoicism, had changed faster than the weather in the Sierra Nevadas. One moment the sheriff's concern had been teaching a value lesson to Hoss and Little Joe, and in an instant it had changed to getting his granddaughter home with an armed escort.

Somewhere out there in the darkness, danger approached, and Hoss walked stiffly up the street, studying each passing pedestrian and each mounted man. His fingers rested casually on the butt of the .44-caliber Russian Model Smith & Wesson at his side. It was a reliable weapon, which felt comfortable in Hoss's big hand but not nearly as comfortable as Sara Ann walking by his side.

"Something terrible is the matter," Sara Ann said, slipping her arm around Hoss's and drawing closer to him. "I've never seen grandfather so worried." Her words were as gentle as her touch upon his arm. She carried her concerns openly, without shame or guile. "What could it be, Hoss?"

Hoss shrugged and felt her shiver against his arm. Was it the cold or was it fear that had caused that tremor? Hoss glanced back over his shoulder, certain someone was following him. Someone was! He could see a large form, one he could not identify by anything other than the hurried footfall. Hoss steered Sara Ann around a patch of window light in their path, then stared back over his shoulder at the indistinct form that gained rapidly on

Sara Ann and himself. His fingers tightened around his revolver, and Hoss gently began to lift the gun from its holster.

"What's the matter, Hoss?" Sara Ann asked, glancing around just as the hurried form plowed through the rectangle of window light Hoss had just sidestepped.

Hoss sighed. That brief instant in the murky light had been enough for Hoss to identify the bulky form as nothing more than an obese woman waddling as fast as she could toward the warmth of her home. The woman gathered her shawl around her as she passed and mumbled a greeting that Hoss saw as a cloud of vapor in another rectangle of leaking light. Hoss let the Smith & Wesson slip from his fingers, then he shoved it snugly into its holster. "Nothing's wrong," he said to Sara Ann.

Both of them knew he was lying.

Near her home, Sara Ann pulled her arm from Hoss's and slipped her hand into the basket which carried her grandfather's dirty supper dishes. She retrieved a skeleton key and offered it to Hoss as they turned up the short plank walk to the house.

Hoss pointed to the glow behind a window with shades drawn. "Did you leave a lamp burning?" His right hand slid casually to his gun until Sara Ann responded.

"Yes, sir. Grandfather always has me leave a lamp burning. It wastes coal oil, I know. And no matter how short a time I'm away, he insists I lock the door. Other than a few mansions, I bet we're the only house in Virginia City that has spent money on a lock."

Stepping up the stairs, Hoss slid the key in the mortise lock, twisted it, then shoved open the door. The house was warm and inviting, the glow of the lamp soft like Sara Ann. Hoss wrinkled his nose at the still fresh smell of apple cobbler and looked about the modest parlor as Sara Ann slipped in and adjusted the lamp. At Sara Ann's touch, the room brightened, and in the light, her smile grew.

"I bet you'd like a dish of cobbler," she said, gliding as gracefully as a dove on the wing through the door at the rear of the parlor.

"Yes, ma'am," Hoss said. He moved to the side door that opened off the parlor into the sheriff's bedroom, and looked around for anything that might be amiss, anything that might give reason for the sheriff's as yet unstated fears. A lamp Sara Ann had lit in the kitchen cast a pillar of light into the back bedroom. Hoss stepped to the door between bedrooms, feeling a flush in his face as he studied Sara Ann's room. Seeing nothing in the dim light that appeared unusual, he spied Sara Ann through the kitchen door. She stooped over the wood stove to scoop out a bowl of cobbler for him. He enjoyed the view of her shapely figure, but worried she might turn around and catch him staring. He retreated to the parlor, confident the house was safe.

Like the sheriff, the house was modest, its four rooms plainly furnished, and the furniture — a rocker, two chairs, corner table, and sofa — was well-used. Worn spots on the back and arms of the sofa were disguised by coverlets crocheted by Sara Ann. The most ornate coverlet, with scalloped edges and an intricate, painstaking design, covered the corner table. Displayed atop the coverlet was a single framed tintype of Sara Ann's parents. Hoss bit his lip, thinking about the tragedy, and felt sorry that Sara Ann had never gotten to know her mother and father. Hoss could understand half the loss, for he did not remember his mother. But he at least had had his father, who remembered his mother fondly and recalled her as a big woman with an even bigger heart.

Hoss seated himself in the rocking chair, noting the adjacent basket of crochet hooks and thread. Beside the basket, a quilting hoop held a section of unfinished quilt. When he looked up, Sara Ann stood before him, offering him a bowl of warm cobbler.

"Let me take your hat," she said with a smile.

Hoss grabbed for his hat, embarrassed he had not taken it off before, but pleased there was no reproach in her voice. She accepted the hat in exchange for the cobbler and carried it to the corner table, where she placed it on the delicate coverlet beside the tintype of her parents. Hoss sucked in the aroma of the cobbler, then attacked it with the spoon, savoring each bite, loaded with sugar and cinnamon and good apples. "Ummm," he said as Sara Ann walked to the rocking chair and picked up her basket of crocheting.

Taking a seat on the sofa opposite Hoss, Sara Ann gathered her crochet hooks and began to knead a length of lacework. Her fingers were long, delicate, and graceful as they manipulated hook and thread. Her work was as orderly and precise as the house she kept.

Hoss scraped the last of his cobbler out of the bowl. "Mighty fine, Sara Ann, mighty fine." He held up his arm when she moved to get up for his bowl. "You just keep your seat." The rocking chair creaked as Hoss arose and stepped for the kitchen. He placed the bowl on the table beside the basket with her grandfather's dirty dishes and noted the wood box was low. "I need to make a trip to the woodpile," he called from the kitchen.

"Maybe later, Hoss. I prefer you stay with me. Something's wrong and your company makes me feel safer."

"There's nothing to be afraid of," Hoss said, doubting his own words as he returned to the parlor. The rocking chair groaned under his weight. For an awkward moment he sat silently staring at Sara Ann, her delicate lips glorified by a sincere smile. "There's nothing wrong," he repeated.

When Roy Coffee came home, his face was dark with concern as he locked the door behind him. Hoss could see trouble in his face, particularly when the sheriff clenched his jaw and stared at his granddaughter.

"Sara Ann," Coffee said, "the Wharton brothers have escaped."

She grimaced and lowered her head. She seemed suddenly vulnerable, especially when she spoke softly, almost inaudibly. "The ones that killed my folks?"

Coffee nodded slowly, deliberately, and Hoss thought he saw a mist in the veteran lawman's eyes. "They've always vowed to murder me and Ben for killing their pa."

"We'll be okay," Sara Ann said, in a voice as smooth as silk.

"It's you I'm worried about, Sara Ann. Your folks were killed the last time they tried to get me. I couldn't stand to see something happen to you. You're all I've got left."

Sara Ann tossed her handwork aside and jumped up from her seat, bolting across the room into her grandfather's arms. "Everything'll be okay," she said, "everything'll be okay."

The barber held the mirror to Little Joe's face. Little Joe stared at himself and grimaced. His curly brown locks had been shorn closer than he enjoyed, but if he were going to California for a few weeks, what difference did it make? He ran his fingers through his hair and shook his head, his frown as deep as his hair was short.

"Something wrong?" the barber asked, slowly dropping the mirror and placing it on the counter at his elbow.

Little Joe shrugged, then clenched his jaw at the sight of his father and Hoss riding up outside. "Pa will like it," Little Joe managed as the barber removed the white drape cloth and shook off the trimmings. Little Joe slid reluctantly out of the chair, fished two bits out of his britches pocket, and pitched the coin to the barber. He retrieved his flat-brim hat and plopped it in place, trying to snug it down, but thanks to the haircut, the fit was wrong. The door rattled as Little Joe pulled it open and stepped outside in the late morning sun. When he nodded to his father and Hoss, his head seemed to wallow around in the hat like a pebble in a tin can. Little Joe felt his face flush at Hoss's laugh.

Ben sat stiffly on his yellow dun, his brow furrowed, his thoughts seemingly miles away. Ever serious, Ben had been downright solemn since the telegram arrived at the jail last night.

Little Joe tipped his hat to his father, awaiting some acknowledgment of his sacrificial clipping. Ben nodded so slightly Little Joe could not be sure it was an actual response.

Hoss just laughed. "An Injun couldn't have scalped you any better, little brother," he joked.

Scowling at Hoss, Little Joe tugged his hat back on his head. As loose as the hat was now, he feared he might have to tie it on his head with a kerchief like a fancy lady on a Sunday excursion. Little Joe untied his reins from the hitching rail, shoved his foot in the stirrup and climbed aboard the pinto. A bundle of new-bought work clothes strapped behind the cantle reminded Little Joe of his impending banishment to California. "I'm ready, Pa."

Ben sat silently in the saddle. His yellow dun flicked its tail occasionally and dipped its head.

Impatient, Little Joe looked down C Street, taking in the men and women scurrying about Virginia City's commercial district. They were an odd mix, these residents of Virginia City. Many were working miners, the best paid in the world, earning four dollars a day for their hard labor in the deepest mines on earth. The miners pulled the wealth from the earth like dentists extract teeth, but the people who profited most were the speculators who made money where none existed and lost other people's money before they lost their own. There were college-educated engineers, self-taught swindlers, illiterate tradesmen, and learned storekeepers. The women, like the men, came in all sorts, from the boardinghouse proprietors to waitresses to saloon women.

The wealth that drew them all to Virginia City was hundreds of feet beneath the street where they trod, on the slopes of Mount Davidson. Virginia City had carved out a canted existence on the mountain's rough-hewn shoulder. Mount Davidson was the richest mountain on earth, but for all its wealth, it was ugly as a faded dowager. With a barren peak, its trees long since cut like whiskers after a shave, it stood naked and pitted from mining's insatiable search for precious minerals. Like Mount Davidson, other mountains for miles around had been denuded to feed the mines' voracious appetite for timber to shore up unstable walls hewn from rock. Timber could still be found within easy riding distance of Virginia City, but only on the Ponderosa and only because one man — Ben Cartwright — had a vision of what western Nevada would have to be once the minerals played out and the miners and their wealth migrated to the next boomtown.

"I'm ready, Pa," Little Joe repeated after adequate pause.

Ben nodded. "I heard you the first time."

Hoss leaned over in his saddle, resting his hands on the saddle horn. "It's the Wharton brothers, ain't it?"

Stroking his chin, Ben licked his lips. "They

bring back bad memories and create new worries, Hoss."

"You worried they'll come for you and the
sheriff, Pa?" Hoss asked.

Ben backed his yellow dun away from the
hitching rail, but instead of turning the gelding down C Street and the route for the Ponderosa, he aimed the animal up the street.
"Roy thinks so, son, but I don't know. I'm not
as worried about him and me as I am about
Sara Ann. We can take care of ourselves, but
you know her. She wouldn't hurt a fly, and
can't accept that anyone else could either."

Hoss and Little Joe turned their mounts in
beside Ben and started up the street beside
their father.

Little Joe had an idea, one that might keep
him from being exiled into California doing
whatever hard work Pa had in mind. He
cleared his throat, but spoke tentatively. "Pa,
I was just thinking."

Ben glanced at his youngest son and nodded
for him to proceed.

"Maybe one of us should stick around,
watch after Sara Ann until these Whartons
are back in prison."

A sliver of a smile escaped Ben's stern lips.
"I was thinking the same thing, Joseph, and
wanted to discuss it with Roy. Any thoughts
who should stay?"

It was working, Little Joe thought. Now he
just had to make it appear he wasn't too

anxious to volunteer. "Well, Adam's tied up with the Bristlecone, and you know Hoss grows bored after a few days in the city."

"That leaves just you, Joseph."

Little Joe shrugged nonchalantly.

"Think you can handle it?"

Little Joe nodded.

"Well, then, it's settled," Ben said, turning from Little Joe to Hoss. "Hoss, you mind staying in town and looking out for Sara Ann Coffee for the next week or so, until the Wharton brothers are back in jail?"

Jerking his hat off his head, Hoss answered with a grin, "I suspect I can, Pa."

Little Joe sputtered, "But what about me, Pa?"

"You'll be working in California, Joseph. I haven't forgotten the incident at the Delta." Little Joe slumped in his saddle.

"I want you to know I appreciate it, Ben," Roy Coffee said. He turned to Hoss, who stood holding his hat in front of his belt, rolling the brim up. "You don't object to keeping an eye on Sara Ann, now do you?"

"Nope," Hoss answered. A gap-toothed smile as wide as his belt creased his face. "Be glad to."

Little Joe, still smarting that he had been denied the chance to squire Sara Ann Coffee around Virginia City until the Wharton brothers were found, sat on his pinto. It galled him not to know what he would be doing in California. If only that sharp in the saloon hadn't swindled him out of a hundred dollars, this wouldn't be happening, he thought.

Ben turned away from the white picket fence around Coffee's modest house and mounted his yellow dun. "You take care of that girl, now," Ben said, just as Sara Ann emerged from the front door.

"I'm not a girl anymore," Sara Ann said, but the smile on her face betrayed the mock anger of the hands on her hips.

"Yes, ma'am," Ben replied.

"Mr. Cartwright, you take care of yourself too. It's you and grandfather who should have a bodyguard, not me."

"What she means, Ben," interjected Coffee, "is thank you."

Sara Ann nodded. "That I do." Then she turned to Hoss. "Now, Hoss, what do you think you might like for lunch?"

"Hmmm," Hoss said, plopping his hat back on his head and starting for the house.

Coffee slapped Hoss on the back. "So that's why you've agreed to give us a hand." Coffee laughed and waved at Ben and Little Joe.

Little Joe nodded weakly and turned his horse about to catch up with his father. "Where we going, Pa?"

"To the mine office to see Adam."

Little Joe sighed and rolled his eyes. Anything Adam was involved in was trouble.

Adam was too serious for his own good. Little Joe wondered if Adam had ever had any fun in his life. Little Joe doubted it, as stuffy as his older brother was.

The two men rode silently down Union Street, then turned on F Street, past the Consolidated Virginia, the richest mine on the Comstock Lode. The Bristlecone Mine, a division of Cartwright Enterprises, abutted the Consolidated and shared in the wealth of the richest silver find in the history of man. The earth trembled with the vibrations of great steam engines powering the hoists that lowered timber and lifted ore from the deepest mines on the globe. The whine and huff of those steam engines provided the anthem of the industrial age. The raw brute strength of industry created a constant attack on the senses, the ears aching from the clatter, the nose burning with the smell of hot metal, the eyes watering from the smoke in the air. Some four dozen trains a day rolled into Virginia City to exchange timber and supplies for tons of ore shipped to the stamp mills on the Truckee River. From there, the bullion was taken to the mint in Carson City, where much of the nation's coinage was produced. The air was filled with the shrill steam whistles of departing trains and the constant clackety-clack of endless ore cars following one another down steel tracks like iron sheep.

Past the four towering stacks that belched

smoke above the Consolidated Virginia's hoist works, Ben and Little Joe approached the Bristlecone offices. Several Bristlecone miners tipped their caps to Ben. "Good day, Mr. Cartwright," called a couple, and Ben touched the brim of his hat in acknowledgment.

Little Joe wondered why no one greeted him. After all, he held twenty percent of Bristlecone stock, as much as either of his brothers. Everyone greeted Hoss because he was so friendly. Miners acknowledged Adam because he was running the operation. But for some reason, he was ignored, Little Joe reflected, and he didn't understand why. Dismounting with his father in front of the two-story wooden office, Little Joe tied his reins over the hitching post and followed Ben inside. The clerks jumped up from their desks and scurried to greet Ben while barely even tossing a nod toward Little Joe, who moved practically unnoticed up the stairs.

Little Joe was at Adam's door before Ben could get past all those who had stood up to greet him and shake his hand. Angered, Little Joe shoved open the door to Adam's office and marched in.

His brother glanced up from a stack of papers on his rolltop desk, his solemn black eyes ablaze. "Do you know how to knock, Little Joe?"

Little Joe swaggered to the table by the window, tossed his hat down and slid into a chair. Leaning back, he propped his feet beside his hat. "I own just as much stock as you in the Bristlecone."

Adam nodded. "But you don't own as many manners."

Little Joe growled and began to rock on the hind legs of his chair until he saw his father standing at the door.

Ben was scowling. "Joseph," he called, and needed to say no more.

Slowly, Little Joe retracted his feet from the tabletop.

Ben greeted Adam, then strode across the room and took a seat opposite his youngest son.

Adam made a couple of notes on a ledger, stood up, and stretched his arms before joining his father and his brother.

Little Joe grabbed his hat and toyed with it, ignoring Ben and Adam.

Ben coughed into his fist, then spoke solemnly to his youngest son. "Joseph, I've been disappointed in you lately, I have to admit."

Little Joe cocked his head and answered only with a sheepish grin.

"I figure," Ben continued, "part of it's my fault for not giving you more responsibilities."

Little Joe rubbed his chin. What responsibilities was his father talking about? Was Ben going to let him run the mine for a while? Then Bristlecone employees wouldn't ignore him when he appeared around the place.

"Adam and I," Ben started, "have talked it over . . ."

If Adam were involved, thought Little Joe, there'd be nothing good to come out of this.

". . . and decided we want to put you in charge of our timber operations on the government lease up in the Sierras."

Little Joe grimaced. "I'm not cut out to be a logger."

Ben's hands knotted into fists and his gaze bore into his youngest son. "At times, Joseph, I'm not certain you're cut out for anything but mischief."

Adam held up his hand at his father and turned to Little Joe. "Am I a miner?"

Little Joe laughed. "You don't like getting your hands dirty."

"Am I a miner, Little Joe?"

"No!"

"And Pa's not asking you to be a logger. You'd be supervising our timber works. I don't trust the foreman we've got, a man named Nat Greer. I'd put you over him."

Little Joe pointed his index finger like a gun at Adam. "You'd put me over him. It's always you that's in charge. I'd have to report to you, when you don't own any more stock in Cartwright Enterprises than I do."

Ben shook his head. "Adam works for his share of stock, carries responsibility. You think herding a few head of cattle to town is responsibility, but Adam has to oversee men, a payroll, purchasing, and the business end of mining."

Little Joe just shook his head. "You're both trying to get me out of Virginia City and into the mountains where I can't have any fun or spend any money. It's not like we don't have enough money to have a little fun when we get to town."

Shaking his head, Adam stood up and walked away with a shrug.

"You just want to put me in charge of something where I won't get in your way. And you won't put me in charge of something important, just a bunch of slow-witted loggers."

Ben stood slowly from his chair. "Nothing important, you say, Joseph."

Little Joe nodded.

"Is the Ponderosa important enough for you?"

"This isn't Ponderosa land where the timbering is."

"Is the Ponderosa important enough for you, Joseph? Answer me," Ben commanded, the anger rising in his voice.

"More than this damned mine and all the timber in California," Little Joe acknowledged.

"Joseph," Ben said, "you'll watch your language so we can have a civil conversation."

"Yes, sir," Little Joe said.

Ben nodded. "If the Ponderosa is important to you, this is the most important responsibility you could ever take on."

Little Joe couldn't help but grin at his father, who was surely putting him on. "Just how's this job so important?"

"You want all the trees on the Ponderosa cut?"

"Not all, Pa, but a few wouldn't hurt."

Ben turned to Adam. "He won't believe me unless I show him." Exasperated, Ben turned back to his youngest son. "Come on, Joseph, maybe between here and the logging camp, you can learn a few things. And when we leave town, get a good look at it, because you won't be returning to Virginia City for a while."

CHAPTER 4

Screened by the tall ponderosa pine on the mountaintop, three men sat on lathered horses and studied the ranch house and outbuildings below. Beyond the ranch headquarters, the waters of Lake Tahoe were as smooth as dark blue silk.

"Was in prison so long," said Vern Wharton, "I forgot there was such a thing as mountains and trees and lakes."

Lem Wharton spat. "Mountains remind me of rocks and rocks remind me of prison. If I don't see another rock for as long as I live, I'll be okay."

Willis twisted around in his saddle and looked back toward Carson City and beyond, toward Mount Davidson, which shaded Virginia City. "We should've gone to Virginia City first and taken care of Coffee."

Lem snarled. "That's what they'd be expecting. Virginia City's got a telegraph and Coffee'll know we broke out. The Ponderosa don't have no telegraph. We might slip up on Ben Cartwright and get him before he knows we busted out."

Willis had a sadistic streak in him. "I kinda wish he'd know we're out, maybe live in fear awhile before we killed him."

The three sat for half an hour, watching the Ponderosa. Except for the smoke that came out of the kitchen stovepipe, the ranch house and the surrounding buildings looked abandoned by men who had chores to do away from headquarters.

The Wharton brothers had the look of human culls. Their skin was sallow from years in prison, their cheeks gaunt, and their eyes murky. Each had dirty brown hair which matched dirty brown eyes. Lem, the oldest and biggest at six-two, was missing the top third of his right ear from a fight with Willis, the youngest. Willis was cross-eyed and his right shoulder rode a few inches higher than his left, giving him an unbalanced appearance which matched his mental stability. Vern Wharton had a flat nose, thanks to Willis and a broken axe handle, and deep-set eyes that gave his face the look of a flesh-covered skull.

Willis kept licking his lips, anxious to ride down on the ranch house and extract revenge for his father, killed at Timberline Pass a dozen years ago by Ben Cartwright and Sheriff Roy Coffee. Lem, though, thought it best to rest the horses in case they had to make a run for it. If they got a chance, they would exchange their stolen mounts for a few of the fine horses dancing about in the big corral behind the Ponderosa barn. The stolen mounts matched the stolen clothes they wore and the stolen guns they fingered.

"Well, boys," said Lem finally, "are you ready to visit Ben Cartwright?"

Willis nodded. "Been ready twelve years."

"We got a plan?" Vern asked.

"Just to kill the bastard that killed our pa," replied Lem, the bile rising in his voice.

"You don't reckon the son of a bitch died while we was in prison, do you?" Vern asked.

Willis growled. "If'n he did, I'll dig him up and shoot him again. You don't think he died, do you?"

"Vern, dammit," said Lem, "don't go asking any questions that'll confuse Willis. He's a hard enough time keeping his head, shoulders, and eyes straight as it is."

Vern shrugged.

"We've waited a long time for this and we can wait a little longer, so let's ride in easy so no one'll think anything's the matter," commanded Lem.

The three men nudged their horses down the slope. The horses were drooping from the hard ride up the mountains and the thin air around them. They had been poor horses to start with, but men who paroled themselves out of prison couldn't be too picky, not when every lawman in the state was likely looking for them.

Lem led the way, then came Willis, then Vern, who had learned to be wary of his younger brother after Willis splattered his nose with the axe handle. Willis just didn't see things the way other men did, maybe because of his crossed eyes or maybe because of the mean streak in him, which he had inherited from their father. The old man had believed in having tough sons, and had beat them plenty to thicken their hides. Those lessons had come in handy in prison, where the hardest and toughest men in Nevada knew to steer clear of the Wharton brothers.

At the base of the mountain, the Whartons picked up the wagon trail and aimed for the ranch house a half mile away. The three men rode abreast as they reined up their horses in front of the fine two-story ranch house made of native timber, squared and fitted, and native stone, precisely chiseled. A high wooden gable gave way to a shingled over-hang that ran the breadth of the house and shaded a long porch. The front door of thick varnished wood stood in the shadow. To the side of the entry jutted the kitchen, a wide room with a door opening out onto the porch and a chimney pipe spewing smoke from the roof.

"Howdy," called Lem Wharton. "Anybody home?" He watched the massive front door and the windows.

"You sure this is the place, Lem?" Willis twisted around in his saddle, looking for some point of reference that would confirm this as the Cartwright place.

"Dammit, Willis, you leave the talking and the thinking to me," answered Lem. "Howdy, anybody home today?" Hatless, Lem squinted at the midday sun, then lifted his hand to shade his eyes. As he watched the front door, the side door opened up from the kitchen and a Chinese man in a neatly pressed apron stepped outside with a meat cleaver in one hand and a dish towel in the other. He nodded meekly at the Wharton brothers.

Lem Wharton spat toward the cook. "Anybody else around, John Chinaman," he snapped, "anybody that speaks English?"

"Hop Sing speak English," he said, bowing humbly.

Lem moved his hand from his brow and scratched his mangled ear. "We're looking for Ben Cartwright. This is the Ponderosa?"

Hop Sing nodded. "Mr. Ben away, Virginia City. A couple days, Mr. Ben return."

Willis eased his horse up to Lem and spoke under his breath. "Let's kill the Chinaman."

Lem grabbed Willis by the arm. "Nothing doing," he said. "We don't want any more trouble than we can handle until we get Cartwright and Coffee."

With his crossed eyes, Willis cast a befuddled gaze toward his oldest brother. "This here Chinaman," he argued, "can't cause us any trouble."

"Dammit, Willis," Lem shot back, glancing toward Hop Sing, who stood smiling as they whispered his fate, "let's not raise a ruckus just yet."

"Lem's right, Willis," interjected Vern.

Willis shrugged.

"Now, John Chinaman," Lem said to Hop Sing, "we're wanting to see Ben Cartwright about work. We'll come back in a few days. Mind if we water our horses?" Lem pointed to the water trough by the corral where fresh mounts trotted about.

"Take water, plenty water. More water in lake," Hop Sing said, waving the dish towel toward Lake Tahoe. He turned about and retreated to his kitchen.

Willis lifted his hand like a gun, pointing his index finger at Hop Sing's back. "Pow," he said, then lifted his finger upright to his mouth and blew away an imaginary puff of gun smoke.

Lem chastised his brother. "You don't do any real shooting until I give the word." Lem jerked his head toward the corral. "Let's go water our horses now." He laughed as he gave his reins a savage tug, his horse whining at the pull of the bit in its mouth.

The brothers rode their horses to the water trough beside the corral and barn. The Whartons dismounted in unison, let their jaded mounts drink, and walked around, stretching their tight muscles, studying the barn and admiring a tack room filled with saddles and harnesses.

Standing in the tack room door and enjoying the aroma of leather well cared for, Vern whistled. "Never seen so many fine saddles outside of a store."

"Help yourself," Lem said, "we'll trade ours for theirs. If we're exchanging horses, we might just as well exchange rigs. Way I figure it, Ben Cartwright owes us a lot for killing Pa and seeing us in prison the last twelve years."

Vern nodded. "Yeah." He glanced over at Willis, who stood in the open barn door, looking at the bundled hay and the ranch wagons. "What are you thinking, Willis?"

The youngest Wharton looked over his sloping left shoulder, his crooked eyes ablaze with mischief. "I was wondering how long it would take this barn to burn to the ground."

"Longer than we've got," Lem replied, pointing to the corral. "Pick out a good mount and a good saddle, then let's get out of here. We'll wanna be on good mounts when we get to Virginia City."

"But what about Cartwright?" asked Willis.

"He'll wait," answered Lem. "Besides, I figure we can find us some female companionship in Virginia City."

"Yeee-haaa," yelled Willis, "let's saddle up and get going."

Ben still simmered from Little Joe's impertinence. The boy had a good mind, if he chose to put it to use on something other than mischief. Maybe Adam was right. Maybe Little Joe did need more responsibility for Cartwright Enterprises. But when Ben tried to give him authority to oversee the timber operation, Little Joe had thought it an insignificant assignment, one beneath his station as a member of the Cartwright family, which owned the wealthy Bristlecone Mine. The timber operation was not the biggest money-maker among Cartwright Enterprises' varied business interests, and Adam believed it was the most inefficient operation Cartwright Enterprises was involved in, but it was likely the most important to the future of the Ponderosa itself.

The mines of Virginia City consumed lumber by the tons to shore up sagging tunnels. Ben knew that in the previous year more than six million cubic feet of lumber had been buried in the mines beneath Storey County. Many times he had been offered exorbitant prices for the Ponderosa and its virgin timber. He had refused the offers because he was a man wealthy beyond his dreams and the Ponderosa meant more to him than anything but his sons. He had seen the pressure coming from the needs of the Bristlecone, and by generous bid had secured a lease, with some difficulty, on federal timber tracts in the Sierra Nevadas of California, across Lake Tahoe from the Ponderosa. The lease, some fifty thousand acres, was to protect the Ponderosa so he would never be tempted to harvest more than the ranch's meager needs for timber.

To Ben the connection between the timber operation and the fate of the Ponderosa was as clear as the waters of Lake Tahoe. Adam, with his business mind, understood it as well. Hoss, who knew nature better than any of the Cartwrights, including himself, Ben knew, could comprehend the connection, though he might not articulate it as well as the others. But Little Joe didn't apply his mind to the connection between the timber leases and the future of the Ponderosa. Worse yet, he seemed not to care.

This expedition, Ben hoped, would educate his youngest son about that connection. Little Joe hadn't understood why he had bought them each a coat in Virginia City, not when the spring days were turning warm. Nor had Little Joe understood why he had borrowed a bedroll apiece for them and thrown in a few supplies for the trail. Ben was taking Little Joe straight to the logging camp around Lake Tahoe.

Outside of Virginia City, where the road joined the one to Carson City and the Ponderosa ranch house, Ben ignored the turn.

"Pa," said Little Joe, a smirk in his voice, "don't we want to go that way?" He pointed to the road they had passed.

"Not today, Joseph. I'm taking you to the logging camp."

Little Joe shrugged. "It's still closer through Carson City."

"I want to show you the Carson River."

Little Joe grimaced, then scratched his head, which still felt unnatural from the barber's sharp scissors. "I've seen the Carson River before."

"You've seen much, Joseph, but understood little," Ben replied without looking at his son.

Now Little Joe really scratched his head, not knowing what to make of his father's pointed words and the sharpness in his voice. Oddly uncomfortable near his father, Little Joe let the pinto fall a few steps behind the yellow dun. After riding silently for several minutes, they eventually reached a rise where the road overlooked the Carson River. Ben reined up his horse and motioned for Little Joe to stop beside him. Little Joe stared. He didn't know what he was seeing, and his father did not speak.

In the distance were the stacks of the stamp mills and sawmills that clung to the riverbanks like grimy leeches. The river was just returning to normal after the annual spring thaw had overflowed its banks. Wide ribbons of mud paralleled the river, and bands of logs, on their way to the sawmills downstream, knifed through the waters. The lumbermen floated their logs, cut high in the Sierras, after the spring thaw rather than before so that the timber would not overflow the riverbed and become marooned on the muddy banks after the waters went down.

"What do you see, Joseph?" Ben asked.

Little Joe shrugged, impatient to be riding and to be done with this lesson. "The Carson River, Pa, just like I have a hundred times or more."

"Anything different?"

"Nope!"

Ben said nothing, just stared at his youngest son.

Little Joe squirmed in the saddle and studied the river, trying to come up with the answer that would satisfy his father. "The river's been flooding, but it does that every spring."

"When I first came here, the river didn't flood like this each spring. Sure it rose some, but not like this."

"We've had more snow in the mountains, Pa."

Ben shook his head. "I don't think so, Joseph, but say we have had more snow in the mountains. Then why does the river turn into a trickle by fall? It didn't do that when I started the Ponderosa."

"A lot more irrigation today in Washoe Valley than in the old days, Pa."

Ben pursed his lips and pointed west toward the mountains and Ponderosa land. "Let's head toward the ranch, sleep out in the mountains tonight."

"It's not much farther to ride to the house, Pa. We can sleep on a nice mattress."

Saying nothing, Ben nudged his horse down the road and toward the Washoe Valley. To Little Joe's dismay, Ben angled the horse away from Carson City, following an old trail that would take them to the southern reaches of the Ponderosa.

Little Joe thought this the toughest trip he had ever made with his father, and Ben seemed to have no interest in making the ride any easier on him. Little Joe sighed and aimed his horse in the same direction as Ben's.

They reached Ponderosa land in the Washoe Valley around mid-afternoon and began the climb into the mountains, gradually working their way into the scrub trees. The sunny warmth of the valley gave way to the shady cool of the mountains as the two Cartwrights moved under a canopy of towering trees, mostly sugar pines and the ranch's namesake ponderosa pines. Here and there patches of hard-packed snow hung like necklaces around the base of the thick trees, and the invigorating air was perfumed with the fragrance of pine.

About an hour before dusk, Ben turned off the trail that skirted the mountains and nudged his horse through thick carpets of snow. Little Joe didn't understand the purpose of all of this. Even if his father were taking him around Tahoe to the California logging camp, it would have been easier on the horses and themselves to stick to the trail.

The coolness of so much snow finally made Little Joe twist around in his saddle, untie his coat and slip it on.

Finally, Ben stopped on a level plot of ground halfway up the mountain. "We'll camp here for the night," he said as he dismounted. "I'll care for the horses. You gather as much wood as you can before dark."

"Sure, Pa," Little Joe said, shivering as a cool westerly breeze slipped unseen over the mountain. He tossed his father his reins and angled up the mountainside, gathering an armload of wood and returning it to camp before heading back for more. By the time Little Joe returned with his third armload, Ben had unsaddled and hobbled the horses, then built a fire. Ben wore his coat now and held his hands over the fire and a coffeepot.

"There's a tin of oysters, if you're hungry," Ben said, pointing to a canvas bag of supplies he had toted from Virginia City. The damp wood gave up a smoky wreath that circled the elder Cartwright, making him almost ghost-like against a clump of white snow on the hillside beyond him.

Little Joe took the tin and a can opener from the bag and ate supper. Ben handed him a cup of coffee when he was done. The coffee warmed him as it went down, but he shivered to think of the cold night ahead. Still, he wondered what all of this was about.

"There's still plenty of snow around," Ben

offered as he reached for a stick of wood Little Joe had piled nearby. Ben shoved the limb between a pair of boulders and pushed against it until it broke in a length suitable for the fire. "We need to break as much wood as we can to get us through the night."

Finishing his coffee, Little Joe stood up and began to split dead limbs like his father.

"That should last the night," Ben said, tossing a final length of wood onto a stack near the fire. "It'll be a cool night."

It didn't have to be, thought Little Joe. They could have spent the night at the ranch house and had Hop Sing cook them a hot breakfast before they headed to California.

Ben wrapped himself in his bedroll and said nothing more. Little Joe threw more wood on the fire, then made his own bed. In spite of the nearby fire, he slept cold and restless, waking several times to toss more wood on the flames. By sunrise the fire was nothing but glowing embers and Little Joe was shivering. He was glad when he heard his father stirring, and he quickly got up, stamping his feet and clapping his hands together against the cold.

Ben picked up his canteen and sloshed the water around inside. "Didn't even freeze last night," he announced.

"I did," Little Joe replied.

Ben coaxed enough of a fire from the glowing embers and the remaining wood to boil a pot of coffee which he shared with Little Joe.

Then the two men gathered their belongings, saddled their horses, and mounted up. Ben pointed to the mountaintop and started his yellow dun that way.

Little Joe steered his pinto into his father's wake. The patches of snow grew bigger until all the ground was carpeted with at least a thin layer. The encrusted snow crackled with each footfall of their mounts, and Little Joe tugged at his coat collar to keep the soft breeze from running down his chest and adding to the chill. Though the sun was climbing, only bits and pieces of warm light made it through the screen of pines that shrouded the mountaintop.

When they had finally reached the peak, Ben gently pulled the dun's reins and the gelding stopped. He looked west toward Lake Tahoe. "Your mother loved that lake, Joseph. She said there was no place prettier on earth."

Little Joe nodded, wishing he could remember his mother. Like each of his brothers, Little Joe had lost his mother in childhood. Though Ben had been lucky in life, he had been unlucky in love. Three sons by three women, not one of whom lived long enough to be remembered by her offspring. "She was right, Pa."

Ben nodded, then pointed to the south. There, at the foot of the mountain on which they sat, ended Ponderosa land. Beyond that invisible property line, the other mountains were denuded, naked in the morning light.

"Remember the Carson River," said Ben, "flooding this time of year and turning to a trickle in the fall?"

"Yes, sir," Little Joe answered, knowing the lesson he was about to receive was the purpose of this out-of-the-way trip.

"There's the reason," Ben said, a touch of sadness in his voice. "When the trees are cut down, there's no shade for the snow and no trees to block the westerly breezes. The first warm spell that comes along, all the snow melts."

Little Joe nodded.

"It melts quickly, Joseph, rather than the slow melt that can last into summer with tree cover." Ben pointed south again. "Look at those mountains. The quick melt erodes the mountains, carrying silt to the river."

"I never thought about that, Pa."

"That's why the logging operation is important to the Ponderosa. Is that how you want the Ponderosa to look in a few years?"

"No, sir."

"Then remember that when you get to the logging operation. It's a big responsibility that's important to the Ponderosa and keeping it as we know it. Think you can live up to the responsibility?"

"I'll give it my damnedest."

CHAPTER 5

For several miles Little Joe and his father followed the trail beside a great flume that clung to the mountainside like a giant wooden millipede. The thud of passing logs banging into the wooden trough rumbled through the mountain air like distant thunder. Occasionally, where the flume curved around the mountain, the descending logs would send a spray of water over the edge to drift across the trail and dampen the faces of Little Joe and Ben. In places the flume was notched to provide a throw gap so troublesome logs could be diverted from the trough into the ground below. Most logs, though, slid down the trough all the way to Lake Tahoe, there to be floated in great lumber barges to the Nevada side, then sent by another flume to the Carson River and the mills downstream.

On some mountains trees stood clumped like soldiers out of formation in brown puddles of snow. Other mountains lay stubbled with jagged stumps, naked beneath the afternoon sun which days ago had melted the winter snow. Occasionally in the narrow shadows of the stumps, Little Joe spotted a teardrop of snow, but mostly he saw eroded topsoil. The

79

sight made him value the virgin lands of the Ponderosa and appreciate the responsibility his father had placed upon his shoulders.

Before Little Joe saw the loggers, he could hear their work, the thwack of axes, the rasp of saws, the clank of chains, and now and then, the crack and crash of huge trees as they collapsed to the ground, rattling the earth. Gradually, Little Joe heard the distant cries and grunts of laboring men and the gee and haw of bull whackers guiding teams of oxen. Riding up a gentle incline, Little Joe and Ben topped out on a plateau, bisected by a dry streambed that paralleled the flume. The plateau abutted a mountain a quarter of a mile ahead. At the base of the mountain a huge earthen dam held back the headwaters that gradually fed the flume. Atop the wide dam, teams of oxen pulled giant logs that were rolled into the reservoir, then herded one by one into the flume.

At the base of the flume stood the logging camp itself, a disjointed collection of shanties, sheds, and three bunkhouses. On the opposite side of the flume was a barn and large corral where a dozen oxen stared at their approach. Beyond the camp and down the adjoining valley, Little Joe could see dozens of men at work on distant ponderosa pines or giant sugar pines.

Little Joe shook his head and turned to his father. "Pa, I don't know anything about logging. What can I do here?"

"Learn, Joseph," Ben replied. "You won't be ordering men around, that's the foreman's job. I just want you to oversee things, make sure all is handled in the best interest of Cartwright Enterprises."

Little Joe nodded, but knew his furrowed brow gave away his lack of confidence.

His father, though, seemed pleased by his doubts. "For once, Joseph, you recognize your limitations."

Little Joe grinned sheepishly. "You've taught me something on this trip, Pa."

"You mean about preserving Ponderosa timber?"

"No, Pa, about how cold spring nights can get in the Sierras."

For a moment Ben stared at Little Joe, and then his stone facade cracked into a wide grin.

"The other too," Little Joe added.

Father and son rode on past a signpost that had been knocked over, likely during the winter, by the look of the spring grass that was sprouting in the post hole. On the overturned sign was painted CARTWRIGHT ENTERPRISES.

Ben shook his head and pointed at the downed post. "Let's see that that sign is fixed."

"Yes, sir," Little Joe answered.

Reaching the camp, Little Joe sniffed the air, wriggled his nose, then picked up the aroma of fresh bread and cooling pies. He turned to Ben. "Smell that? I knew you should've sent Hoss up here. He could've guarded the food while I guarded Sara Ann Coffee."

Ben laughed as he reined up his horse in front of the camp's squat office. "That would've been the fox guarding the chickens here and in Virginia City." Dismounting, he took Little Joe's reins and his own and tied them to a metal ring embedded in a tree stump.

Little Joe slid out of his saddle and stretched his arms and legs as he studied the camp that would be his home for a while. Beyond the camp office were three long wooden bunkhouses, windowless and dark. Stovepipes at the end of each bunkhouse spewed wood smoke and the aroma of supper. In addition to three shanties for the foreman and his two assistants, the other buildings were toolsheds, storage huts, a blacksmith shop, a harness shed, a laundry shack, and outhouses. Little Joe watched a dozen or more pigs, all with narrow hocks and small bellies, scavenging among the buildings.

"Not enough bacon on those pigs to make Hoss a good breakfast, Pa," Little Joe said with a toss of his head.

Ben nodded just as the door of the camp office swung open.

A man the size of an ox emerged, the frown on his lips accentuated by his drooping handlebar mustache. His shoulders were as wide as an axe handle and his arms thicker than the hocks on those skinny pigs. With dark eyes he studied Ben and Little Joe, then planted his balled fists on his narrow hips. He scowled at Ben, then spat a stream of muddy tobacco juice toward Little Joe.

"What brings Ben Cartwright out here?"

"Nat Greer, isn't it?" Ben asked. "My son Adam says you're the foreman."

"That's right, I'm the bull of the woods, the one in charge," Greer said, his frown deepening.

Ben pointed his thumb over his shoulder at the overturned signpost. "See that our sign is fixed, if you're the boss."

Greer licked his lips slowly. "Tomorrow. I'll see to it when my men aren't exhausted from a full day's work. You ride all the way up here just to tell me that?"

Studying Nat Greer, Ben Cartwright shook his head. "From now on," answered Ben, "you'll report to my son Joseph instead of Adam."

"Just call me Little Joe," said the youngest Cartwright, extending his hand.

Greer spat more tobacco juice, but ignored Little Joe's outstretched hand. "Don't matter to me who I report to," he replied. "You should've sent word by the mail rider. Foolish both of you riding up here just to tell me that."

Now Ben smiled. "I'll be heading back in the morning, but Little Joe's staying with the operation."

Nat Greer's face reddened and his eyes

boiled with anger. He answered with a single word that came as a growl from his throat. "What?"

"Little Joe's to oversee the timber operation, learn logging."

"I ain't got time to nursemaid junior here." Greer glared at Little Joe.

"Find time or find another job," said Ben, standing with feet wide apart and his arms across his chest. Ever since he was a sailor in his younger days, Ben knew how to stare down a man. That could mean survival on a ship at sea, for there was no place to run on the ocean.

Greer's anger softened around the edges but never disappeared. The edginess was smoothed over with a look of chicanery. This was a man, thought Little Joe, who could not be trusted.

Slowly, Nat Greer nodded, his lips straining under a forced smile that was not reflected in the darkness of his eyes. "Logging's dangerous work," he said, more as a threat than a caution. "A man can get hurt once he leaves camp." Greer glanced back over his shoulder at the office door, where a slender man in wire-rimmed glasses had appeared. At Greer's glimpse, the man evaporated inside. "We can give you a broom, let you sweep up the bunkhouses."

"I'm here to supervise," said Little Joe adamantly.

Greer shrugged with a sinister sneer. "You're the boss, but I'm the bull of the woods. I decide where crews cut and what they cut. The men answer to me, not to you. They take my orders, not yours."

"That okay with you, Pa?" Little Joe asked.

Ben pursed his lips, studying Greer intensely. "A man needs only one boss, and Greer'll be it as long as he understands he answers to you."

"We've one boss too many now," grumbled Greer, who spun around and started for the nearest bunkhouse. He stopped suddenly, then called over his shoulder. "It okay, boss, if I check the cooks before I head back into the woods to see that the men work until quitting time?"

"Go ahead," Little Joe called, then grinned at his father. "Let me know if you need my help."

Greer stalked away, his profane mumblings audible but indecipherable.

Ben stood silent, watching. "He's a dangerous man, Joseph. Watch out for him."

Little Joe lifted his hat and ran his fingers through his brown hair. "He's an ornery one." As he spoke, Little Joe, out of the corner of his eye, glimpsed a rail of a man standing just inside the office door, the one with wire-rimmed glasses who had appeared briefly before. Little Joe nodded. "Howdy."

The man stuck his head outside, first looking to see if Greer was nearby, then marching outside, his hand outstretched, his smile as friendly as his eyes. "C. C. Livermore's the name. I'm what they call the 'ink slinger.' I keep up with the books, the payroll, and the logging records."

Little Joe grabbed Livermore's hand and shook it warmly as he studied the bookkeeper. Barely five feet tall, he was a mere bug compared to Nat Greer, and he stood with his chin thrown back as he looked up at Little Joe through his glasses. His soft grip was that of a man who spent his time with pencil instead of axe, and his pale skin that of an indoor rather than outdoor man.

As Little Joe released Livermore's hand, the bookkeeper turned to Ben and spoke with reverence. "I wondered how long it would take someone with your business mind to send his own man up here to oversee things." Livermore kept glancing over his shoulder in the direction that Greer had disappeared. The bookkeeper shook Ben's hand vigorously. "Yes, sir, I'm glad to meet you, and know that ultimately I work for an honest man."

"Perhaps we should have a talk," Ben answered as he released Livermore's hand.

The bookkeeper glimpsed back over his shoulder again and froze at the sight of Greer staring back at him. Livermore paled and his lip trembled. "No, sir, Mr. Cartwright, I've probably said too much already." With that,

Livermore retreated into the office.

Then Greer turned away and marched toward the thudding noise of axes and the rasping sounds of saws.

"Something odd's going on here," Little Joe said.

Ben nodded. "That's what Adam thought, though he couldn't put his finger on it. That's why Adam and I wanted you here, Joseph."

Little Joe jerked his head around toward his father. "Adam wanted me here?"

"It was his idea, Joseph."

Little Joe shook his head in disbelief. "I never figured he would trust me with anything."

Ben smiled. "Adam's always thought you had the brains for it, but not the commitment. Sure, you could learn a few things from Adam, but he could learn some from you about taking time to enjoy life."

For once in his life Little Joe felt on an equal footing with Adam, even though he knew Adam had the better business mind. Still, it was comforting to think his oldest brother had faith in him. Little Joe took a deep breath and felt his chest swell with pleasure.

"Don't just prove to *us* you can handle the responsibility, Joseph, prove it to *yourself* as well. That's just as important."

"Yes, sir," Little Joe replied.

A moment of silence passed between them, reaffirming an unspoken bond between father and son. As Ben stepped away from Little Joe, C. C. Livermore poked his head out of the office. "You're staying the night, aren't you Mr. Cartwright?" the bookkeeper asked Ben.

Ben nodded.

"Supper's at nine. Eat at the first or second bunkhouse," Livermore said, lowering his voice and pointing at the nearest two barracks, "but not the third. Greer keeps his special crew there. Little Joe, make your bunk in the bunkhouse, not in one of the shanties, and especially not if Greer offers you a bed." Livermore's head disappeared back inside the office.

Though both Cartwrights had questions about Livermore's instructions, neither said anything. Ben pointed to the corral, and both men untied their horses and walked them toward the stock pens, passing beneath the flume and reaching the corral just behind a bull whacker with a yoke of oxen.

"Evening," Ben said. "Mind if we put up our horses for the night and give them a little feed?"

"Fine with me," answered the bull whacker, "but you best get Nat Greer's okay first."

"I'm Ben Cartwright and this is my son, Joseph. This is our camp."

The bull whacker grinned. "Then I guess you're about the only men around here that don't have to get Greer's okay to spit." The bull whacker extended his hand to Ben. "Roe

Derus is the name." Derus stood six feet tall and seemed as sincere as his smile. He had a close-cropped beard and graying hair that topped his broad, powerful physique.

Derus opened the gate, then whistled. "Yi-hi," he yelled, and the yoke of oxen trod past him, followed by Ben and Little Joe leading their horses. "Feed's in the barn, and a couple empty stalls as well." The bull whacker closed the gate behind him, then proceeded to remove the yoke from the oxen.

Ben and Little Joe led their mounts into the barn and, shortly, Derus joined them, driving a gray ox with drooping head. "There's plenty of hay in the far corner," Derus offered as he maneuvered the ox into a stall, then wedged a plank behind the animal to prevent its escape. Derus quickly began to curry down the animal, paying close attention to the shoulders for sore spots and the neck for blisters. "A man has to keep the collars clean and watch for loose harness rivets that can rub a cut into the hide," he explained. "With the loads these animals pull, you've got to keep them healthy."

After unsaddling and rubbing down his yellow dun, Ben carried a couple of pitchfork loads of hay to the animal's trough, and walked over to the bull whacker. Draping his arm over the stall walls, Ben studied Derus's gentle work.

"You sound like you don't enjoy working for

Nat Greer," Ben said.

Derus shrugged. "He lacks a lot for a bull of the woods."

"Then why d'you stay?" asked Little Joe as he walked up beside his father.

Derus looked over the ox's back at Little Joe and studied him a moment. "Skinny pigs," Derus answered.

"Huh?" asked Little Joe.

"When pigs are so skinny they look like ugly dogs, it tells you the cooks don't throw out much food. Skinny pigs tells me the cooks make a good spread on the table."

"But Greer?" asked Ben.

"I do my job and mind my own business. Let's just say Greer plays favorites. The crew in the number three bunkhouse he works separate from everybody else."

"What about —" Little Joe began, when Ben grabbed his arm.

"Thanks for leveling with us," Ben said to Derus, then glanced at Little Joe. "It's time we look around camp and find us a place to bunk."

"You two fellows don't talk too loud around here," Derus warned. "Sometimes it's like the trees have ears."

"Thanks again," Ben said as he turned to leave, Little Joe right behind him.

They emerged into the murky light of dusk and said nothing until they reached the flume. Then, standing beside one of the high trough's spindly legs, Ben whispered instructions to Little Joe.

"We've a crew of a hundred twenty men at this camp," he said, "and Adam's not sure they all put in a good day's work, no more timber than we're getting out of this lease. He wants you to give him an estimate on the time it takes to cut down a pine and the average size of the trees they're chopping."

"How come, Pa?"

"It's information Adam needs to evaluate what kind of job they're doing and what they're capable of doing."

Little Joe made a mental note of Adam's questions.

"Send the information by the first mail rider you can. After we get it, we'll make decisions about who runs the camp."

What Little Joe had first seen as just an excuse to get him out of Virginia City was taking on real importance. As he thought of the responsibility, he realized something had changed in the air. The noise of axes and saws had stopped. The crews were coming in for the night. From the north, men came in by wagon over a road that angled by the reservoir.

These men seemed birthed by a separate human race. They were big and muscled and, by this time of day, exhausted. Over their broad shoulders they carried their tools and chains. In their hands they held springboards or cans of lubricants. The spikes on the soles of their caulked boots kicked up dust as they walked along the worn trails, raising a brown fog that gave the loggers a ghostly appearance in the failing light of day.

Little Joe and his father walked under the flume and headed toward the second bunkhouse. As they drew closer, several men began to point at them. As they passed a pair of loggers, Little Joe heard one of them mention Ben as the man who paid their wages.

One by one the men finished washing up and marched inside the bunkhouse. Little Joe and Ben went in with them.

The building was long and dark, the front half crammed with bunks. Behind a rough wooden partition was the dining room, and beyond it was the kitchen. The tables were piled high with roasts, flapjacks, potatoes, bread, and pies.

Little Joe grinned. "This would be heaven for Hoss."

"Not quite," answered Ben. "Too much competition for plates."

Little Joe laughed as he slid onto a bench at the corner of the nearest table, Ben taking a seat across from him. The more men that walked into the room, the quieter it seemed to become. Little Joe glanced at the fellow who had taken a place beside him. "I'm Little Joe Cartwright." He offered his hand to the logger.

The logger turned and shook his hand

briefly. "No talking at the table," the logger whispered.

Little Joe regarded him with a puzzled look.

"This is the time to fill up, not swap stories," the logger whispered, looking around to make sure no one was watching. "As long as there's no talking, there's no complaining about the food. That keeps the cook happy." The logger nodded. "I'm Jack Chaney."

The moment he said his name, Chaney froze and sat stiffly on his bench. Little Joe studied Chaney's honest face and his muscled arms, then glanced at the dining hall door. There stood Nat Greer, his arms crossed over his chest, his dark brooding eyes as threatening as storm clouds.

Late-entering loggers slipped meekly past Greer and took places around the room, not saying a single word or grinning at a soul.

Satisfied that all the men were present, Nat Greer stepped down the aisle between the two rows of tables. "Men," he bellowed, "I'd like you to meet Little Joe Cartwright." Greer motioned for Little Joe to stand.

Embarrassed, Little Joe rose from his seat and nodded around the room.

"Now, Little Joe is representing Cartwright Enterprises and its head man, Ben Cartwright, his pa, who's also with us." Greer's flinty eyes stared at the two Cartwrights. "Old man Cartwright'll be leaving tomorrow."

As Little Joe sat down, he saw the anger in his father's eyes.

Greer sneered at the two Cartwrights. "But Little Joe is staying with us. He's going to be my boss."

A chorus of laughter arose around the room, and Little Joe, his face flush with anger, started to rise.

"Joseph," said Ben, "don't let him rile you."

Little Joe slid back down on the bench. Beside him he heard Jack Chaney's whisper.

"Nobody cares for Greer except the crew in the number three bunkhouse. He eats with them and works them at a different site from the rest of us."

"Tomorrow," Greer threatened, "we'll see what kind of man Little Joe is." The foreman spun around and marched out of the dining hall.

Little Joe thought he heard several sighs of relief, but he could not be certain, especially as he looked down the table at huge platters of roast meat and giant bowls of baked beans or potatoes among lesser bowls and plates of greens, hotcakes, oatmeal, dried fruits, camp-baked bread, cookies, puddings, and pies. This was a table spread that Hoss could appreciate, and these were men carved from the same timber as Hoss, big powerful men, though leaner and, by their looks, meaner than his amiable giant of a brother. Other than the bookkeeper, C. C. Livermore, Little Joe figured he was the smallest man in camp.

The cook came out of the kitchen and banged a skillet with a metal spoon. Instantly the men began to fill their tin plates with food and their tin cups with coffee. They ate without speaking, though it was anything but silent, not with the clink of their forks and knives against the tin plates.

Little Joe and Ben took moderate helpings of meat, bread, and potatoes, and a few refills of coffee. Both finished the meal off with a thick slice of apple pie.

"You fellas should eat up," whispered Jack Chaney. "After all, you're paying for it."

"Where can we stay the night?" Little Joe asked.

Jack Chaney nodded. "There's room in this bunkhouse, if you can tolerate the lice."

"It beats Greer," Little Joe replied.

When Chaney stood up from the table, he whispered to Little Joe, "You be careful around Greer."

"Why?" Little Joe asked back.

"He's a hard man." Chaney hid his lips behind his uplifted coffee cup.

"I'll watch my step."

"And," warned Chaney, "don't hang around me too much. Greer'd get suspicious I'm talking about him. That would be dangerous for both of us."

CHAPTER 6

Well before five o'clock the cook got up to start breakfast. By the time Nat Greer barged in the door at six, the bunkhouse was filled with the aroma of flapjacks, bacon, and biscuits.

"Get up, you lazy sons of bitches, you've work to do," Greer growled. "You too, Cartwright, if you're gonna learn logging."

Little Joe arose slowly and saw his father on the adjacent bunk, pulling on his boots. "Last night reminded me of my sailing days," Ben said. "I'd forgotten how loud tired men can snore."

Ben and Little Joe washed their faces before treading to the breakfast table. All around them loggers stretched and yawned until the cook entered and banged an iron skillet with a metal spoon. Instantly they attacked the food, gobbling it down greedily, then shoved away from the tables and marched outside. By the time Little Joe and Ben had finished their breakfast, the cook's helpers were clearing the tables. Outside, Ben and Little Joe watched the loggers, saws and axes on their shoulders, climb into wagons that would carry them into the woods.

Ben pointed at the wagons. "Last night they walked in after a hard day. If Greer can provide wagons to get them to work, he can see they have wagons to get back to camp. Make sure he does that, Joseph, and has the sign fixed."

"Sure thing, Pa," answered Little Joe, still stretching and yawning as they marched past bunkhouse number three and the hard crew that was loading in wagons there. Like Greer, this crew wore malicious scowls as Little Joe and Ben walked by.

Little Joe shivered at the spray of water that doused his face as he walked beneath the flume and angled for the corral. Ben stopped midway between the flume and the barn, where bull whackers were yoking oxen for another hard day of work.

"Remember, Joseph, to send Adam his information as soon as you can. We're paying for three crews of forty men. That doesn't count the foreman, his assistants, the cooks, the teamsters, the blacksmith, and the boys that handle the odd chores."

"Sure thing, Pa."

"And, Joseph, watch out for Greer. He's a hard man and this is mean work. A lot of ways a man can get hurt from it."

Little Joe grinned. "It goes with the responsibility."

Ben laughed and started for the barn, Little Joe at his side. They found Roe Derus in the stall saddling Ben's yellow dun.

"Morning," Derus said, "I heard you were leaving, Mr. Cartwright, so I figured you wouldn't mind me tending your mount."

Ben smiled. "I'm grateful."

"You be careful on the return trip," Derus said to Ben as he cinched down the saddle. Derus nodded to Little Joe. "You watch out for things around here too."

Little Joe shook his head. "Seems the few who'll talk to me are all saying that."

Derus led Ben's horse out of the stall. "Nat Greer doesn't like someone looking over his shoulder." He offered the reins to Ben.

Taking the leather bands, Ben walked the dun outside and mounted. With his lips tight and his eyes narrowed, he studied his youngest son for a moment. "You take care."

"Yes, sir, Pa," answered Little Joe as Ben aimed his gelding toward Lake Tahoe.

Little Joe watched his father ride beside the flume until he disappeared down the slope. Little Joe knew he was now actually in charge of the camp, if not the men. And while he never remembered feeling prouder, he was never any more unsure of himself. Could he deal with these hard men, Nat Greer especially, and could he provide the information Adam needed?

As he stood mired in his thoughts, he heard a growl behind him. "Did you come here to learn the logging business or to stare at the scenery?"

Slowly, Little Joe turned around to find Nat Greer with legs apart and balled hands on his hips, his jutting chin defiant.

"You're free to go with crew number one or number two," Greer said. "I oversee crew number three. They're cutting in rugged terrain that's more dangerous for a babe in the woods like yourself."

"I thought I was your boss, Greer," said Little Joe, stretching to his full height to answer Greer's challenge.

"You got any orders?" Greer mocked.

Little Joe nodded. "A couple. Why do the men get wagon rides to the work sites in the morning?"

Greer smirked. "To get their butts to chopping timber as soon as possible."

"And why don't they get rides back in the evening?"

Greer laughed. "Once it's too dark to work, it's not my problem how they get back."

"It is now," answered Little Joe. He spotted Roe Derus standing nearby, catching every word. "From now on, send wagons for them at dusk, even if you have to drive them yourself."

Then Little Joe pointed to the overturned sign. "See that the post is set today on that sign."

Greer's scowl deepened at this second order. He spat. "Cocky little son of a bitch, ain't you? You just remember you ain't got your pappy here to look out for you now." Greer tried to cow Little Joe with his hard gaze.

Little Joe felt the withering glare, but it made him buck up. He was a Cartwright, and he was not about to back down from a man of Greer's ilk.

Realizing the futility of his intimidation, Greer shook his head. "Which crew, number one or number two, are you going out with, so I can notify the crew boss?"

The bull whacker Roe Derus stepped forward. "He told me he was going with me for the day."

Greer nodded. "Just make sure he stays out of the way of me and my men, Roe."

Derus shrugged. "That won't be a problem."

Greer took a couple steps toward camp, then stopped and turned around. "And remember, Roe, nobody goes with the number three crew unless I say so."

"I know the rules, Nat."

Greer strode angrily away.

"Obliged," Little Joe said.

"The foremen on both crews are Greer's men. You'll be better learning a few things from me than them. Once I get a team of oxen hooked up, we'll head out." Derus disappeared into the barn.

Little Joe walked over to the fence and propped his arms on the top rail, watching the sky as a good morning light began to take hold. The warmth of the soft light began to ease the morning chill. Gradually, in the distance, the noise of axes and saws began to pick up.

Shortly, Roe Derus whistled and a team of oxen trod out of the barn, six yokes in all, strung together. "Get the gate, Little Joe," Derus ordered. "Gee, gee," he yelled at the team, and the animals moved to the right, straight for the gate.

After the team had passed, Little Joe shut and latched the gate, then jumped in beside the bull whacker, who controlled the team by his whistle and his language, "gee" meaning right and "haw" meaning left. Little Joe had never seen a team this large handled so precisely. "You're good at this."

"Feed your animals well and make sure they don't get sores, and they'll take to training and work. Haw, haw," he called. The team skirted the camp, then hit the trail the loggers had followed into the tall trees.

For half a mile the trail wound around jagged stumps before straightening out and moving into the trees. By his voice and whistle, Derus maneuvered the team adroitly ahead until the trail split in two directions.

"The upper road goes to number one's site and the lower to number two's," Derus said matter-of-factly. "They're both pretty good crews."

"What about crew number three?" Little Joe asked.

Derus shrugged. "Gee, gee," he yelled, then

said, "As bad a collection of thugs as you'll find in the woods. Probably a good thing Greer keeps them apart from the rest of the men."

The thud of axes and the grind of saws grew sharper, and the sounds of men grunting at hard labor mingled with the noise of their tools. As the oxen trod down the lower trail, Derus explained the operation.

Two-man crews of cutters, he said, work together on every tree, first notching out an undercut and then chopping into the timber from the other side until the tree falls under its own weight. A good faller, as they were called, could position a stake in the ground, then drop a tree atop it. Because the swell at the base of a sugar or ponderosa pine was often great, the fallers would cut into a tree head high or higher. To reach that far up a tree, fallers carried a five-foot-long, eight-inch-wide metal-tipped springboard which they drove into the side of the tree for a narrow perch from which to attack the trunk. Danger was constant. A misstep and the faller could tumble to the ground. A solid swing of the axe might jar a dead limb — appropriately called a widow maker — loose from its tenuous hold overhead to crash down upon the ax man. When a logger miscalculated or failed to jump in time, the falling tree could crush or maim him.

The fallers had to have stamina for a day of swinging a four-foot, straight-handled western axe with a narrow, double-bitted, three-pound blade at its head. The fallers were known not only for their stamina and their accuracy in pinpointing the direction of a fall, but also for their accuracy with an axe. A smooth undercut was especially important because a rough cut could cause the tree to twist as it fell, jarring it off target, endangering men for hundreds of feet around.

"Timmmm-berrrr," came a cry down the skid road, and Little Joe looked up in time to see a giant sugar pine begin to topple. He heard the crack of splintering timber and the swish of the accelerating tree as it plummeted to earth. The tree hit the ground and bounced up, shaking the earth all around.

"That was Jack Chaney's tree," Derus said. "I can tell by the voice."

"How long does it take to chop a tree?" Little Joe asked.

"Depends," said Derus as he aimed the oxen at a line of downed trees. "A ponderosa pine can grow four foot or more in diameter and a hundred fifty feet tall, while a sugar pine can grow seven to eight foot across and up to a hundred seventy-five foot high. A broad sugar pine can take a crew all day, while a ponderosa could take four or five hours from the time the chips start flying until the dust settles."

Little Joe would remember those figures so he could relay them to Adam.

"These are mostly ponderosa pines, so a

day's work ought to average out at a little over two trees per crew," Derus said. As he maneuvered the oxen around, then backed them to a downed tree, Derus explained the duties of the other men.

Buckers, he said, were men who attacked downed trees with eight-foot saws to cut the timber into designated lengths, depending on their intended use. Most of the wood on this lease was intended for shoring in the mines and cut in sixteen-foot lengths. Other uses might require lengths of twenty-four, thirty-two, or forty feet.

After the buckers finished their work, the choke setters took over, attaching cables and chains to the tree segments. The choke setters helped the bull whacker hitch the logs to the team. Skid greasers carried pails of grease and swabs to spread lubricant over the wooden skids buried at twelve-foot intervals along the trail, so no matter where a team might stop along the trail, the logs rested on at least two skids.

Roe Derus backed the team up to the logs, and the choke setters hooked the chains to the oxen rig. Derus whistled and the oxen strained against their yokes. A couple of animals slipped until the huge log budged and began to slide forward, the skid greasers darting from skid to skid to do their job.

"Haw, haw, haw," yelled Derus as he started back to the camp and the flume which would send the logs hurtling toward Lake Tahoe. Little Joe tagged along behind the bull whacker, amazed at how Derus could steer the oxen. "It's monotonous work," said Derus, "up here and back for the logs, walking the same old trail over and over again."

Glancing back over his shoulder, Little Joe saw that not just one, but a half-dozen lengths, all chained together, were being pulled by the oxen.

On the way back to camp, Derus directed the oxen up a high trail that led out onto the earthen dam holding back the headwaters for the flume. Atop the dam stood loggers Derus identified as loaders and pigs. The pigs carried peavey sticks, long poles with a hinged hook attached to a metal spike, for shepherding logs in the reservoir and lining them up for the flume. The pigs balanced atop floating logs and aimed them for the chute like an artillery-man providing shells for a breech-loading cannon. Loaders at the flume chute positioned the logs, then released them for their run to Lake Tahoe.

When Derus brought the log train to a stop, the logs were perfectly aligned along the rim of the reservoir. The skid greasers put down their pails and swabs and began to unhook the oxen rig and remove chains from around the logs. Meanwhile, one logger used an odd-shaped tool to strike the end of each log. Little Joe couldn't explain the purpose of the long-handled tool, which the logger swung like an axe. However, instead of a blade at its head, this tool had a metal triangle at the end. Once when the logger threw the tool aside, Little Joe sauntered over and picked it up. He was surprised at what he saw, a replica of the Ponderosa brand. A vertical rail with two angular rails spreading out from the top point out toward the bottom. This was the Ponderosa brand, made to represent the ponderosa pine. Like the brand on a new calf, the mark on the end of the log determined ownership. This log belonged to Cartwright Enterprises. Once Derus moved the team out of the way, pigs and skid greasers tied into each log individually with a pulley chain and rolled the timber into water.

Little Joe followed Derus back down the trail toward the timber cutting. What was surely a monotonous morning to Roe Derus was an education for Little Joe. The lesson in logging was interrupted only by lunch, which was brought out in wagons to the loggers. As with all meals, the loggers ate quickly and without conversation. Joe trailed Derus all afternoon, picking up more and more about the timber business, and all the time feeling there was so much more to learn. Little Joe's only rest came when the choke setters were hooking up timber to the team or when Derus would take a break and visit with loggers beyond Little Joe's hearing.

Gradually, more and more men tossed Little Joe casual smiles. If it wasn't acceptance by them, it was at least tolerance.

Come dusk, Little Joe had lost count of the round trips he had walked with Derus. His muscles ached from the exertion, and his feet hurt most of all. His boots were made for working in the saddle, not for walking on mountainside skid roads. After the final load, Little Joe followed Derus to the corrals.

"Head on back to the bunkhouse and get the hitch out of your gait," Derus said. "Maybe tomorrow we can find you a pair of logging boots."

Little Joe shook his head. "I figure the least I can do is help with the oxen."

Derus slowly shook his head. "No, sir, you've done more than you'll ever realize."

Little Joe shrugged. "What are you talking about?"

"Nothing," Derus said, "just let me tend my animals. It takes me longer than the other bull whackers because I'm particular with my animals."

Little Joe grinned as he opened the corral gate. "I've learned not to argue with a stubborn man."

"Especially not a stubborn man as hungry as me," replied Derus, waving Little Joe back toward the bunkhouse. "See you later."

Little Joe ambled to camp, passing under the flume. As he neared the number three bunkhouse, he noticed something that sent the anger rising in him. The sign at the head of the camp had not been repaired, as he had instructed Greer.

Forgetting his soreness, he picked up his pace, glancing around for Greer. Just as Little Joe reached the number two bunkhouse, a wagon filled with loggers arrived and began to unload. One of the workers spotted Little Joe.

"Let's hear it for Little Joe Cartwright," he yelled.

"Hip, hip, hurrah," they shouted in unison. "Hip, hip, hurrah!"

Little Joe was taken aback. What was going on? No sooner had the question entered his mind than several loggers were upon him, shaking his hand. A second wagon pulled up, and men from bunkhouse number one unloaded and joined the rest of the men in thanking Little Joe.

Still, Little Joe did not understand until Jack Chaney explained. "The men appreciate you ordering Greer to send wagons for us in the evenings. That's been a sore spot with us ever since we signed on, especially since the number three crew always had a wagon to ride in."

Little Joe didn't know what to think about the number three crew. Maybe Greer gave them the ride because their work was in more rugged terrain and perhaps more dangerous.

Maybe he just liked number three better.

Virtually all the men from the number one and number two crews shook hands with Little Joe or patted him on the back. Gradually they wandered away to drop off their axes and saws at the blacksmith shop for sharpening, to wash their faces, or to collapse into bed for a few restful moments before supper.

Little Joe remained outside, looking for Nat Greer. Seeing nothing of the foreman, he retreated to bunkhouse number two and washed his hands and face at the line of washbasins on a shelf outside the door.

As tired as he was, it took great effort to put one leg in front of the other and march past the bunks and into the dining hall. As before, the more people who entered, the quieter the room became. When it was almost full and the coffeepots had been scattered around the tables, the cook entered the room, banged his metal skillet, and smiled as the loggers attacked his fare. Little Joe had a hardier appetite than last night, and now understood why these men could polish off so much food in so little time. Little Joe ate twice what he had the night before and didn't feel the worse for it. When he was done, he eased back into the bunk room and began to pull off his boots on the deacon's bench at the foot of his bunk. He rubbed his socked feet and considered having the cook heat him a pail of water he could soak his feet in, but decided the loggers would think him soft.

As he massaged his feet, a man stepped up in the lantern light and dropped a pair of logging boots at his feet. Little Joe looked up and saw Roe Derus. "See if those'll fit well enough to get you by."

"Obliged," Little Joe answered as he gingerly put his feet inside. The caulked, or spiked, boots were a little loose, though Little Joe thought he could solve that problem by tying the leather laces tighter. "They'll do just fine."

Derus nodded and marched over to his bunk, just as Jack Chaney marched in and took a seat near Little Joe.

"You gonna start felling trees tomorrow?" He grinned.

"I ache too much to even laugh at that," Little Joe replied, removing the logging boots and massaging his toes again.

"That's a logger's life."

"Why'd you take it up?" Little Joe asked.

"A man's gotta eat."

"Why'd you join this outfit? I gather Greer's not liked by many loggers."

"Greer's reputation is bad, but the Cartwright name's always been good in these parts. I heard Cartwright Enterprises was paying a dollar and a half a day, but I heard wrong."

Little Joe scratched his head. "Cartwrights don't go back on their word."

Chaney shrugged. "Somebody did. All I get is a dollar a day, same as everybody else in this room. At least the Cartwright camp doesn't charge for room and board like some camps. The things I could . . ." The words died on Chaney's lips when the door banged open and Nat Greer walked in with two men behind him.

"Where's Cartwright?" demanded Greer.

A couple of loggers pointed at Little Joe, and Greer strode in that direction, his two henchmen following him.

"Cartwright," said Greer, "from now on, you go to the work sites with one of our supervisors." The two men stepped beside him. Greer pointed to the taller of the two. "This is Ben Tull. He's in charge of the number one crew. The other here is Ted Karnes, who's in command of this bunkhouse. They can teach you all you need to know about logging."

"Who's in charge of the number three crew?" Little Joe asked.

Anger seemed to flare in Greer. "I am."

"I want to go out with you, then."

"Too dangerous," Greer said, shaking his head. "You go with who I say you go with."

Little Joe shook his head. "You're forgetting I'm giving you the orders, not the other way around."

"I'm in charge of the men," Greer shot back.

"But I'm in charge of you," Little Joe replied. He stood up to meet Greer's challenge. "I told

111

you this morning to repair the sign out front. Why wasn't it fixed?"

"My men were too busy."

"Then you fix it."

Greer scowled and stepped toward Little Joe. "I've had about enough of your cockiness." Greer lifted his fists.

Little Joe grinned, but wondered how long he could survive against a man Greer's size. Before he had to answer that question, Tull and Karnes each grabbed one of Greer's arms.

"Back off, Nat," Karnes said, "you've got too much to lose beating up the owner's kid."

Little Joe didn't back down. "Let him loose, let him fight."

Greer backed away and shook his arms free from Tull and Karnes.

Little Joe pointed his index finger at Greer's nose. "Fix that sign before dawn. Either do it yourself or have one of the men from bunkhouse number three do it."

Greer twisted about and stormed out the door. Behind him, the loggers congratulated Little Joe and talked until bedtime about the incident.

Come morning, Little Joe stepped outside the bunkhouse and looked toward the rutted approach to camp. Someone had replanted the signpost overnight. Little Joe smiled.

CHAPTER 7

Somehow it seemed appropriate that Ben stop by her grave. After all, it was her son he had left in the Sierras beyond Lake Tahoe. He dismounted reverently and tied his yellow dun to graze on the fine spring grass that made a green velvet carpet in the clearing. Ben took off his hat before he walked the last fifty yards to the top of the knoll where he had buried Little Joe's mother, Marie. She had loved this view as much as she had loved the Ponderosa, and she loved the Ponderosa almost as much as she loved Little Joe and his older brothers.

Ben saw the simple stone that marked her grave, and his fingers tightened around the brim of his hat. How could a man be so lucky to have had three wives as different and as loving as Marie and Inger and Elizabeth? How could a man have been so unlucky as to lose each one? For all the success that Ben had managed in life, he could not understand why he had failed to keep a wife much beyond the birth of a son. He sometimes wondered if those sons had not yet married out of fear that early death was the natural fate of Cartwright women.

Though Ben had aged, Marie survived forever young in his memory, a dark-haired beauty. He saw much of her in Little Joe's smile, his lively eyes, his engaging laugh and his hard-headedness. Ben approached the grave, the late afternoon sun casting his long shadow across the simple marker. He wanted to tell her about his worries and admit his fears for Little Joe back in the logging camp, even if it was a decision that had to be made. For Little Joe's own good and his success as a man, he had to learn to accept responsibility. Little Joe didn't have to work, nor did Hoss, nor Adam. Since the Bristlecone had struck the Big Bonanza, the Cartwright fortune was multiplied beyond Ben's wildest expectations. But great wealth brought greater responsibility, and Ben knew he must prepare Little Joe for that responsibility.

Ben wanted to tell Marie all, but he knew there was no need. She would know. He felt a wisp of a breeze against his face and knew it was Marie's caress. He heard the call of a songbird he did not recognize and knew it was Marie's sprightly answer. She would watch after Little Joe even when he couldn't, Ben thought.

He smiled at the memory and at the veil of spring flowers that covered her grave. The colors were as bright as her personality and the petals soft as her manner. Ben turned away, fighting back a tear for all three of his wives and ever grateful that each had left a living monument to her life through the son she had borne into this world. Ben felt honored to have shared each woman's love and each woman's son.

As he walked back to his dun, Ben heard the songbird's trill and saw a flash of yellow, Marie's favorite color, as the bird flew from a high branch back into the shadows of the tall trees. He let the gelding graze a few more minutes before mounting and turning toward the ranch house. Though these visits to Marie's grave were tinged with sadness, they also revived the many good memories, and Ben smiled as he thought of her all the way back to the ranch house, the home that Marie had wanted but had never seen completed.

No sooner did Ben dismount and tie the reins to the hitching rail than the door from the kitchen flew open and Hop Sing darted out, his loose blouse and baggy pants bouncing with each stride.

Hop Sing bowed his head. "Hop Sing glad you return, Mr. Ben. Much excitement in your absence. Three men come, ask for you."

Ben felt a shiver run up his spine. The trio could only have been the Wharton brothers returned to avenge their father's death.

"Mean men," Hop Sing continued, breathlessly fast, "steal three horses. No one else around. I cannot stop them. Stay inside with shotgun."

"Good job, Hop Sing," Ben said, shaking the cook's hand. "Nothing else you could have done."

"Hop Sing try, Mr. Ben, but Hop Sing scared."

Ben nodded as he glanced toward the barn. "They stole horses from our corral?"

Hop Sing nodded. "And saddles, Mr. Ben, they took saddles."

Ben looked at the sun sinking behind the mountains across Lake Tahoe. He must get word to Roy Coffee back in Virginia City, but it was too late to get there before dark. Were the Whartons still on the ranch or had they headed for Virginia City? Ben didn't know, but he did know they were bound to return for revenge. Bad seeds don't fall far from the tree, and the Whartons were the definite progeny of their old man.

"I'll stay the night here, Hop Sing, then leave for Virginia City in the morning. I've got to let Sheriff Coffee know."

Hoss pushed himself back from the table and patted his stomach after another good meal. "Hmmmmm, you sure know how to cook."

Sara Ann tossed her head, her auburn hair bouncing sprightly, and smiled. "You make a woman feel good the way you put away her cooking."

"Maybe so, Sara Ann, but your cooking is

about the best I've ever had."

Sara Ann looked at the single slice of pie remaining in the pan. "Sure you don't want the final piece of cherry pie?"

At first Hoss shook his head, then finally nodded his change of heart and stomach. "Maybe just part of it."

With the pie server in hand, Sara Ann scooped out the remaining piece of pie, its golden crust glistening like frost with sugar, and pushed it off on Hoss's plate. "Just take it all, Hoss."

He needed no more encouragement.

"Mind if I ask you something, Hoss?" she said. Her smile was as inviting as her cherry pie.

"Nope, go ahead," Hoss answered, jabbing at a bite of pie.

"Do you see me as a girl or a woman?"

The fork with its pie stopped short of Hoss's mouth, then retreated to the plate. How could he answer that? Hoss had taken to her after her parents' death, always thinking to bring her pinecones or flowers from the Ponderosa every trip he made to Virginia City with Pa. He had thought of her, in a way, as the sister he never had. But then suddenly Sara Ann changed. She was no longer a girl, but a woman, and Hoss found himself attracted to her not just for her unwavering spirit, but also for her womanly beauty. He had to admit he enjoyed watching the movements of her lithe body, the swell of her breast and the life in her brown eyes.

As much as he enjoyed the woman in her, he could never forget the girl she had been. Here he was, more than a decade older than her. What would people think if he courted her? What would her grandfather say? And he was six-four and she only five-two. Would people laugh at them? At times like these, he felt as awkward of tongue as he was of foot. The right words always seemed to come so easily for her, and with such difficulty for him. Like now. He toyed with the cherry pie.

Sara Ann reached for his large hand and patted it gently. "I didn't mean to embarrass you, Hoss."

"Yep." Hoss nodded, thinking that that was part of the problem. She was not a girl anymore, but an attractive young woman with plenty of suitors.

"I've been thinking, Hoss, that you've been keeping watch over me for four days now and haven't even been out of the house except to escort me on my errands and dinner runs to grandfather. Maybe you'd like to get out of the house for an hour or two this afternoon."

The idea was tempting to Hoss, even though he knew he should stay, just in case the Whartons came calling on Sheriff Roy Coffee. Stretching his legs sounded good. So did downing a cold beer at the Delta Saloon without Little Joe around to cause any trouble.

Hoss took a bite of pie as he cogitated.

"Good," Sara Ann smiled, "you're eating again."

Hoss felt his face blush.

"There's no danger here, Hoss, and you need to take an hour or two each day for yourself."

"You sure you don't mind?" he asked between bites.

"Not at all," she said, "but I would ask you to do one thing for me." She turned her eyes away from Hoss as if she might be asking too much of him.

"Sure," he said, "anything."

She looked up at him with her wide brown eyes. "Since you've been watching out for me anyway, I thought maybe you could take me to the Masonic Hall Saturday night."

"What's going on there?"

"A dance," Sara Ann replied innocently.

Hoss stopped chewing. She had connived him into going to a dance, but he didn't feel at all tricked. In fact, he felt rather pleased that she would, in her roundabout way, get him to go with her without him having to ask. "I'd be pleased to escort you, Sara Ann, but you know I dance like a beer barrel."

"And you're twice as handsome." Sara Ann grinned.

Hoss blushed again. He'd never been called handsome by a woman, not that he could remember, at least. He liked the feeling, in spite of the blush of embarrassment it brought to his face. Hoss envied Little Joe for his ability to charm the women with his words. All he could counter with was sincerity. "A little fresh air might do me good," he admitted.

"You do that and take an hour or two," she said, standing up and taking his empty plate. "I won't go anywhere."

"You promise?"

She smiled. "As long as you promise to take me to the dance."

"I promise, Sara Ann, as long as you won't force me to wear a tie Saturday night." Hoss stood up and stretched. "Another fine meal."

He walked around the table and into the front room, grabbing his hat. Sara Ann came out of the kitchen and opened the door for him.

"Run along for a while and enjoy yourself. I'll be here when you get back."

"Latch the door," Hoss said as he marched out and away, "and I'll see you in a bit." He exited the waist-high picket gate and started down the walk to C Street and the Delta Saloon.

The saloon was crowded but not packed, it still being a while until the shifts changed in the mines. A few men, mine speculators by their greedy looks, abandoned a table, and Hoss slid into one of the chairs. No sooner had he settled in than a red-haired woman sidled up beside him and bent low to give him a peek down her blouse. Hoss recognized her as the saloon girl who had held Little Joe's money before he lost his hundred-dollar bet.

"What'll it be, honey?" she asked, dipping low over the table again.

"The coldest beer in the house."

"Good as done," she answered. "You leave junior at home this time?"

Hoss nodded. "Sent him out of state until he grows up."

"Honey," she replied, "a lot of men live to be old codgers without growing up."

After dispensing her jaded wisdom, the redhead moved toward the bar. She returned shortly with a frosty mug of beer.

Hoss flipped her a silver dollar. "When this one's empty, bring me another, then keep the difference."

"Thank you, honey. You sure there's nothing else I can get for you?" She let her question hang as an open invitation, even after Hoss shook his head. She retreated across the room to another patron and another prospect.

Hoss enjoyed the cold beer and watched the ebb and flow of the Delta patrons. Among them he saw Blake Tipps, the sharpster who had conned Little Joe with his hat trick. The patrons, though, suddenly began to point at the clock and head out the doors in groups. Hoss had forgotten about the saloon girl, so was pleased when she approached with his second mug of beer.

"The drinks aren't that bad, where's everyone heading all of a sudden?" he asked.

121

"Honey, you never know for sure with men, but I hear there's a cockfight scheduled down in the red-light district."

Hoss grabbed the new mug and gulped down the beer, wiping the foam from his mouth.

"Don't tell me you're going too," the redhead said.

"Just as well. I've got a little time to kill."

She smiled invitingly. "I'd be glad to take the time off your hands."

Hoss finished his beer and stood up. "No thanks," he answered as he strode to the door.

"Remember," she called after him, "the invitation is open after the fight too."

Hoss burst out the Delta's doors and started downhill for the red-light district, which paralleled the main line of the Virginia and Truckee Railroad. Though he didn't know the precise location, he followed the stream of men moving in that direction. They all walked with excitement, talking about the upcoming fight. From what Hoss overheard, two birds, each with a half-dozen victories, had been matched for the fight. One was named Honest Abe and the other Chow Chow.

Just beyond a two-story brothel known as Fran's Boardinghouse, commonly called by its frequenters Fran's Hoarding House, Hoss saw a throng of men, five hundred or more, gathered around a pit, shouting among themselves and waving money they intended to bet. In the ring, two men circled the perimeter, holding over their heads two fighting cocks with sharp metal spurs banded on the back of their heels. The roosters' feathers were clipped in fighting trim. One of the handlers was a Chinese man with a long braid of hair hanging down the back of his baggy blouse. The other handler was an Irishman whom spectators called McTeague.

Several Chinese men wandered amid the throng of spectators, taking bets on Chow Chow. Southerners among the crowd had a real problem, not finding it in their unreconstructed hearts to put anything on a bird named Honest Abe, yet unwilling to bet on a bird trained by a foreigner.

Hoss had a couple of dollars in his pocket and was game. He studied both roosters as best he could from twenty feet and decided to go with Chow Chow, which seemed much more aggressive. A Chinese man strode up to Hoss and offered to bet. The man seemed totally confused when Hoss said he was betting against Honest Abe and on Chow Chow.

"Good bird, Chow Chow, and you good man," the Asian man said, then walked on. Hoss turned around to look for someone to bet with and found himself facing Blake Tipps, the sharpster from the saloon.

"Where's your brother?" Tipps asked. "I'd rather bet him because it's a sure thing."

Hoss laughed. "He's in the Sierras, thanks to you."

Tipps grinned. "He should be as smart as you and know when not to bet. You betting on the Chinaman's bird?"

Hoss nodded. "He's a winner."

"Nope," Tipps replied. "The real winner is tomorrow. A Virginia City cock called Goliath is fighting a bird from San Francisco, one named Fireball. Between them, they've fifty or more wins. Some are saying it'll be one of the greatest matches in the history of cock-fighting, rivaling some of the classic fights of England even."

Hoss pointed at the pit. "They're about to start."

"It's easier for a tall man like you to see."

"Are you taking my two-dollar bet?" Hoss asked.

"It's small change for what I normally bet, but I guess I owe it to you since I made an easy hundred dollars off your brother."

In the ring, the two cock handlers circled each other, holding the roosters chest high and thrusting them at each other. A referee circled the pit with the handlers. Around the ring, bettors called for final wagers and began to shout for their favorites. The cocks began to squirm and dart their heads at one another, their spindly legs with the metal spurs at the heels churning, the metal blades flashing.

With the roosters fighting mad, the handlers backed to the edge of the ring. Honest Abe, a dark gray cock with muscled chest, lunged for the ginger-red Chow Chow. For an instant Chow Chow seemed tentative and his handler screamed at him in Chinese. At the signal, both handlers threw the cocks to the ground. The roosters hit with their clipped wings flapping and their feet churning.

A roar cut loose from the crowd as the cocks lunged for one another.

After a lunge that missed, the red rooster turned and ran, Honest Abe giving chase.

Blake Tipps shouted and cheered like all the others who had bet on Honest Abe. Tipps nudged Hoss in the side with his elbow. "Your chicken's chicken."

All the Chinese men groaned and cursed in their native tongue. Hoss was angry at himself for going against a bird with as patriotic a name as Honest Abe.

"Your luck's no better than your brother's," Tipps said, rubbing it in.

Honest Abe chased Chow Chow around the ring, but just before the referee was about to raise his hand and declare a default, the red rooster spun around and jumped in the air, his feet flashing the razor-sharp metal spurs. His momentum too great to stop, the surprised Honest Abe ran full speed into the sharp metal, which slashed, then punctured his chest. It happened so fast that for an instant the spectators stood silent until they understood what had just transpired.

The Chinese men took up a great cheer,

while the losers groaned and tossed their bet money at the victors.

Now Hoss elbowed Blake Tipps. "How quick did my luck change?" he taunted.

"You know, a man's gotta be a fool to bet on a damn chicken." Tipps shoved his two dollars at Hoss. "How about a rematch tomorrow when Goliath goes against Fireball? I'll double today's bet, go four dollars against you, and you can pick whichever bird you want."

"Maybe," Hoss said. "Just depends if I've got business to attend to tomorrow."

Hoss stared down at the pit where two more handlers were coming in with their fighting cocks. "We could bet on these."

Tipps shook his head. "Fellow, these are only culls, not worth a damn as fighters. If I'm going to bet money on a chicken, I want it to be a damn good chicken. Honest Abe wasn't bad, maybe a bit stupid, and the Chinaman's bird is developing a reputation, but nothing like Goliath and Fireball."

Hoss shook his head. "I ain't betting on no San Francisco chicken. I either take Goliath or I don't take any chicken at all."

Tipps grinned. "I prefer the San Francisco bird. Then it's a bet?"

"Sure," Hoss answered, "and if I don't make it here tomorrow, I'll settle up with you at the Delta later."

"I'll be around."

Hoss turned and elbowed his way through

the crowd, knowing he had probably left Sara Ann alone longer than he should have. He walked briskly back up the inclined street, breathing hard from the exertion. At the head of the block he could see the house, but something was wrong. The front door was wide open!

He raced up the street, looking all around him for any sign of the Wharton brothers. Had they hurt Sara Ann? Was she still inside? Why had he ever left her alone?

Hoss bolted up the walk, barged through the swinging picket gate and raced inside the open door. "Sara Ann!" he shouted.

No answer.

He raced from room to room.

She was nowhere to be found.

He spun around and there she stood. In the doorway. Holding a cup in her hand.

"Hoss, what's gotten into you?"

"I thought something had happened to you, the Whartons had taken you."

"No, silly," she said, "I just ran next door to borrow a cup of sugar from Mrs. Coker."

CHAPTER 8

Whew-wee," said Willis Wharton as he stepped on the balcony of Fran's Boarding-house and collapsed in a chair beside Lem Wharton. "After twelve years in prison, I've got a lot of catching up to do."

Lem jumped out of his chair, drew back his fist and blasted Willis's nose, drawing blood.

"Dammit, Lem," Willis sputtered, "why'd you do that?"

Lem leaned over him and pointed his finger at his youngest brother's nose. "Keep your damn mouth shut, you son of a bitch," he threatened. "I've waited as many years as you for this, and I don't want your big mouth ruining our chance to settle the score for Pa."

"Nobody heard," Willis groaned.

"These girls hear more than you think, you fool," Lem whispered.

"They like me," Willis answered.

"Sure they like you, until your money runs out," Lem replied.

Willis just shook his head. "We can rob some more fellas just like we got all our money since we broke out of prison."

Instantly, Lem punched Willis in the mouth, then leaned over and snarled in his ear. "You mention prison one more time, Willis, I'll kill you." Lem slid back in his chair as Willis spat blood.

Vern Wharton stepped shirtless onto the balcony, a wide grin on his face. "These ladies know how to treat a man," he said. He stopped when he saw Willis. "What the hell happened to him?"

"One of the ladies," Lem answered, "knew how to treat him."

Willis sulked.

"Come on, Lem, what happened?" Vern implored.

"Your brother," said Lem, "doesn't know to keep his mouth shut. Once we settle our business and get out of Nevada, he can talk all he wants. Until then, he best not open his mouth except to eat and ask a woman upstairs."

Vern stepped to the balcony railing and stretched his arms, glancing down at the throng of men gathered across the street. "What's the crowd about?"

"A cockfight, boys," came a smirking female voice behind them.

Fran strode onto the balcony, weaving among the three Whartons. Her dress was out of fashion and tight in the wrong places. She tried to hide her lost beauty behind the caked powder and thick rouge upon her cheeks, but the cosmetics only accentuated her age. In spite of her long years in the profession, she strode about with her arrogant nose in the air, as if she were superior to all men.

She looked at Willis and shook her head, then strode by Lem before turning to Vern. "I know you boys are in trouble, I just don't know what. And even if I did, I wouldn't tell a soul as long as you don't bruise my girls or bother my regular customers. You may be the three that's robbed a few men the last couple nights, then you may not be. It don't matter to me as long as you stay paid up. My girls know that's the rules."

From across the street a roar went up from the crowd.

"I like a good cockfight, boys." She turned to Lem. "Care to join me?"

Lem shrugged, but she grabbed his arm and pulled him toward the balcony. Whatever made the ugly madam happy was fine as long as she kept her mouth shut.

Willis struggled to get up.

"No soap for you," Fran told him. "I don't want any of my customers seeing your blood-ied face. It might be bad for business."

Lem reached the balcony railing in time to see the two handlers throw their roosters to the ground. The roosters lunged for each other, then the red one turned and ran, the gray one giving chase until the red spun about and slashed it to death. A loud groan followed by a feeble cheer went up from the crowd.

Fran enjoyed the blood sport. "It's a shame

the cock didn't last longer. It'd been a better fight."

Lem shrugged. "It's settled. I'd like to settle all my affairs that quick," he said, thinking of Roy Coffee and Ben Cartwright.

Fran slid her arm around Lem's waist. "Sounds like you need one of my girls to cheer you up."

Lem shivered at her frigid touch. A block of ice would have been warmer than her cold hand and colder heart. "Nope, but my brothers do." He reached in his pocket and pulled out a wad of stolen money. "See that a couple of your girls occupy them for the rest of the day and night."

"And what about you?" Fran asked.

"I've business to attend to."

Fran laughed. "Another robbery, is it?" She spun away from him and disappeared inside. A few minutes later two scantily clad ladies came out for Vern and Willis, quickly persuading them both to go inside where things were cozier.

Lem sat in the rocking chair until after dark, not the least bit amused by the fast tunes of the player piano downstairs and the creaking bedsprings, gasps, and squeals upstairs. When it was dark enough, he stood up and retreated inside Fran's Boardinghouse, down the stairs and out the door, toward the sheriff's office. Last night he had seen a big man and a young woman bring a basket of

131

supper to Sheriff Roy Coffee, who stayed late in his office. Tonight, he would follow the pair and see if they led him to the sheriff's home. Lem recalled the unsuccessful ambush on Coffee's place a dozen years ago, but Virginia City had changed and the sheriff could have moved.

About dusk the big man and the young lady appeared as they had the night before, taking Coffee a late supper. Lem stood in the shadows, out of the glow of just-lit gas lamps. Through the barred jail window, yellow with lamp light, Lem watched Coffee eat his supper and converse with his visitors. He fought the urge to ambush Coffee now, but knew an escape from Virginia City could be difficult, especially with his two brothers.

He knew he had to lure Coffee away from Virginia City, and the young woman just might be the bait he needed. He recalled again the unsuccessful ambush on the Coffee residence and remembered the cries and screams of a young girl. At the trial, he learned the girl was Coffee's granddaughter. Could this young woman be her twelve years later?

When the young woman began to gather up the dishes, Lem pried himself away from the building where he had been leaning and slipped down the street in the direction from which the young woman and big man had come.

Staying on the opposite side of the street,

he was half a block away when he saw them leave the sheriff's office. After pulling his hat down to hide the ear that Willis had maimed, Lem waited until they drew even with him, then he crossed the street and fell in behind them, slowing to their easy pace. A couple of times the big man glanced over his shoulder, but didn't seem to notice him.

When the couple turned on a side street and started up the shoulder of Mount Davidson, Lem stuck to their shadowy trail. As he advanced, it reminded him of that night a dozen years ago when he and his brothers had come up this street to avenge their father's death. They had failed that night. They would not fail again!

As the couple reached their destination, Lem recognized the house as the one he and his brothers had shot up years ago. Surely this woman was Coffee's granddaughter and this man her husband. He must be a lazy son of a bitch, Lem thought as the couple let themselves in, to marry a woman and then mooch off her grandfather. Lem walked past the house and hid in a clump of bushes up the street. He would wait now to see if Sheriff Roy Coffee would return here. He didn't care how long he had to wait, because a man in prison grew accustomed to waiting. This would be short compared to the twelve years he had spent hoping for this day.

In about an hour he saw a solitary man

coming up the street. As the figure passed a gas lamp, Lem recognized Roy Coffee. The sheriff opened the gate in the white picket fence, then shut it behind him. He marched up on the porch and let himself in.

Lem smiled to himself as Coffee disappeared. By the time Lem had emerged from behind the bush, the plan had come to him. Abduct the girl and take her to Timberline Pass, where Coffee and Ben Cartwright had killed his father! Then leave word where Coffee and Cartwright would find her. It was a good plan because it would take him and his brothers away from Virginia City and bring Coffee and Cartwright to them.

Lem strode back to Fran's Boardinghouse. Now all he had to figure out was a way to take the girl and get her out of town. The cover of darkness would make it easier to remove her unseen, but it would make it harder for the three of them to pick up the trail to Timberline Pass. Too, they had to do something to get her husband out of the way, particularly if he had nothing more to do than sit around the house all day with his wife and sponge off her grandfather.

When he reached Fran's, the madam greeted him at the door. "Well, how'd your job go tonight?" she teased.

Lem shrugged. "How about a woman?"

"My oh my," said Fran, "you must have rolled a rich one. I'll pick out the best for you."

"What about you, you bag of bones?"

"I'm saving myself for someone special," she shot back.

They both laughed, a laugh of evil.

Ben Cartwright left the Ponderosa just after good sunlight. He held his dun at a steady pace and made the ride to Virginia City in a couple of hours. Along the entire journey, he cautiously scanned the trail ahead and studied the cover along the way in case the Wharton brothers were in ambush. Regularly, he glanced over his shoulder to make sure no one had slipped in behind him. The ride went without incident, and by mid-morning Ben had the gelding trotting through Virginia City, headed for Roy Coffee's office.

Tugging down his hat, Roy Coffee emerged from his office just as Ben reined up to the hitching post.

"Howdy, Ben," Roy said as he stepped onto the boardwalk. "I didn't expect to see you for a few more days."

"The Wharton brothers," Ben said, dismounting slowly.

"Haven't seen nor heard a thing about them," Coffee replied, a look of relief on his face.

Ben shook his head. "They visited the Ponderosa, stole three horses and saddles."

Coffee's face was quickly overcast by worry. "I should've known better than to think they'd forget and just disappear." He shook his head.

"I'm glad Hoss is around to look after Sara Ann."

Ben smiled. "Me too. Anything unusual the last few days, Roy?"

Coffee shook his head. "Robberies seem to have picked up over the last week, but those things go in cycles. I don't make much of it."

"It's possible," said Ben, "that the Whartons are holing up somewhere else, waiting for the right opportunity to come to town."

"You mean to come looking for us, Ben?"

Ben nodded. "I figure it's the same thing."

Coffee let out a long sigh of futility. "It's always the uncertainty, never knowing what's about to happen. I'm getting too old for this. Should've retired years ago." He ran his finger across his graying mustache, then dropped his head and looked at his vest and the six-pointed star pinned below his heart. "I'm losing my hair, Ben. I can't hear out of my right ear from so many gunshots over the years. And now I can't escape the past. Makes you wonder if there's any justice in life."

"Absolutely, Roy."

Coffee took a deep breath and looked up and down the crowded street. "Any of those fellows could be the Wharton brothers."

"You'd remember Lem, the one missing the top half of his ear."

The sheriff shook his head. "My memory's going right along with everything else," said Coffee. "I'd forgotten about that."

"His little brother's the one that bit it off, remember?"

Coffee laughed. "That's right. Fine, upstanding group of boys old man Wharton raised. I think I'd remember Lem, if I saw him now."

Ben grinned. "As old and ugly as we've gotten, Roy, the Whartons may not recognize us."

Coffee shook his head. "Guess there are some advantages to growing old."

"Yes, sir." Ben laughed, slapping Roy on the shoulder. "But we've been smart enough to live this long, unlike a lot of other men who were smarter and more dangerous than the Wharton brothers."

Coffee grinned. "This wise old man's got rounds to make."

"I figure one of those stops'll be by the house to let Sara Ann and Hoss know the Whartons came by the Ponderosa."

"You can read me like a book, Ben, and you're welcome to join us for a bite of lunch around noon. Sara Ann will have something prepared, though with Hoss at the table, it's hard to know if there's gonna be enough to go around."

Ben took off his hat and ran his fingers through his silver hair. "It's a good thing the Bristlecone hit the Big Bonanza so we can afford to keep Hoss in the groceries, Roy. In fact, our earnings have been going up daily since we sent Hoss from our table to yours."

Roy laughed. "I can believe it, but the invitation for lunch is open."

"Thanks, but I need to discuss business with Adam, and he'll probably want to eat at the Washoe Club."

"Good enough, Ben, but just keep an eye open for the Whartons."

"Same for you, Roy," Ben said, then started for his dun as Coffee ambled down the walk, tipping his hat to a couple of women.

Ben mounted and aimed the gelding for Union Street, which sloped down toward F Street and the offices of the Bristlecone Mine. Below him, he could see the four stacks of the Consolidated Virginia mine works, which claimed most of the Big Bonanza. The Bristlecone Mine held claim to the fringes of Big Bonanza, but even a fraction of such a large deposit was worth a fortune. The Cartwright mine earnings did not put Ben and his sons in the same category as the Big Bonanza kings John Mackay and James G. Fair, but they did make the Cartwrights among the richest men associated with the Comstock Lode. The mine earnings augmented Ben's solid business income from his livestock, timber, and railroad interests.

Granted it was more money than any one man needed, but Ben wanted to put it to good use, and most of all, to make sure the unbridled wealth did not destroy his sons as easy money had destroyed the children of many mining magnates. Ben was worried most about Little Joe, and he thought of his youngest son as he passed the commercial district on C Street, then the red-light district along D Street. Across from Fran's Boardinghouse Ben saw men setting up bleachers around a fighting pit. Ben figured someone had scheduled a dog- or cockfight, a barbaric sport but one that attracted men with money in their pockets and time on their hands.

At F Street Ben turned for the Bristlecone office. He never made this trip without amazement at the brute strength of the industrial age. The giant stacks of the mine works belched smoke from the fires that powered the machinery that gave Virginia City a constant roar. The very earth seemed to vibrate with that strength. Mining was a cruel business, its vagaries enough to break a man's spirit and his bank. Ben had been lucky, making his claim years ago, when the prevailing thought had the great ore bodies trailing away from rather than toward the Bristlecone property. But the ore-bearing lodes had gone deeper into the earth, then doubled back toward the Bristlecone. Virginia City held claim to the deepest and richest mines in the world, the Bristlecone among them.

As Ben neared the mining property, Bristlecone employees greeted him. As he dismounted in front of the office, one of the

139

men walked over and took his reins to tend his horse. When he walked in the front door, every employee stood up out of respect. Ben motioned for them to sit down, then wandered among them, greeting them all by name before striding up the stairs toward Adam's office.

He knocked on Adam's door, then entered at Adam's invitation. His oldest son sat at the table by the window, studying a stack of financial papers. "Yes," he said, without looking around.

"Morning, Adam," Ben said, and instantly Adam turned around in his seat.

"Didn't expect you back so soon, Pa. You get Little Joe squared away at the timber lease?"

Ben nodded, took off his hat and hung it on the hook by the door. "I don't feel right about him up there with those hard men," he admitted, "but if he's ever to grow up, he needs to be on his own for a while, take on responsibility like you have. Even so, I'm not comfortable with him at the timber operation."

Adam's face was drawn and his lips tight as he nodded. "I can't put my finger on it, but I'm not comfortable with our lumber operation either."

Ben moved across the room to the table and took a seat opposite his son. "That Nat Greer's a hard one."

Adam bit his lip for a moment. "You need a tough man to run a lumber operation, but you need an honest man as well."

"Greer's a tough one," Ben admitted.

"But I'm not sure he's an honest one. Look at this," Adam said, passing Ben a couple of sheets of paper with his ciphering on it.

Ben glanced at the papers, uncertain what he was looking for. He shrugged at Adam. "What's it mean?"

"Several things," Adam said. He took his pencil and pointed to various sets of figures on the paper. "We spent more than two hundred thousand dollars on a flume to get our lumber from the lease to Lake Tahoe. The flume was finished more than four months ago, and I can't show that it's resulted in any increase in our lumber production, though we've got three crews out there now. No more lumber's reaching the mills than when we moved it all the way to Tahoe by oxen, and that was the point of the flume."

Ben looked at the figures, though he knew Adam would never have voiced his suspicions had he not been certain of the numbers. "Looks like we do have a problem."

"Yes, sir," Adam said, "and one I can't figure out by myself. You did tell Little Joe to send me back information on how many trees a crew can cut in a day and the average size of a tree?"

"He was told," Ben admitted, "but you know him. Sometimes he'll remember, sometimes he'll forget."

Adam rubbed his chin. "He should remember this time since there are no young ladies in camp."

"What do your numbers show us losing, Adam?"

"Well, Pa, I've figured it a couple ways, and with the number of men we've got out there, I figure at best we're managing only three-fourths of the trees we should be. It may be we're getting no better than two-thirds."

Ben whistled. "Let's hope Little Joe is responsible enough to give you the information you need."

"Pa, what I don't understand is, we set wages at a dollar fifty a day, that's fifty percent more than other camps. We're paying them the best in the Sierras and they're performing worse than an average crew."

"Could you be overlooking something, Adam?"

Adam let his hands fall to the table. "I don't know what it could be, Pa. I just wish I had the time to see for myself how things are going."

Ben nodded. "Though I suppose we've got to let Little Joe take care of himself and our business on this one."

"Is Hoss still with the Coffees?"

"Yes, and he'll need to stay there awhile longer."

"Why?" Adam shrugged. "No one's seen the Wharton brothers, have they?"

"Afraid so, Adam. They came by the ranch, looking for me, stole three horses and saddles."

Adam whistled. "That's all we need."

CHAPTER 9

Sara Ann Coffee was as pretty as a button in the red gingham dress and her perpetual smile. In fact she was so pretty that Hoss could think of no job better than keeping an eye her. It was as good a job as a man could have, and at the same time, as bad a job as imaginable. He couldn't overcome his feelings for her or his guilt because of them, him being years older than her and more than a head taller. What would people think? Sometimes he wished he were more like Little Joe. His younger brother didn't care what people thought, and most people tended to like him. Hoss sat in the hard-back chair across from Sara Ann and just wished he knew the proper thing to do. And he was getting nervous about Saturday night and the dance. What would people think? Him and her? He wondered if tongues would wag because he had been staying with her when her grandfather was away from the house. That would scandalize some, but he couldn't really explain he was guarding her, because both his father and Roy had thought it best not to advertise the potential danger.

Hoss squirmed in the hard-back chair. In

his hands he held a frayed copy of the *Enterprise*, but he wasn't in the mood for reading, not when Sara Ann was so near. Another fine lunch had long since settled in his stomach, and he needed to do something, needed to get away for a bit, just to get his mind on something other than Sara Ann. At lunch Roy had told him of the Whartons' visit to the Ponderosa. Hoss knew the Whartons might be around, but even that possibility didn't seem as important as getting away for a while so he wouldn't make a fool of himself by admitting his feelings for Sara Ann.

"A penny for your thoughts," Sara Ann said from her rocking chair, where she sat darning a pair of her grandfather's socks.

Hoss's thoughts were so entwined with his feelings for Sara Ann that at first he did not hear her.

"A penny for your thoughts," Sara Ann repeated. "Hoss, a penny for your thoughts."

Finally her words seemed to register. Hoss wrinkled his nose and stumbled over his answer. "I was, ah, had to be, ah, just thinking a bit."

"About what, Hoss?"

He shrugged and grinned sheepishly. "Nothing."

Sara Ann cocked her head at him. "Now, Hoss Cartwright, I know better than that."

"Huh?"

"You've been sitting there for half an hour,

holding the paper and just staring blankly over it, never reading a line."

Hoss grimaced. She was right, but what could he say? "Just thinking," he replied. "A man like me don't have many profound thoughts."

"Now, Hoss," she chided, "you quit running yourself down. You don't give yourself enough credit."

"Credit? For what?" Hoss frowned again.

Sara Ann shook her head and dropped the socks and darning needle in her gingham lap. "Credit for being a decent and well-intentioned man. Very few men would've been as good a gentleman as you over the last few days."

Hoss shrugged. "It's what's right," he replied.

"But not all men know what's right, Hoss."

The longer this conversation continued, the more uncomfortable Hoss became. He folded his paper and dropped it on the floor, then stuck his finger down his unbuttoned collar to loosen it further. "Not all men have Ben Cartwright for a father."

Sara Ann pursed her lips and shook her head before chastising him. "There you go, Hoss, not giving yourself the credit you deserve. You've been a perfect gentleman the whole time."

Hoss coughed into his fist. "I haven't been thinking like a perfect gentleman," he admitted, then blushed at what he had said. He glanced at Sara Ann, expecting disgust on her face. Instead he was surprised by a soothing smile and a pert toss of her head which sent her auburn hair to bouncing gaily.

"That's the nicest thing you've admitted to me, Hoss," she said, her voice as smooth as Lake Tahoe on a windless day.

Hoss shook his head in total confusion and turned away from Sara Ann. He stared at the table clock, its tick much steadier than his heartbeat. It was half past two, just thirty minutes before that cockfight scheduled between Virginia City's Goliath and that San Francisco bird called Fireball.

"I didn't mean to embarrass you, Hoss."

Hoss stood slowly from his chair and paced about the room, pinching the bridge of his nose between his thumb and his forefinger. "Sara Ann," he began, pausing in his pacing, "I'm just not good about these kinds of things."

Sara Ann squirmed in her chair and her face clouded over for an instant. Then the smile returned, as comforting as ever. "Hoss, that's one of the reasons I'm fond of you."

Hoss felt his cheeks redden with embarrassment — and pleasure.

"I don't intend to make you uncomfortable, but I'm fond of you the way you are," she continued.

Hoss paced the room faster. "Sara Ann, I'm, ah, ah, fond of you. Always have been, ever

147

since you were just a little girl."

Sara Ann smiled. "I'm not a little girl anymore, Hoss." She gathered her darning materials from her lap and placed them on the table at her side, then stood up.

"But I still think of you as a little girl, Sara Ann, one that wouldn't let Roy tie a bow in your hair because he couldn't do it as pretty as you. And then you'd tie some of the ugliest bows around, but nobody'd tell you otherwise."

Sara Ann slid over to Hoss, took his arm, and pulled him toward her. Standing on her tiptoes, she kissed him on the cheek. "I'm fond of you, Hoss, always have been, from the days you used to bring me flowers and rocks from the Ponderosa."

Hoss sighed, totally confused as to what to do next. He needed to think. He needed a distraction. "I'm fond of you, Sara Ann, but I've gotta get away for a few minutes and think on a few things." Before Sara Ann could say no, Hoss bolted for the door. "I'll not be gone more than an hour," he said. Instantly, he was outside. The hot sun burned into his face and he realized he had forgotten his hat. Without the courage to go back and face Sara Ann, Hoss charged down the hill toward C Street. He headed for the Delta Saloon, knowing he would wind up at the cockpit.

Out of breath when he reached the Delta, Hoss sidled up to the near empty bar and requested a beer of the stocky bartender. The bartender shoved a mug under a spigot and filled the glass, then slid the frothy beer down the bar to Hoss, who grabbed the mug and downed it without coming up for air.

"Wish all my customers would drink that fast," the bartender said.

"Yeah," Hoss said, "I bet you do." Hoss spun around, headed back out the swinging doors and aimed down the hill for the cockfight. Even above the rumble of the mines, Hoss could hear the excitement of the sportsmen gathering two blocks away to wager on the fighting roosters. Hoss trotted down Union Street, the quick beer jostling in his belly.

When he turned onto D Street, he was shocked at what he saw. A crowd of two thousand men, some four times as many as yesterday, had gathered. Men were feverishly wagering with one another, miners with mine owners, merchants with lawyers, railroaders with gamblers. Hoss drew up short of the throng and stood with hands on hips, looking for Blake Tipps.

Hoss didn't see the gambler and he didn't really care if he did or not. He knew he just had to get away from Sara Ann for a few moments to collect his muddled thoughts. Oh, how he had wanted to throw his arms around her and answer her kiss with one of his own, but that would be ungentlemanly. And he knew he could probably stand here all day and not resolve his feelings for her and his feelings about the relationship.

"Ten minutes until the feathers fly," shouted the referee. "Virginia City's own Goliath," he called to a chorus of cheers, "against the bird from San Francisco, the bird that some call the best in the world, Fireball." Several Goliath fans booed.

Hoss edged a little closer to the ring, but he was too late to get a good view. It wasn't that important anyway. Now at least he had time to think about himself and Sara Ann. He was still thinking when the fight began and the throng erupted in great cheers.

Lem Wharton leaned against the balcony rail at Fran's Boardinghouse and watched the gathering crowd. Fran herself stood beside him, reeking of so much perfume that it made Lem's nose twitch.

"You smell like an outhouse," he told her.

She smiled. "You really know how to sweet-talk a girl, don't you? Was that how you got your ear bit off?"

"You've a big mouth for such an ugly bag of bones," he told her.

"If you keep sweet-talking me, you'll just sweep me off my feet." She moved in closer when she realized her perfume made his nose twitch.

Lem sneezed. "Back away, woman, back away."

"Hush that sweet talk."

Lem started to shove her away, but froze instead. Approaching the perimeter of the crowd was the big man he had seen escorting the sheriff's granddaughter last night. The man seemed to be looking for someone, more than getting close to the fight. This would be his chance to get the girl, the bait to draw Roy Coffee and Ben Cartwright to Timberline Pass.

Lem put his arm around Fran and pulled her next to him.

"Oh, sweet talker, what you got in mind?" Her voice came out as a hiss.

"How long before the cockfight starts?"

"Ten or so minutes," she answered.

"Good." He shoved her away. "Me and my brothers want to go down and get a close look." Lem spun around and raced back inside the brothel, banging on a closed door. "Vern, Willis," Lem called. "Come on, it's time for us to go."

Willis's voice came from one of the girl's rooms. "Just a minute," he yelled.

"No, now," he shot back, flinging open the door.

Willis was half dressed, and the woman he was with fumbled for the covers out of reflex, more than modesty. She had raven hair and big blue eyes that were wide with terror. She said nothing to Willis and seemed scared by him and his wild look, made all the more frightening by his swollen nose and fat lip from the punches Lem had landed yesterday.

Lem tossed Willis his hat and shirt, then kicked his boots toward him. "Hurry, we've got to get the girl," Lem said before he realized he had divulged his plan in front of the soiled dove. Lem approached her, and she tugged the covers higher to her neck. He pointed at her nose with his finger. "You best not repeat anything you heard here or we'll come back and carve you up like a whittling stick. Do you understand?"

She nodded as meekly as a scared bunny.

"Willis, dammit, hurry and grab your belongings so we can get out," Lem commanded, then spun around and barged out into the hall, barreling over Fran. "Stay out of my way," he grumbled.

"You son of a bitch," she spat back. "I hope whoever you saw at the cockfight that scared you catches up with you and gives you a taste of your own medicine." Fran laughed insanely and retreated down the stairs.

"Vern," Lem yelled, "we need to be moving on."

"Down here," Vern replied.

Lem ran down the stairs, shoving past Fran, and cursed as he saw Vern seated on a plush sofa between two of Fran's girls. "Get off your butt when I call," Lem screamed, lunging for his brother and grabbing him by the shoulders. Lem jerked him from the grasp of the two girls vying for his attention.

"Why the sudden urge to leave, Lem?"

"We've got business to do for Pa, remember?"

Vern nodded. "I ain't forgot."

Lem maneuvered Vern away from the girls. Once beyond hearing distance, Lem whispered for him to go get their horses out of the livery stable and have them back at Fran's as quickly as possible.

Vern shot out the door just as Willis came down the stairs. He had a wild look in his crossed eyes and a grin that was as crooked as his lopsided shoulders.

"Is it the law?" Willis mumbled, reaching for the holstered pistol at his side.

"No need for gunplay, Willis," soothed Lem. The girls had slipped a bit closer, and Lem knew they were eavesdropping. "Soon as we get our horses, we'll head for Reno, catch a train back east," Lem lied to throw the girls off.

"Huh?" Willis scratched his head.

"Nothing to worry about just yet," Lem said.

Lem walked over to the gun case where Fran made customers store their weapons. Lem, though, had — at the point of his revolver — sweet-talked Fran into letting him and his brothers keep their sidearms. Lem took the two carbines he and his brothers had stolen off their robbery victims, then grabbed another one, which until that moment hadn't belonged to them. He tossed one at Willis and held onto the other two as he stepped up beside the door and waited. After five minutes, Vern rode up leading two saddled horses.

"Come on, Willis, let's go," Lem called, and as soon as he and Willis were out the door, he heard clapping and cheering from the women in Fran's brothel.

"Good riddance," Fran called from somewhere down the hall.

Willis glanced angrily back over his shoulder.

"Ignore them, Willis," Lem cautioned. "Just take it easy so we can get out of here."

"Where are we going?" Willis asked in a whisper.

"We're going to start avenging Pa," Vern said.

"Yeeee-haaaa," Willis shouted. His yell was lost in the commotion across the street.

Lem and Willis approached Vern and the horses, mounting quickly and aiming the mounts toward the house of Sheriff Coffee. Lem glanced back once over his shoulder and saw that the big man was intently scanning the crowd, as if he were still looking for someone.

"What's the plan, Lem?" asked Vern.

Lem said nothing.

"We don't have a plan, do we?" Willis said.

Lem scowled. "While you two have been playing with the ladies, I've been figuring out what we'll do."

"So, what's the plan?"

"We'll steal the sheriff's granddaughter and take her to Timberline Pass. That'll draw Coffee and Cartwright away from here, where we can kill them like they did Pa."

Quickly, they rode toward Coffee's house. Lem pointed it out and issued instructions. "Vern, go around to the back of the house and make sure she doesn't leave by the back door. Willis and I'll see if we can get in the front door. You two understand?"

Both Willis and Vern nodded.

"And another thing," said Lem, "don't hurt the girl. For now!"

Sara Ann heard the knock on the door and jumped from her chair. How could she apologize to Hoss for putting him on the spot? That had not been her intention. She had just wanted to let him know that she was fond of him. She wanted to deal with him honestly, not to trick him as she had when she got him to agree to escort her to the dance Saturday.

The knock came again, harder.

Sara Ann glanced at the mirror and patted her hair in place. She licked her lips to put a little gloss on them, even if only temporarily. At the door, she twisted the key in the lock and pulled it open. "Hoss," she said, then jerked her hand to her throat. It wasn't Hoss!

Before her stood a man over six feet tall with brown hair, brown eyes, a man she did not recognize until she saw his ear. The top third was missing. Then she knew who it was.

This was one of the men who had killed her parents!

She started to scream, but cat-quick the man was on her, his callused fingers covering her mouth with one hand and jerking her arm behind her back with the other.

"Now listen to me," whispered Lem in her ear. "You don't cause any trouble and we'll not hurt you." He accentuated his demand by jerking her arm up her back.

Sara Ann grimaced and whimpered at the pain.

"Do you understand? If you try to scream or anything, I'll put you in more pain than you thought possible."

Sara Ann forced herself to nod.

"Willis," Lem ordered, "find the back door and let Vern in." Then he turned back to Sara Ann. "When'll your husband be back?"

Sara Ann shook her head as Lem released his hand from her mouth. "I'm not married," she replied.

Lem jerked back on her arm and Sara Ann let out a delicate cry. "I've followed you the last two days. Where's your husband, the big man?"

Tears came to Sara Ann's eyes, tears from the pain and from the irony of being thought Hoss's wife. "I don't know when he'll be back," she replied. "He didn't tell me where he was going."

"He's at the cockfight betting some of your grandpa's money, I figure."

Sara Ann nodded, certain that her only hope was to play along with the gunmen's every notion. "He should've stayed here instead of sneaking off," she said, stalling for time, desperately trying to figure out how to outsmart these three murderers.

Lem released her arm and she edged toward the door, but he grabbed her wrist. "If you try anything, you'll end up with a bullet in your head."

Sara Ann caught her breath as she heard a noise outside. Hoss was returning!

Lem also heard Hoss's approach, and before she could scream a warning, he covered her mouth and pulled her with him into the kitchen. "Willis, come with me. Vern, you get behind the door, and once he comes in, shove your gun in his back."

Sara Ann felt her heart pounding. She was helpless to do anything but wait and hope they didn't hurt Hoss.

She heard the front door swing open. "Dad-blame-it, Sara Ann, you shouldn't leave the door unlocked like this, not with the Whartons on the loose."

Lem Wharton leaned close to her and she could smell his acrid breath as he whispered in her ear, "Tell him you're back here."

"I'm in the kitchen," she called, not mentioning his name so the Whartons wouldn't connect him with Ben Cartwright.

She heard the front door close, then Hoss's surprised voice. "What the hell?"

"I got him," called Vern Wharton, "and his gun."

Lem laughed and dropped his hand from Sara Ann's mouth. "Then bring him on back here with his wife."

"Wife?" Hoss said as he entered the kitchen, a scowl on his face. "It's my fault, Sara Ann, for leaving you alone."

"Shut up," Lem ordered. "Now, fellow, what's your name?"

"Cart—" started Hoss.

"Carter," interrupted Sara Ann.

Lem laughed. "Well, I see who wears the pants in this family."

"My husband, Eric Carter, wears the pants in this family," said Sara Ann.

Hoss stood with a puzzled look on his face.

"Well, Carter, do you know who we are?"

Hoss nodded, but said nothing else.

"Who?" demanded Lem.

"The Wharton brothers," Hoss replied.

"Yep, that's right," said Lem. "We've spent twelve years in prison just waiting to get out and settle our score with Roy Coffee and Ben Cartwright."

"Then why you bothering me and . . ." Hoss paused and looked straight in Sara Ann's worried eyes. ". . . my wife?"

Sara Ann sighed, relieved that he hadn't divulged who he really was.

"She's the bait," Lem replied.

"Why you need bait? Roy Coffee's just down the street, and Ben Cartwright stays out at his ranch."

Lem laughed. "We've already been there. We went a-calling on Ben Cartwright and he wasn't around to greet us. So, we just figured we'd invite them to come see us."

"Let Sara Ann go, take me as bait instead."

Lem laughed again. "Who'd want to rescue a big, ugly brute like you?"

"I would," said Sara Ann meekly.

"Shut up," ordered Lem.

"What do you want me to do?" Hoss asked.

"Your job is to tell Roy Coffee and Ben Cartwright to come to Timberline Pass if they ever want to see your wife alive again."

Hoss nodded. "I'll be with them."

"Come ahead, you'll make a big target." Lem grinned wickedly, then nodded at Vern, who stood with his gun behind Hoss. "Whenever you wake up from this!"

Vern lifted his hand and sent the butt of his revolver crashing into Hoss's head. Hoss stood for a dazed moment, then toppled forward onto the floor.

"Hoss," Sara Ann cried, bending to tend him.

Lem grabbed her wrist. "We've got to ride. You give us any trouble and we'll kill you."

CHAPTER 10

Her blue eyes were wide with fear and her cheeks were wet with tears. She leaned against the brick wall outside the sheriff's office and waited, knowing that it was close to supper-time, when business picked up and when Fran wanted all her "boarders," as she called her girls, around to entertain customers.

When a man on a yellow dun rode up and dismounted, she stepped away from the building and tentatively approached him. He was an upright man with thick silver hair peeking out from under his hat. He wore a brown leather vest, blue shirt, and brown corduroy pants. As he dismounted, she advanced to the hitching post.

"Are you the sheriff?" she asked softly.

"No, ma'am, though I expect him shortly because his horse is here," he said as he tied the reins of his dun around the hitching post. "Can I help you?"

She shrugged. "Maybe," she said, looking both ways down the street and pausing at the approach of another man.

Ben glanced down the walk and saw Roy Coffee. "There's the sheriff now," he said. "Roy, this lady needs to talk to you in a hurry."

The sheriff broke into a jog and quickly reached his office, unlocking it and swinging the door open for the raven-haired woman to enter. "Come on in, Ben," the sheriff offered. No sooner had the door shut than the woman began to tell her story.

"Three men are in town talking about stealing a girl," she cried. "I don't know who the girl is, just that they're mean men."

Roy looked at Ben then back at the woman. "Was one of them missing half an ear?"

She nodded. "I can't stay long."

"Where are they?" Roy asked.

"Fran's Boardinghouse is where they were. They left in a hurry mid-afternoon, said something about getting a girl, but I didn't take it to mean one of the boarders."

Ben and Roy looked at one another.

"Sara Ann," they said simultaneously.

"I just couldn't let mean men like those roam around town. Fran could, but I couldn't."

"Yes, ma'am," Roy said, "you run on. We've got to check on this girl. If we need you, we'll come to Fran's."

Her eyes widened and her cheeks paled. "Don't let her know I was here. She thinks it's bad on business when we tell the law about some of the bad men."

Roy opened the door and ushered her out, then he and Ben dashed for their horses, untied the reins, jumped onto the saddles, and raced away, drawing the stares of several passersby. Down the street they turned their horses up the road leading to Coffee's house. They were there quickly. Both slid out of their saddles and tossed the reins over the picket fence.

The house was dark and the front door ajar.

"Dammit, Ben, they can't have hurt her. She's all I've got left."

"Hoss wouldn't let anything happen, Roy," Ben replied, wishing he believed that himself.

Roy shoved the cracked door open. "Sara Ann! Sara Ann, where are you?"

Only silence answered.

"Sara Ann," Roy called again.

"Hoss, you here?" Ben shouted. He heard a groan from an adjacent room.

Ben darted into the dim kitchen while Roy lit a lamp. Ben could make out a large form on the floor. "Hoss," he said, kneeling beside his son.

Quickly, Roy brought the lamp into the kitchen. Hoss's eyes fluttered, then he lifted his hand to shield them from the light.

"They got Sara Ann, Pa. They took her with them."

"Where?" Roy broke in.

"Timberline Pass," Hoss managed, through a voice scratchy with thirst. "Water."

For a moment Coffee and Ben stared at one another.

"Timberline Pass, where it all began," Ben said.

Roy turned away and cursed, placing the lamp on the table, then got a tin of water from the drinking barrel. He handed the cup to Ben, who lifted Hoss's head and helped him sip the water.

"Ben, I should've killed the sons of bitches years ago when I had the chance. I wanted to. God knows I had reason enough to, but this damned badge kept me from it. I was sworn to uphold the law, not to become judge and jury."

"I know, Roy," Ben answered as Hoss finished the water and tried to rise.

Ben gave the cup back to Roy and helped Hoss to his feet. He supported Hoss as he stumbled into the parlor and fell into the rocking chair; Sara Ann's rocking chair.

"They jumped me, Pa. I'd been out for a few minutes, and when I got back they were waiting. Damn their lousy stinking hides," Hoss said, spitting out the words, then grabbing his head. "They said they'd be waiting for you at Timberline Pass."

Roy Coffee moved next to Ben and grabbed his hand. Roy took off his badge and slipped it into Ben's palm. "I'm going after them, Ben."

Ben grabbed his arm. "Not tonight, Roy. You won't be able to do any good, not in the dark, not in your state of mind. They've got a longer lead than you can make up in the dark, and you're not going alone. I'm going with you."

Hoss struggled to get up. "Me too."

Ben pushed him back down in the chair. "Nobody's going tonight." He turned to Roy. "Get Dr. Martin for Hoss, Roy, and after he looks over Hoss, I'll get provisions for our ride to Timberline Pass."

Ben offered Roy his badge back, but the sheriff shook his head.

"Keep it. I don't want it between me and my own brand of justice." Ben slipped the badge into his vest pocket.

Roy stepped away from Ben and out the door. In a moment Ben heard the sheriff's horse gallop off.

"I'm sorry, Pa."

Ben nodded. "Nobody's blaming you, Hoss."

"But I'm to blame, leaving her here alone."

Ben sighed. "Had you been here, they might have killed you, killed Sara Ann."

"I'm fond of that girl, Pa."

Ben nodded. "I think she's fond of you as well."

A broad smile crossed Hoss's face. "How d'you know that?"

"Sometimes it's easier for others to see."

"I promised her I'd take her to the dance, Saturday night."

Ben patted Hoss on the shoulder. "Save your strength. You'll need it when we ride out for Timberline Pass."

The tick of the clock seemed to ricochet around the room. Even the industrial noise of

Virginia City did not intrude upon the parlor and the thoughts of Ben and Hoss.

Within minutes Roy Coffee returned with Dr. Paul Martin, a physician wise in the ways of medicine and men. The doctor marched in, nodded at Ben and went straight to Hoss. Bending over his patient, Martin touched the side of Hoss's head to get a good look at the knot sprouting in back.

Hoss grimaced. "Ouch."

"Nasty bump you got there, Hoss," the doctor said. Putting his hand under Hoss's chin, the doctor lifted his head. "Your vision blurred or anything like that?"

Hoss shook his head and squinted his eyes. "Nothing, except the light hurts a bit."

"That's to be expected," the doctor replied. He held up his index finger in front of Hoss's nose. "Now follow my finger."

With that, Dr. Martin began to move the finger left and right, then up and down in front of Hoss's face. Hoss's eyes followed the doctor's movements.

"Fine, Hoss," the doctor said, "you can relax now." He turned to Ben. "A nasty bump, but it didn't seem to cause any permanent damage. His head'll be tender for a few days and it won't be easy wearing a hat, but he'll recover as handsome as ever."

"Doc," Hoss said, "it won't be no problem for me riding tomorrow, will it?"

Martin shrugged. "An extra day's rest

would do you good, but you should be able to manage. If you get dizzy, just pull off the trail and rest for a while. You'll be okay."

"A little dizziness ain't gonna stop me from going to Timberline Pass."

Roy Coffee moved away from the door to Martin. "Doc, I'd appreciate you not letting word out about this. I especially don't want word getting to the papers, particularly that damned Billy Makovy with the *Enterprise*. He's lower than a snake's belly."

Martin nodded. "Sure, Roy, I understand. You just take care of yourself and get Sara Ann safely back home." The doctor turned to Hoss and patted his shoulder. "Send someone if you need me, Hoss."

"Thanks, Doc," Ben said, escorting Martin to the door.

When the doctor left, Ben said to Hoss, "We'll put you to bed, while Roy and I get things together for tomorrow."

Hoss waved the offer aside. "I'll manage. You two get what we need so we can ride out before daybreak." He pushed himself up from Sara Ann's rocking chair and walked gingerly into Roy's room, aiming for the mattress that had been thrown on the floor for him while he stayed with Sara Ann. He collapsed on the mattress and went limp from exhaustion.

Ben turned to Roy. "I'll go to a mercantile and get us supplies enough for the three-day ride to Timberline Pass, and a pack animal to

166

carry them. Anything else, Roy?"

"Yeah," the sheriff answered, "plenty of ammunition."

They were vicious men, the Wharton brothers, and Sara Ann hated them, not just for killing her parents years ago, but also for hurting Hoss. She prayed he was okay and hoped he didn't blame himself for this, though she knew he would. That was the way he was. The Whartons had tied her hands with a stiff hemp rope that had cut into her flesh. When she complained of the pain, the one called Lem produced a knife from a scabbard in back of his gun belt. Then he grabbed a handful of her auburn hair and sliced it off.

"Don't bellyache," Willis had sneered, his crossed eyes seeming to stare everywhere but at her, "or he'll cut your head off."

Lem tossed the handful of hair on the ground and moved on.

The Whartons had smuggled her out the back of her house and forced her to ride double with Lem. She sat in the saddle and he was behind her, his hands wrapped around her waist and holding the reins so as to hide her bound hands from prying eyes. They stuck to the back streets and made it out of Virginia City in broad daylight.

It was a three-day ride to Timberline Pass, and Sara Ann knew she could not last that long on a shared saddle. Lem's acrid breath against her neck almost made her gag. Her body ached from discomfort, with him so closely pressed against her. She felt a wave of revulsion when he occasionally rested his pointed chin on her shoulder.

Just before dark the three brothers encountered a solitary rider approaching them on the trail.

"Howdy, friend," Vern Wharton called, "you wouldn't happen to have a match on you, would you?"

The man stopped and dug into his pocket, fishing out a tin of matches as Vern rode up.

Sara Ann wanted to scream and warn the man, but Lem was so close behind her that he could almost read her mind.

"Don't say a thing," he whispered.

Laughing, Vern drew up to the man. "I don't have the makings for a cigarette. Guess I don't need a match after all."

The man glanced from Vern to Willis, who now rode up to him too, then at Lem and Sara Ann, before realizing something was amiss. His realization came too late.

Vern pulled his pistol and shoved it in the man's ribs. "I don't need your matches, friend, but I'll take your money and your horse."

"No," the man yelled. He tried to kick his horse into a gallop, but not before Willis grabbed the reins.

"You shouldn't a tried to do that," Willis snarled.

Vern drew back his pistol and slugged the innocent man across the ear. The rider tumbled like a rock from the saddle.

"There's your horse, woman," Lem said, shoving Sara Ann out of the saddle to the ground.

Sara Ann hit hard, losing her breath, but not her composure. She would not let them destroy her spirit.

Vern jumped out of his saddle and jerked the sidearm from the holster of the downed rider. Then he rifled the man's pockets, shouting when his hand pulled out a roll of money.

"Keep it down, Vern," Lem ordered. "We don't want the whole county knowing we're around."

Vern spat toward Lem. "There's a couple hundred dollars here, at least."

Lem nodded. "We'll need it for supplies, if we'll be at Timberline Pass for a while. We'll find us a store tomorrow and buy what we need, but tonight we need to keep riding and put some distance between us and Virginia City so old Coffee doesn't pick up our trail and cut us off before we reach the pass."

Sara Ann grimaced, but rose gamely to her feet and stumbled toward the horse. She put her narrow foot in the stirrup, and the horse shied away from her. Sara Ann tumbled backward to the ground.

Willis laughed, holding up the reins of the downed man's horse. Sara Ann cursed him silently. He had jiggled the reins when she tried to get her boot in the stirrup, and made the horse shy away from her. Sara Ann said nothing, knowing Willis was trying to break her spirit.

She walked around the horse, jerked the reins from Willis and moved to the stirrup. With her tied hands, she grabbed the saddle horn as best she could, stuck her foot in the stirrup and pulled herself atop the tall mount.

Vern was trying to count the roll of money when Lem rode over and demanded it. "I'll keep it," he said, bending over in the saddle and yanking it out of his brother's hand.

Vern scowled, scratched the front of his pants, then hobbled back to his mount and climbed gingerly aboard.

Lem turned to Sara Ann. "If you try to run away, the first thing we'll do is shoot the horse. If you survive the fall, then we'll slit your throat."

Sara Ann nodded, but said nothing. These men were crazy.

Lem pointed toward the Sierras, their peaks dark outlines on the horizon. "Let's put some more distance between us and Virginia City. Then we'll bed down for the night."

"It won't be as much fun as at Fran's," Willis said, and glanced at Sara Ann. "But it won't be as bad as prison either, because Red there can entertain us, I bet."

"Not until I give the word, Willis," Lem shot

back. "Once we get her grandpa, then we can do what we want with her, but I don't want her damaged until then, you follow me?"

Willis grumbled indecipherably.

"What was that, Willis?"

"Okay," Willis answered.

The anger buried in his one word answer didn't give Sara Ann much comfort.

"Let's ride," commanded Lem, "time's a-wasting."

Vern took the lead, and Sara Ann guided her mount in line after him. Willis and Lem followed.

They rode for three to four hours, Sara Ann figured, though she realized her fear of these three and the pain of the ropes digging into her flesh had scrambled her sense of time. When they said they were stopping for the night in a grove of trees near the Carson River, she moaned with relief and stumbled out of the saddle. She collapsed on the ground near a tree, craving sleep more than food, water, or anything else but freedom.

Still, she forced herself to stay awake for a while so she could watch her abductors. Though she pretended to sleep, for a half hour she listened to them talk, in case it might give her some idea about how to escape or how to help her grandfather and Ben Cartwright avoid an ambush. Too, she worried greatly about Hoss, hoping he was okay.

The Whartons unsaddled the horses, took

some jerky out of the saddlebags, and ate it as they pitched their bedrolls in the darkness.

"I sure got an itch in my britches," Vern complained, hobbling around the camp.

"I told you," Lem said, "we aren't touching the girl until after Coffee's dead. She's our bait, and I want her alive until then."

"It ain't that," Vern replied. "I must've picked up something back at Fran's, 'cause things sure burn down there. Makes it hard on a fellow to walk or ride."

Willis scratched himself. "I thought maybe it was just me, but I've been having some itching myself."

Lem laughed at his brothers. "Maybe you two should've stayed in prison, then, where the girls wouldn't give you more than you can handle."

That was the last thing Sara Ann remembered before she dozed off.

Come morning, Lem wasn't laughing anymore. He too was walking gingerly around the camp, and grimacing like his groin had been scalded when he sat in the saddle.

With the packhorse trailing behind them, Roy Coffee, Ben, and Hoss slipped out of Virginia City before sunrise, so as not to be seen by very many people.

They rode grimly, each weighted down with ammunition and thoughts of Sara Ann and how vulnerable she must be in the clutches of the Whartons.

"What is it that turns a man bad, Roy?" Ben asked on the road.

Roy shrugged. "Ben, in my business I think the question is what is it that makes a man turn good. Seems like there aren't enough good ones in anything anymore."

Hoss sat silently in the saddle, his regrets, if not deeper, then at least more personal than Coffee's or Ben's. He faulted himself for not protecting Sara Ann better. Periodically he would pat the .44-caliber Russian Model Smith & Wesson revolver at his side, or the .44-caliber Henry rimfire carbine beneath his leg.

"You can't brood about it all day, Hoss," Ben finally said.

Hoss shook his head, then frowned at the tingling pain from the still tender lump the Whartons had given him. "Not much I can say."

"Don't blame yourself, Hoss," Roy said, "we'll get her back just fine."

Hoss nodded. "If they lay a hand on her, they'll regret it the rest of their short lives."

By nightfall the three men had made it to the south end of Lake Tahoe. They made camp and ate tins of peaches for supper.

Ben thought of Sara Ann and of Little Joe, less than a day's ride away. The trail to Timberline Pass would take them near the timber lease, but Ben knew they wouldn't have time to stop, at least not on the way up. He hoped his youngest son was holding his own against those rugged loggers. Little Joe certainly had something to prove to Adam and to Ben. But, Ben wondered, didn't Little Joe have something to prove to himself most of all?

Ben said a prayer for Sara Ann. And one for Little Joe.

CHAPTER 11

In the days since his father left camp, Little Joe had learned a considerable amount about the logging industry and the life of the logger. The most important bit of information came from Jack Chaney, who gave him some plugs of chewing tobacco.

"I don't chew," Little Joe said, "but thanks anyway."

"It ain't for chewing. It's for your bed."

Little Joe scratched his head and took the tobacco that Chaney pressed in his hand.

"Chop it up, then grind it between your hands until it's fine, then spread it over your blankets. It'll help keep lice out of your bed, and believe me, lice can make your life hell."

That information had made Little Joe's life easier. The information he was gathering for Adam might make Adam's life easier too. From talking to the bull whacker, Roe Derus, and the faller, Jack Chaney, he had learned that a ponderosa pine can grow more than four feet in diameter and up to a hundred fifty feet tall, while the sugar pines can spread up to eight feet across and a hundred seventy-five feet in the air. On average, a crew of two men could cut at least two trees a day and possibly three, depending on whether they were ponderosa or sugar pines. There were three crews of forty men each, not counting the teamsters, flume operators, blacksmiths, cooks, and assorted other men necessary to keep the camp running. Of each forty-man crew, thirty men worked as fallers in two-man crews, while the remaining ten were buckers and choke setters. Little Joe had paid close attention to those details and planned to forward them to Adam to make sense out of them, since Adam was so good with numbers.

One thing that continued to bother Little Joe was Jack Chaney's comment that he had signed on with the Cartwright timber operation for the promise of a dollar and a half a day. Though Chaney wasn't charged room and board, like most logging companies assessed their crews, Chaney was only getting a dollar a day. It didn't make sense. Little Joe wished he could talk to Adam to help resolve his confusion, but it would be days before that was possible. After all, his father hadn't said when he would return.

With paper and envelope borrowed from the bookkeeper, C. C. Livermore, Little Joe sat down the night before the mail carrier was to arrive and wrote down his findings. Little Joe knew he had to give the letter to Livermore to add to the camp's mail. Likewise, he knew Nat Greer would probably go through the mail and open any correspondence he had with

Adam. Thinking the situation through, Little Joe decided to address this letter to Lucia Sinclair, Adam's woman friend. Lucia worked at the Storey County Courthouse and could be trusted to get the information to Adam. Little Joe scribbled a note to Lucia atop the letter to Adam, asking her to see that his brother got the information. Then he wrote a second letter to Adam as a decoy, hoping Nat Greer might intercept it and disregard the more important letter to Lucia.

This second letter was perfunctory. Little Joe told Adam that he was learning the logging business and had been out with two of the three crews to date, as well as with the teamsters. For fun, Little Joe called Nat Greer an "odd duck" who ran the camp like his personal kingdom. After finishing that letter, Little Joe addressed both envelopes, then found a candle, which he lit for wax to seal the envelopes. He put a few spots of wax on Lucia's letter, then plenty extra on Adam's envelope to make it look all the more secretive. He smiled at his cleverness. He just hoped it was enough to outfox Nat Greer.

Little Joe walked out of his bunkhouse, toward the camp office. In the distance he could hear the thuds of axes and rasping of saws. Since it was mail day, he had stayed in camp so he could deliver his letters not too long before the scheduled arrival of the mail rider. Though he hadn't seen Nat Greer all morning, Little Joe doubted the foreman was out in the woods. He figured he was ensconced in the office, checking all mail that went out, to ensure none of it could damage him. Little Joe stepped up to the office door and barged in. He was right. Nat Greer was standing over a nervous-looking C. C. Livermore. The bookish Livermore seemed disturbed by Little Joe's arrival.

"Morning," Little Joe said. "I've got mail to send. Today is mail day, isn't it?"

"Yes, sir," Livermore replied.

Greer only grumbled, then motioned to the counter. "Leave it there and we'll take care of it."

"Just a letter to my brother, but it's not as important as the one to my girlfriend. That's the only bad thing about working out here so far from Virginia City."

"It's a real shame," Nat Greer said out of the corner of his mouth, his fingers tapping impatiently at the desk beside the bookkeeper. "Maybe you ought to head back to Virginia City and pester her instead of us." Greer twirled the end of his handlebar mustache and eyed Little Joe like a hungry mountain lion watches a lamb.

Little Joe forced himself to grin at Greer. "She's a damn sight better looking than you two. No offense, Livermore."

The bookkeeper answered with a faint smile.

Greer stood up to his full six-four height and looked down at Little Joe. He spread his legs apart and planted his balled fists on his hips. "Now, are you gonna leave so we can get some work done, work you Cartwrights want done?"

"You keep forgetting who's your boss, Greer," Little Joe answered, his chin jutting forward in defiance.

Greer licked his lips. "You're forgetting who's bigger, Cartwright," he replied, his words dripping with challenge and sarcasm.

"Maybe I should be going," Little Joe answered.

Greer nodded triumphantly, as if satisfied that he had cowed Little Joe.

"Now," Little Joe continued, "would be a good time to visit the work site of the number three crew."

Greer's ruddy face turned a deeper shade of red and his dark eyes flared with anger. "I told you to stay away from the number three crew."

"Why?" Little Joe said. "Cartwright money pays them, and I'm representing the Cartwright interests."

"I've told you, it's too dangerous. The terrain is rough and my men don't have time to be nursemaiding the owner's kid. If you get hurt, I'll have hell to pay."

Little Joe considered stalking out the door for the work site of the number three crew, but held back. If he did, Nat Greer would follow, maybe even try to stop him physically. Little Joe figured Livermore had been ordered not to let any mail leave the camp without Greer first looking it over. Above everything else, he wanted to make sure the letter to Lucia Sinclair made the day's mail run.

Little Joe lifted his finger and pointed it at Greer's nose. "I'll catch the number three crew another time."

Greer sneered. "You're getting smarter, Cartwright."

"You're not, and won't until you understand I'm your boss." Little Joe shook his finger at Greer's nose. "Until you get that through your thick head, we're going to have trouble."

Greer flinched in anger, his balled right fist hitting the open palm of his left. "We're gonna have trouble, all right, Cartwright. You may be my boss, but you don't run things around here. I do, and you better remember that."

Little Joe answered Greer with his hardest stare and silence.

"You two need to cool off awhile or somebody's gonna get hurt," Livermore said nervously.

Little Joe nodded at the bookkeeper. "There's some things I've been meaning to ask you, Livermore."

The bookkeeper swallowed hard, his Adam's apple bobbing in his throat like a cork on rugged water.

"What do the fallers make a day?"

Livermore grimaced and looked from Little Joe to Greer and back.

"What's it to you?" interrupted Greer, striding toward the counter and Little Joe.

"Some men say they aren't getting what they were promised."

Greer's eyes narrowed and his brow furrowed as he leaned over the counter toward Little Joe. "I don't know what the men say they were promised. I just know what they make."

"Which is?"

"A dollar fifty a day," Greer answered.

"All the fallers?"

"All of them," Greer replied. "Dammit, if you don't believe me, I'll have Livermore show you the books."

"Do," Little Joe shot back.

Greer sneered as he picked up Little Joe's letters for the mail. "Livermore," Greer commanded, "get out the pay ledger and show Cartwright. Let him see for himself. We've got the records. You think I'm trying to steal or something?"

"I'm getting to know the business," Little Joe replied as Livermore retreated to a shelf and pulled out a bound leather volume which he toted to the counter.

The bookkeeper tossed the ledger in front of Little Joe and flipped through the lined pages to a section marked wages.

"Who's complaining, so we can look under his name?" Greer asked.

Little Joe smiled at the trick. "Several of the men in the number three crew," he answered.

Livermore fidgeted and coughed uneasily as Little Joe thumbed through the pages, lingering over several so as not to give away Jack Chaney when he came to that logger's entry in the ledger. Beside the name of every faller, a dollar fifty was recorded as pay for every day he worked. Jack Chaney was no different.

"You see any problems?" Greer asked.

Little Joe shook his head. "Nothing that I see. Guess I'll have to tell my acquaintances in number three to quit badmouthing you."

Greer snarled. "They wouldn't complain. They're my best crew. I work them hard and give them the most dangerous tasks."

Little Joe nodded. There had to be something else special about crew number three. Maybe it was special privileges. Maybe that was why Greer kept them segregated from the rest of the loggers.

With the letters in his hand, Greer turned away from Little Joe toward a back room that served as a private office in the day and Livermore's room at night. "Let him look at that ledger all day long," he commanded Livermore.

"Don't walk off with my letters," Little Joe shot back.

Greer chuckled. "I've got a couple of my own to add to the packet." Greer disappeared for a few minutes, then returned, waving Little Joe's letters and a few others in the air. Greer seemed to make sure Little Joe saw both the front and back of the letter to Lucia, as if trying to prove there had been no tampering. However, he only showed Little Joe the front of the letter to Adam.

Little Joe was certain that he had out-smarted Greer. "You can be okay," Little Joe said sarcastically, "when you follow orders."

Greer dropped the letters in the mail pouch and retreated to the back room again.

When he disappeared, Little Joe leaned closer to C. C. Livermore. The bookkeeper couldn't hide his eyes behind his thick glasses, though he seemed to want to. Little Joe whispered a question at the bookkeeper. "Are the figures here accurate?"

Livermore's lips quivered and his eyes seemed to overflow with doubt. He coughed into his fist, then stared straight at Little Joe. "The totals add up," he said, "the totals add up."

"But are the figures accurate?" Little Joe whispered.

"The totals add up," Livermore repeated, then wiped away the sweat beading upon his forehead.

Little Joe reached across the counter and patted him on the shoulder. "Thanks, Livermore." He headed for the door, certain that the bookkeeper had been lying. Little Joe saw it in his eyes. But even more than deceit, he had seen fear in Livermore's eyes. Livermore could never talk, not as long as he was under Greer's thumb. It seemed Greer had a lot of secrets at this camp, the greatest being the duties of the number three crew.

Little Joe walked past the bunkhouses and up toward the earthen dam that held back the headwaters for the flume. The teamsters were hard at work, dragging the logs from the woods and rolling them into the water for the loggers to load into the flume. At first the men loading the flume were cordial with him, telling him how much morale had improved since he had ordered wagons to pick them up at the end of the day.

"How much do you fellows make a day?" Little Joe asked.

"Same as most loggers," replied a chute man at the flume, "dollar a day."

"Any of you offered a dollar fifty a day?"

Several of the men laughed.

The chute man nodded. "Rumor started early on that Cartwright Enterprises was paying a dollar fifty, but nothing came of it. Nobody I know got any of that money."

Little Joe shook his head. The books showed otherwise. Was Greer siphoning money off into his own pocket? Or was the fear in Livermore's eyes the panic of a swindler with someone on his tail? Little Joe couldn't see Livermore swindling money from men twice his size.

"Why you ask?" said one of the men as he helped guide a log in place.

Before Little Joe could answer, Nat Greer's two supervising lackeys, Ben Tull and Ted Karnes, approached.

"Shhhh," one of the men whispered, "the idiots are coming."

Tull was tall and lean, mostly arms and legs, which caged amazing strength. Karnes was a stockier fellow, with a flame of red hair and an odd curl to his lips.

"Cartwright," Tull called from the foot of the earthen dam. "You're distracting the men. Come on down."

Karnes seconded Tull's instructions. "Yeah, we're about to ride out with the lunch wagon. You can ride with us and learn more about the business."

"I'm learning plenty up here," Little Joe said, curious as to why they wanted to get him away from the flume. He held his ground, and Karnes and Tull advanced toward him. Little Joe just smiled at their frowns.

"They're mean men, just like Greer," the chute man said under his breath.

Little Joe nodded and waited, watching the line of logs being dragged by teams of oxen from the work sites of both the number one and number two crews.

Then it struck him!

Since arriving at the logging camp, he had seen hundreds of logs pulled from the one and two sites to the west, but not a single one from the northern site worked by the number three crew. He looked across the pond to the trail taken each morning by Greer's special crew and realized it was nothing but a couple of wagon ruts. The loggers headed in that direction every morning and came from that direction every night, but where were the logs they should have been cutting each day?

Little Joe scratched his chin as Tull and Karnes reached the top of the dam.

"You shouldn't be bothering the men," Tull said.

"Yeah," Karnes echoed, "it could distract them and let a log through at the wrong time, damage the flume."

Little Joe grinned, knowing now their reluctance to let him watch the flume too long.

"I'd feel a lot better," Little Joe said, "if you two were out watching the crews and directing their work instead of mine."

Karnes shrugged and ran his fingers through his red hair. "Our job is to keep you out of the way."

"So you don't get hurt," interjected Tull.

Little Joe crossed his arms over his chest. "And I'm in the way up here."

"Look around," Karnes said, "work's stopped while we take care of you."

Little Joe glanced about, and sure enough, all activity had halted. "Seems to me they were doing plenty of work until you two showed up."

"Seems wrong, Cartwright," Tull answered, a growl in his throat.

"You want to walk down," Karnes broke in, "or do you want us to throw you down?"

Little Joe grinned. "Well, fellows, what are we waiting for?" He lifted his elbows, giving each man a chance to slide their arms in his and escort him down the dam like some old matron at a social. Tull and Karnes doubled their fists.

Behind him, Little Joe heard the snickers of the loggers, a merriment that died when both Karnes and Tull glanced back over their shoulders. "Get your butts to work, now," Karnes yelled.

Little Joe angled down the dam, Karnes and Tull following, cursing all the way.

At the foot of the dam Little Joe waited for them. "Anything else you fellows — or Greer — don't want me to do, just let me know," he said. "But I promise you this, I'll figure out what you're hiding from Cartwright Enterprises."

"We don't know what you're talking about," Tull answered. "All we're trying to do is help Cartwright Enterprises get what it's paying for, a decent day's work out of all the men on the payroll. We figure that's something you ought to be thanking us for."

Little Joe turned away from the two men and started back to camp just in time to see a man mounting a horse outside the office. A half-dozen canvas pouches were flung over the horse's rump. It was the letter carrier. Little Joe whistled and waved his hands, then broke into a run.

A lean whippet of a man, the mail carrier looked Little Joe's way, then waved him on in.

Tull and Karnes broke into a run behind Little Joe and were close enough to hear Little Joe's question when he reached the mail carrier.

"You got a letter for me to take?" the mail carrier asked.

"Nope," Little Joe answered, just as Tull and Karnes ran up. "I want to check and make sure you got the letter for my girlfriend in Virginia City."

Behind him, Little Joe thought he heard Tull and Karnes sigh in relief. Perhaps they were just breathing hard from the run.

"I got it if they put it in the pouch inside."

"It's important," Little Joe said. "I've asked her to marry me. If she says yes, I'll be leaving logging."

The mail carrier twisted around in his saddle and loosened the top pouch on the stack. He opened it up and pulled out a handful of envelopes, calling off the names of a few suppliers and several men before reaching the name of Lucia Sinclair.

Little Joe smiled. The back of the envelope had not been tampered with. "That's it. Thanks."

"Sure thing," the mail carrier replied, shoving the correspondence back in the pouch and tying it back on the horse's rump. He grinned. "Maybe I'll bring her answer back from Virginia City."

Little Joe nodded. "That'd be nice." He turned around to face Tull and Karnes. "Why're you two so interested in what I had to say to the mail runner?"

Tull sneered. "We figured you were gonna slow down his work like you're doing to all the other men around here, you being the nuisance that you are."

"This nuisance," said Little Joe, "owns twenty percent of Cartwright Enterprises, the outfit that you work for."

Both men laughed. "I don't care how much you own of Cartwright Enterprises. We work for Nat Greer and you best remember it, because you don't carry no sway with us."

Little Joe pushed his way between them and headed back toward the bunkhouse. They followed him, and he knew they would for the rest of the day. There was no sense in trying to explore the trail taken by the number three crew. He would have to do that later, when he might slip away undetected. He wanted to have another conversation with C. C. Livermore, when Greer wasn't around. That wouldn't be possible either, not as long as Tull and Karnes were shadowing him.

Little Joe walked toward the bunkhouse and slipped inside, pulled off his normal boots and replaced them with the spiked logger's boots that Derus had provided him. He might just as well ride the lunch wagons out to find the number one and number two crews.

When he emerged from the bunkhouse, he found Tull leaning beside the door, sucking on a cigarette. Tull whistled twice, then fell in behind Little Joe.

As Little Joe cleared the corner of the bunkhouse and headed for the lunch wagon, he saw Karnes turn the corner from the back of the bunkhouse. They had been guarding both doors. Little Joe wished he had gotten his revolver from the saddlebags under his bed, just in case.

He climbed in the back of the wagon amid the pots and pans the cooks were loading.

Wordlessly, Tull and Karnes joined him.

Little Joe knew he had stumbled onto something, something that scared Greer and his men. Now, he just had to find out what it was.

CHAPTER 12

When the cook rang the bell to signal lunch, the woods that had been alive with the whack of axes and the low grating of crosscut saws went silent and men streamed in from their trees. They moved quickly, grabbing tin plates and heaping them with beans, potatoes, roast pork, and bread. They picked up tins of coffee the cooks had set out on the wagon's tailgate, then moved to stumps and downed logs, where they sat and gobbled down their meals. They didn't say much. They didn't have time to waste on conversation, not when they only had twenty minutes for lunch. Most men liked to scarf down their food, then lie down for a few minutes of rest from the bone-grinding weariness of work.

After the loggers took their plates, Little Joe grabbed one and piled it with grub. He was pleased to see the bull whacker Roe Derus coming in from the skid road. Derus was one Little Joe could trust. Without Tull or Karnes noticing, Little Joe caught Derus's eye and with a nod of his head invited the bull whacker to join him.

Little Joe walked away from the wagon, aware he was being watched like a hawk by

Karnes and Tull. He wasn't sure whether or not Roe Derus had picked up his signal, so nonchalant was the bull whacker, but after gathering his food, the teamster ambled over to Little Joe and sat down on the log beside him.

Under his breath and between bites, Little Joe whispered questions.

"You ever seen where the number three crew works?"

Derus shoved a bite of bread in his mouth. "No," he replied.

Little Joe watched Tull and Karnes staring at him. He lifted his coffee cup to his mouth, holding it a moment to hide his lips. "The skid road doesn't circle from here around the mountain to their camp, does it?"

Screening his mouth with a forkload of meat, Derus answered, "No," then took the bite and began to chew.

From beside the wagon, Tull and Karnes watched, evidently unaware of the conversation.

Little Joe lifted his arm to his mouth. "I can't understand why no logs ever come from the number three section to the camp." He drew his sleeve across his mouth to wipe his lips.

Derus nodded slightly. With a wad of bread, he sopped up bean juice from his plate. "Neither can most of the men, but be careful."

Picking up his coffee tin between both hands instead of by the handle, Little Joe raised it to his lips and blew in it like it was too hot. "How come?"

Derus placed his clean tin plate and empty coffee cup by his side on the log and slid down onto the ground, leaning back against the log and pulling his hat down over his face as if to shade it. "The last man that asked that question aloud died in an accident the next day," he whispered.

Little Joe dug deep into the coffee cup, draining it of the strong liquid, then took a deep breath. He didn't like the sound of this. He wished he had paid more attention to this timber lease when it was discussed by the rest of the family. There were fifty thousand acres under lease, as he recalled, but he did not remember the boundaries of the lease or where this camp was situated on the property. It didn't make sense, one crew disappearing every working day and returning with nothing to show for a day's pay.

Little Joe stood up, stretched, and carried his tin plate, cup, and eating utensils to a big pot where men placed their dirties. The cook looked around the wagon, then rang the bell that had brought the men in from their work sites. The loggers got up begrudgingly, made their way to the wagon and dropped off their dishes. A couple of men grabbed pieces of cherry pie or cookies to eat on the way back to their back-breaking work. Little Joe didn't envy them.

Soon the air was filled with the sounds of axes and saws and men shouting. The cook and his helpers gathered the scattered pots and plates left by a few loggers and loaded up for the return trip. As soon as they got back, they would need to start preparing another meal, a bigger meal for supper.

Just as the cook was climbing into the wagon, Ted Karnes called to him. "You wouldn't have an extra axe, would you?"

The cook reached over behind the spring seat and picked up an axe, which Karnes grabbed instantly, a wide smile crawling across his face like a centipede.

Shortly, the wagon was rolling back toward camp, leaving Little Joe face-to-face with Ben Tull and Ted Karnes.

"We've been talking," Tull announced.

"Yeah," said Karnes, "we've been figuring how to help you understand logging a little better."

"You've been learning it from the top instead of from the bottom like everybody else around here."

"Most of us," Karnes put in, "weren't born rich like you Cartwrights." He brandished the axe like a weapon as he advanced toward Little Joe.

"We won't start you out on the very bottom, like some choke setter, no sir," mocked Tull.

"We'll let you handle the job that pays the best among the loggers, a faller."

Little Joe watched them carefully as they drew nearer. This would not be the place for them to make a move against him, because there was the potential for too many witnesses, but he knew by the glimmer in their eyes that they had come up with a scheme that could do him harm. "I'm not afraid of work . . . or you."

Tull shrugged innocently. "No, no, we aren't trying to scare you off."

"Not at all," seconded Karnes. Stepping toward Little Joe, he flipped the axe in the air and caught it near the blade, offering it handle first to Little Joe.

Little Joe took the axe, uncertain what their angle was, but certain they had one. One that wasn't in his best interest.

"We want you to fell a tree, to see what hard work it is, dammit," said Tull.

"It's man's work," said Karnes.

"You want to win our respect around here, the respect of the loggers," Tull started. "Then show them you can down a tree."

"I can handle it," Little Joe answered.

"Then follow us," Karnes said, moving down the slope away from the other loggers.

Little Joe wondered if they were just trying to get him out of sight from the other men so they could attack him.

Tull seemed to read his mind. "Where we're

taking you, you can work by yourself and not worry about killing someone if the tree falls the wrong way."

Karnes corrected Tull. "You might worry about killing yourself if the tree falls the wrong way."

Both men laughed as if this were an inside joke.

Karnes and Tull walked with their eyes cast upward, looking for a tree the right size.

"There's one for you, Cartwright." Tull pointed to a sapling that didn't even reach Little Joe's chest.

Finally, Karnes stopped beneath a ponderosa pine that was maybe seventy-five feet tall. It grew in the shadow of other trees and its upper branches seemed matted with fallen limbs that had snagged there.

Little Joe estimated the tree was two and a half, maybe three feet in diameter. It wasn't the biggest he had ever seen, but he knew he had never cut down a tree this size before.

"You man enough to try it?" Tull asked.

"Work doesn't scare me," Little Joe shot back.

"Yeah, well you ain't ever spent half a day swinging three pounds of steel at the end of a four-foot axe handle," Karnes answered. "That's work."

Little Joe felt the anger rising in him. "If this is the tree you want chopped, get out of my way."

Both men laughed.

"Just like a sapling," Karnes said.

Tull nodded. "Don't know how to cut it, but he'll get started right away. Now listen to me, Cartwright, and I'll explain how you do this." Tull glanced up at the treetop, then looked at the ground terrain and the adjacent trees. He pointed down a narrow, shady tunnel that stretched between neighboring trees. "That's where you want to drop her, in that clear space."

Karnes marched around to the side of the tree facing the clearing and glanced quickly up to the tree. "To do that, you want to place an undercut here." He pulled out a pocket-knife, opened the blade and notched the bark. "You want to angle out a section of wood about a third of the way into the tree. Do a flat lower cut and then an upper cut at a forty-five-degree angle. Keep the cut smooth. If it's rounded on the top or bottom, the tree'll roll off target when it falls and can bounce up and hurt you."

Tull motioned for Little Joe to come to the back side of the tree. "When you've finished the undercut, come around to this side and start your back cut. Chop into the tree until it begins to tilt. When that happens, yell 'timber' and get out of the way."

"Yeah," Karnes nodded. "We don't want you to get hurt."

Both men laughed again.

Little Joe knew it was some kind of joke they were playing on him, but he couldn't figure it out.

"Have at it," Tull said.

"See if you can have it down by dark," Karnes said as both men turned away and started back toward the skid road.

Angry at their condescension, Little Joe spat in their direction as they retreated. He lifted the axe, drew it back over his shoulder and slammed it into the tree. It stuck with a thunk. He released the handle and paused a moment to roll up his sleeves.

Overhead a gentle breeze meandered through the tall trees, setting the pines to whispering and swaying, the slight motion releasing a pinecone, which thudded to the ground beside Little Joe. Birds twittered all around.

Little Joe grabbed the axe handle and worked it out of the pine, then marched around the tree and began the undercut. He put his anger into each toss of the axe, but soon his ire was dissipated by the exertion, and his muscles began to scream with the pain of drawing back the three-pound axe head and flinging it into the tree.

Gradually an angled notch of pulpy white wood began to appear in the tree. The cuts were ragged, not the smooth cuts the experienced loggers made, and that angered Little Joe because he knew Tull and Karnes would laugh at the cut. They might laugh at his lack

198

of skill, but they wouldn't make fun of his hard work. He would down that tree before supper and even whittle it into toothpicks if that's what it took to prove to Greer's two supervisors he could do a man's job.

The work was long, hard, and sweaty. Little Joe finally removed his sweat-stained shirt, which stuck to his arms and chest as he attacked the tree. The soft breeze against his sweaty chest sent a shiver coursing through his body, and his muscles seemed to tighten up on him for a moment before he worked out the kinks with the repetitive motion of chopping. Wood chips flew out of the notch and whizzed by his ear or stung his bare arms with each swing of the axe.

Little Joe lost his sense of time, his existence measured only by the repetitive swings of the axe. Occasionally, between swings, he heard a low grinding growl from somewhere overhead. Little Joe shrugged off the noise and continued attacking the tree, which seemed to shudder and vibrate more and more with each thud of the axe.

By mid-afternoon Little Joe had finished the undercut and stood back, taking a breather and thinking. As he stood trying to figure out the motive of Karnes and Tull, he ignored the scraping noise overhead. He wanted to give his arms and shoulders a rest before he began the back cut. Thirsty, he walked among the trees, looking for a clean patch of snow that he could use for water.

When he found a suitable swath of white at the base of a sugar pine, Little Joe scooped up a handful of the crunchy snow and fed his thirst. The ice melted slowly in his throat, his whole body seeming to soak up the moisture. He sat back on the ground and leaned against the sugar pine, letting his muscles rest and still trying to figure out what Tull and Karnes were up to. It wasn't any good, whatever it was. Little Joe was certain of that, if nothing else.

Then, a few minutes later, he understood. He heard the sound of someone approaching. He stayed seated, eating snow from the clump beside him, as Tull and Karnes, oblivious to his whereabouts, approached the ponderosa pine Little Joe had been attacking.

"Where is he?" asked Karnes.

"Has it fallen?" Tull replied, with a glance up at the treetop.

Karnes, too, looked at the top of the tree, and shook his head. "It's still up there."

Little Joe didn't understand what they were referring to. It was obvious the tree hadn't fallen.

"Well, where'd the son of a bitch go to?" Tull asked.

Little Joe stood up. "Here's the son of a bitch," he scowled.

Both men flinched with surprise at Little Joe's voice.

"We didn't hear your axe," Karnes said.

"Yeah," Tull added, "we were just checking on you to make sure nothing had happened to you."

Little Joe started toward them, holding his axe with both hands. "Check the undercut."

"It looks fine," Karnes said, without moving any closer to the tree for a better look.

"Maybe a little rugged," Tull added, "but better than most new fallers." Tull, too, did not venture any nearer the tree.

Little Joe could not escape the feeling that the two men were scared of something, but he could not figure what it might be.

"We've got work to do," Karnes said. "We just wanted to check on you when we heard the chopping stop."

Little Joe grinned. So that was it. If they put him to work chopping a tree, they could keep up with him by listening for the sound of his axe falling. If he stopped chopping for long, they knew he had abandoned his job and might be snooping around, spying on things they didn't want him to know about.

"We'll check on you later," Tull called over his shoulder as the two retreated up the incline toward the skid road.

Now Little Joe knew for sure that his every move would be watched by Greer's men. He would have to be careful not to be seen, especially when he tried to find the work site of the number three crew.

That would come later. Now he just wanted to down that tree. Little Joe approached the pine from the opposite side and began the back cut. He grimaced and cried out from the pain a couple times as his muscles, which had stiffened during the break, began to loosen up and fall once more into a steady, if not entirely comfortable, rhythm.

His hands ached and a blister had developed between his thumb and forefinger. Sometimes he grunted at the blister's pain as the axe thudded into the tree. Other times he just gritted his teeth. He would show Tull and Karnes his mettle.

With his determination and pain growing with each swing, Little Joe attacked the tree with a fury. He worked hard, taking little more than momentary breaks all afternoon. As the sun went behind the mountain peaks, the air turned instantly cool, but Little Joe kept working. As his intensity increased, that grinding growl increased overhead. He glanced up once, but so focused was he on the tall pine that he dismissed the noise as his imagination. He slammed the axe time and time again against the tree, the wood chips flying all around until he stood on a carpet created by his axe.

Then the tree began to quiver slightly, then shudder vigorously. Little Joe stepped back. The grinding growl overhead grew to a screech. By instinct, Little Joe tossed down his axe and ran away from the pine just as a huge limb crashed into the ground where he had been standing. The falling limb could have killed him!

He didn't have much time to think about it, because the pine began to quiver. The pine shuddered again, then gave up a crack that resounded like a gunshot through the woods as the last hold on stability was broken. The tree began to lean into the undercut and tilt forward.

"Timmm-berrr," Little Joe yelled. He jogged farther away from the pine as it lost its balance and fell forward, snapping limbs off adjacent trees. The breaking lumber popped loudly as the tree fell toward the ground.

When the top of the uneven undercut hit the beveled bottom of the cut, the tree wobbled off the stump and hit hard against a ponderosa pine bordering the clear swath where Little Joe had hoped to place the tree. Several limbs were sheared free and many more dead limbs that had snagged in that pine fell free as well, showering the swath.

The tree hit the earth with a crash that roared like thunder through the woods, then bounced up, as if it were trying to regain its footing, and writhed back toward the stump and Little Joe.

Although he was out of danger's way, Little Joe backed up even farther, waiting for the dust to clear.

It had all happened so fast, it took Little Joe a moment to replay the events in his mind.

The tree had begun to shudder. He had backed up. Then the screech came overhead. He had tossed his axe down. The tree had started to lean. He'd run away. The huge branch had crashed into the ground beside the tree.

"Damn them," Little Joe shouted.

He raced to the fresh tree stump, which was partially covered by the twisted form of the broken limb. Little Joe kicked at the limb. It was a foot thick in places, with several smaller branches jutting out from it. The limb had landed on his axe. He squatted down, grabbed the head of the axe and pulled part of it from under the limb. The handle was snapped in half.

Little Joe studied the limb and cursed again. The limb was dead. That meant it had been snagged overhead, a constant danger the whole time he had been working. That explained why neither Tull nor Karnes had approached the tree when they came to check on him. They knew the limb might fall at any time. Little Joe knew he was lucky the snagged limb had held until the tree began to topple. Otherwise, he, rather than the axe handle, might have been under that limb.

"Damn them," Little Joe repeated.

He grabbed the other half of the axe handle

and started up the incline toward the skid road. He realized it was late and that the work had quit except for a solitary axe man somewhere. Little Joe tried to dash up the incline, but he was too tired. Instead he saved what energy he had left for Karnes and Tull.

At the skid road he headed toward the wagon, where several of the loggers had taken seats. A couple of them clapped for him, giving him a wide grin of encouragement.

Tull and Karnes, though, weren't smiling. They stood at the wagon tailgate, betraying no emotion, save possibly disappointment that he hadn't been hurt.

Near the wagon, Little Joe tossed both ends of the axe down and charged Tull, striking him full in the nose before the supervisor could react. Little Joe screamed from the pain in his fist but was so overcome with fury that he could not stop himself. Though a bigger man, Tull was caught by surprise by Little Joe's sudden outburst and could do little but try to protect himself as Little Joe pummeled him in the face, stomach, and side.

For a moment Little Joe felt a hand grab his shoulder, then he felt the hand being wrenched away and heard the welcome voice of Jack Chaney. "It's one on one, Karnes. You just stay out of it."

Finally comprehending his predicament, Tull began to fight back, but his punches were wild because he was unable to see much for all the blood splattered on his face.

"You tried to kill me," Little Joe yelled.

Tull staggered backward into the wagon, then collapsed on a skid in the middle of the road.

Little Joe moved in to attack him, but Jack Chaney grabbed him and wrapped his powerful arms around him.

"Take it easy, Little Joe, you don't want to kill him."

"Yeah, I do," Little Joe spat out. "He tried to kill me. Karnes did too."

"Liar," Karnes said. "I don't know what he's talking about." Karnes moved over to help Tull, who was still shocked by the sudden fury of Little Joe Cartwright. "He wanted to learn logging," Karnes continued, "so we sent him down the slope to cut down a tree."

Chaney glared at Karnes. "Was it the ponderosa pine that had the big widow maker on top?"

"Widow maker?" Joe asked.

"A dead limb that's hung up in the branches, a limb that could fall and kill a man."

"That's it, that's the tree," Little Joe said, trying to break free of Chaney and attack Karnes.

Chaney turned to the wagon. "Somebody go check if it was the dangerous tree. You know the one I mean."

A couple of fallers jumped from the wagon

and darted down the slope. In their absence, everyone was silent except Tull, who mumbled curses as he wiped the blood away from his face.

When the two loggers returned, their somber expressions told all the men that the accusation had been true.

Chaney shoved Little Joe aside and marched up to Karnes. "Did Greer put you up to this?"

Karnes stood defiant. "I sent him down there so he wouldn't kill any of you loggers. He picked out his own damn tree to cut. Tull and I had nothing to do with it."

"That's a lie!" Little Joe shouted, and charged Karnes, but the two loggers who had just returned grabbed his arms.

"Did Greer put you up to this?" Chaney repeated.

Karnes just snarled. "You better be careful, Chaney, or you'll be looking for a job with some other outfit, and I'll put the word out you're nothing but a troublemaker."

"Did Greer put you up to this?"

Karnes spun around and helped Tull up. Without another word the two supervisors hobbled back down the road toward camp.

Chaney pointed Little Joe toward the wagon. "Climb in," he said.

Little Joe managed to pull his body into the wagon despite the soreness from all the work and the fight. Several loggers patted him on the back to show their approval of his pugnacity. Their touch didn't make his body feel any better, but it helped his spirit to know he had allies in camp.

CHAPTER 13

As always, supper was eaten without conversation. The only noise was the clink of utensils against tin plates and grunts of hungry men. Little Joe never felt hungrier. He had seconds and thirds of fried beef, boiled cabbage, canned tomatoes, and hash, sopping it all up with a half-dozen pieces of fresh bread and washing it down with five cups of black coffee. It was a meal that would have matched Hoss's portions, and Little Joe could have eaten more.

Though no one said a word during the meal, Little Joe knew his fight with Tull was on the minds of every man seated around the tables. He figured he had come up another notch in their estimation for whipping Tull. He could tell it by the looks in their eyes or the set of the lips or their nods when his gaze met theirs.

Little Joe wondered what Nat Greer's response would be when his two henchman reported to him that he had not only escaped unscathed from the dangerous chopping assignment, but had also beaten Tull. Something odd was going on here at the camp, and Nat Greer was behind it for sure, but what exactly was it?

A few men were standing up and stretching or carrying their plates to the wash pan when Little Joe decided a large helping of apple cobbler would be just right to finish his meal. As he slid off the bench and headed for the dessert table, what little noise there was in the dining hall died instantly.

Little Joe turned around to see Nat Greer standing at the door. Behind him stood Ted Karnes and Ben Tull, his face swollen and bruised. Greer stood akimbo, his massive arms angling out from his thick upper torso, his balled fists planted firmly on his hips. He wore a scowl hard enough to scratch steel.

Little Joe continued to the dessert table and helped himself to a bowl of apple cobbler, taking his time about it, feeling the hard stare of Nat Greer in his back.

"I want everybody to sit down and listen," Greer boomed.

The loggers who had stood slid onto the nearest benches and stared at the hulking figure.

Little Joe turned around, slowly ambling back to his place, taking his time to enrage Nat Greer.

Greer lifted his hand and aimed his finger at Little Joe. "You think you're above the rest of the loggers, don't you, Cartwright?"

"I stay in the bunkhouse with them, Greer. That's more than I can say for you and your two monkeys." Little Joe plunked his dish of cobbler on the table for emphasis.

"You ain't been nothing but trouble since you came here, Cartwright," Greer shouted across the room. "You've stirred up the hired help and you're gonna get a lot of these loggers fired."

"Greer, you're forgetting that you're hired help too. I can fire you," Little Joe shot back.

Greer took a step toward Little Joe, shaking his fists. "I'm not gonna have you riling my men again like you did today."

Little Joe nodded. "You want to fire men, go ahead, but you start with every man in the number three crew. I don't know what the hell they're doing, but they're not bringing in any lumber here."

"You bastard," Greer yelled, unbuttoning his sleeve and rolling it up his beefy arm. "I'm gonna get you for that." Greer lunged across the room toward Little Joe.

Karnes and Tull both grabbed him. "Think what you're doing, Nat," Karnes implored, but the big man charged past a table.

Little Joe jumped from between his table and bench and squared to meet Greer's charge. All around the room men stood up, clenched their iron fists, and moved toward Little Joe.

By the time Greer came within striking distance, a dozen loggers were lined in an arc beside him, their fists raised to take on the bull of the woods.

Jack Chaney stepped between Little Joe and Greer. "You better back off, Greer. Little Joe's made friends around here. You don't have any outside of the number three crew."

Karnes and Tull caught up with Greer and grabbed his arms again. "Nat, you've got too much to lose," Karnes said.

Tull stared past Jack Chaney at Little Joe. "You won today, but you won't win again. Not in this camp, not against me."

From the door came another voice, and Little Joe looked past Greer and his henchmen to see Roe Derus, his arms crossed. "You won't be fighting just against Cartwright," Derus said as he stepped into the room. "There'll be a lot of us you'll have to fight."

"This ain't your affair, Roe," Greer called over his shoulder, his eyes still burning at Little Joe.

"Maybe not, Nat, but if you want a fight, start with me. I'm your size."

Greer turned around. "You know I don't want to fight you."

Derus lifted his fists to his face, crouched over and leaned forward onto the balls of his feet. "You sure?"

Greer nodded, his face so red with humiliation that it appeared his cheeks might explode.

"Then get out of here, now," Derus ordered.

Quickly, Greer started for the door, Tull and

Karnes behind him.

Jack Chaney turned around and grinned at Little Joe. "Roe there is a former bare knuckles champ of the Pacific Northwest. That's why Greer can't bully him around."

Little Joe nodded. "Thanks, fellows."

Several of the men slapped him on the back. "He can't fire you," said one.

"But he can kill you," interjected another.

"I don't know what's going on here," Little Joe said, "but I intend to find out." He turned to Jack Chaney. "How much did you tell me you made?"

"Huh?" Chaney said, confused by the change in conversation.

"How much are you paid?"

"A dollar a day," Chaney answered, his face wrinkling with bewilderment.

Little Joe turned around and went from logger to logger. "How much do you make? And you?" he asked.

A dollar a day or a dollar plus room and board came the answer each time.

"Why?" Chaney asked finally.

Little Joe crossed his arms over his chest. "Because Livermore's pay ledger shows each of you getting a dollar fifty."

The loggers grumbled to each other like sailors before a mutiny.

"I think it's time we visited Livermore," Little Joe announced, starting for the door.

The grumbling loggers fell in behind him as

they marched out of the dining hall, through the bunk room, and out the door into the darkness. They angled for the camp office where Livermore kept his bunk in the back room. He hadn't joined them for supper tonight, which was not unusual for him, because he wasn't a big eater. What was unusual, though, was the darkness in the office window. On most nights Livermore would be up working over the books way past this hour.

Little Joe led the mob across the grounds, scaring several of the skinny pigs that ran free around the camp. "Livermore," he called, "we need to talk to you."

"Yeah, yeah," screamed the loggers.

No answer.

"Livermore," Little Joe shouted.

Again no answer.

Little Joe knocked on the door once and it swung eerily forward, then stopped against something.

"What is it?" Jack Chaney asked, turning about to quiet the men.

Little Joe pushed against the door, trying to widen the opening enough to get in. "Something's blocking it." He shoved and the door budged, then gradually gave before his exertion. Whatever was blocking the door screeched as it scraped against the rough-hewn floorboards.

Entering, Little Joe stepped on something, then something else that broke and crackled

214

beneath his caulked boot. He reached over-head for the lamp that should have been hanging from the ceiling, but it was gone. His nose caught the greasy smell of coal oil.

Behind him, Jack Chaney lit a match, which flared for a moment and then gave a pall of light bright enough for Little Joe to see that the office had been ransacked.

"Careful," Little Joe said, "there's coal oil on the floor."

"Somebody run and get a lamp," Chaney called out behind him. The word was passed among the men, and a couple ran off for lanterns.

Little Joe stood motionless. "Livermore," he called softly. For an instant he thought he heard a groan, but he could not be certain because of all the murmurings outside. Through the open door he saw yellow glows approaching and spotted a lantern being passed from man to man and finally to Jack Chaney, who held the light inside.

Little Joe shielded his eyes from the bright glare. As his eyes adjusted, he saw the wreck before him. The counter had been turned over and Livermore's desk smashed. Papers and records were scattered across the floor as well as ledgers, much of the paper soaked with coal oil.

"Someone was planning to set fire to it all," Little Joe said to Chaney, who eased into the room.

Outside, several men shouted questions. "Shut up," Chaney answered, "we don't know anything yet." He looked at Little Joe. "You see anything of Livermore? He was too puny to do all this."

Shaking his head, Little Joe moved toward the back room, then stopped, pointing to the floor. "There's his glasses." Little Joe gritted his teeth. Drops of blood had run down the lenses like red tears. He motioned for Chaney to bring the lantern nearer.

Behind them a couple more loggers squeezed into the room.

Chaney waved at them to stay where they were. "We may have found Livermore."

Little Joe stepped to the door to the back room, the lantern's ball of yellow light casting a pall like death over the room. Little Joe knew what to expect, but he was still shocked when he saw Livermore sprawled across the floor, crimson stains draining from gashes in his body. On the floor near his leg was the axe that had mutilated him.

Little Joe looked from the floor to Chaney and shook his head. A draft of cold air flowed through the window over the bed at the far wall.

"The killer escaped through there," Chaney said, then called out to the front room, "Livermore's dead."

Word passed from man to man as the excitement and the noise grew.

Little Joe was about to step out of the room, but something caught his ear, a slight wisp of a noise. It was Livermore! "Tell them to shut up," Little Joe yelled, "tell them to shut up. He's alive."

Little Joe leaned down over the bookkeeper and felt a wisp of a breath. Livermore batted his eyes, and the exertion seemed to drain him of his last ounce of strength.

"Who did this to you?" Little Joe asked.

Livermore struggled weakly for breath, then grimaced. "Books," he gasped. His chest rose from the floor as he tried to get up. "Two books." His chest sank to the ground and he went limp, his eyes staying open and staring into a distance that only the dead can see.

"Damn," Little Joe said. He pushed himself up from the floor, his hands now sticky with Livermore's blood.

"What did he say?" Chaney whispered.

"Don't tell anybody else, but 'books, two books' were his last words. That make any sense to you?"

"None of this makes sense to me, except that Greer's involved somehow."

"Just what I was thinking. You'd figure the bull of the woods would be at the office checking on the commotion, wouldn't you?"

Little Joe and Chaney retraced their steps to the front office after motioning for those who had entered to leave. Little Joe ordered two men to stand watch over the office and raise a commotion if anyone came near. He ordered another pair to stand by the back window so no one could slip inside that way. Then he ordered everyone else to follow him. He ran back to his bunkhouse and rushed inside to his bed. Bending over, he pulled out his belongings to get his revolver and his carbine.

They were gone!

"Dammit," he cried.

"What is it?" Chaney asked.

"Someone's stolen my guns."

Chaney shook his head. "They're staying one step ahead of us."

"Not for long," Little Joe replied. He left the bunkhouse and stood before the loggers from crews number one and two. A few of the men had lit torches, which cast eerie shadows in the cool night air.

"We'll do what you want," one of the men yelled, and his offer was affirmed by shouts of all the others.

"Follow me to Greer's place."

"Yeah," went up their voices, almost as one. With Joe in the lead, the mob moved to Greer's quarters, a two-room shanty that looked much like the office building. It was dark. Little Joe called once for Greer to come out, then pushed open the door, and he and Chaney made a quick search of the place. It was empty. Then Little Joe led the mob toward the one-room shanties of Ben Tull and

Ted Karnes. Again, both were vacant.

Little Joe spun around and marched away, his anger rising with each step. "They've got to be at the number three bunkhouse," he scowled. "Follow me, men."

They started at a walk, then picked up the pace as they covered the distance to the bunkhouse.

Up ahead they could see a big fire by the shed where the men took their weekly baths on Sunday. Silhouetted against the fire were the shadowy forms of the men of the number three crew. By the set of their feet and the angle of their arms, Little Joe could tell they held axes and peavey sticks at the ready for battle. He wondered which of Greer's men had his guns.

Little Joe slowed and the loggers behind him did too as they saw the men of the number three crew brandishing the tools of their livelihood like weapons. Little Joe stopped twenty feet short of the hard men who stood before him.

Ben Tull stepped out to challenge him. "You should've listened to me, Cartwright, because you won't win against me again."

"Where's Greer?"

"What's it to you?"

"Livermore's dead."

"You don't say."

"Now where's Greer?"

Behind Tull came a shout that Little Joe

recognized as Greer's voice. "Over here."

Little Joe's eyes focused on a figure in a big black wash pot.

"I'm taking a bath," Greer scowled, "trying to wash the filth off from being around you."

"You sure it's not the blood from killing Livermore?"

Greer shook his head. "Is Livermore dead?"

"I figure you were the first one to know."

"You figure wrong, just like on everything else you've stuck your nose into," Greer barked back.

"Where are the clothes you were wearing?" Little Joe asked, hoping to inspect them for blood. Livermore's blood.

Greer pointed to the fire that was heating more water. "I burned them." He laughed.

"Because of the blood?"

Greer feigned shock. "Lice. The lice got so bad I had to burn them. Don't tell me you're so clean you don't get lice."

Little Joe knew he was whipped. Greer had outfoxed him at every turn. He wondered if the same fire that consumed Greer's blood-stained clothes also had burned the records that could help Adam sort this whole mess out.

"Come on, men," Little Joe said. "Let's go clean up the office and start building a box for Livermore." He turned back over his shoulder. "The number one and two crews won't be working tomorrow until after Livermore is buried."

"If they don't work, neither does crew number three," Greer shot back.

Little Joe and his somber allies strode to the office, a few hanging back to make sure Greer's men didn't charge them.

"Greer did it, didn't he?" Chaney said.

Little Joe nodded. "I just want to know what else he's been doing."

At the office, Little Joe asked for a couple of volunteers to remove Livermore's body and to start building his coffin. He and Chaney began to pick up the camp records.

"You seen Roe?" Little Joe asked Chaney as he gathered an armload of papers.

"Not since he backed down Greer in the bunkhouse."

Little Joe scratched his head. "I thought he would be in with us."

"I figure he is," Chaney replied, "but Roe looks after those animals in the stalls. I figure he thinks he ought to keep an eye on them while everybody else is watching each other."

Little Joe nodded. Maybe that was a good idea, especially since his pinto was there. He would need that horse well fed and rested when he had to make his run back for the law.

Little Joe sent another man to the bunkhouse to bring back some wooden crates to store the remaining camp records and papers in. Then he and Chaney righted the overturned counter and tried to make the smashed desk usable again. It took a couple of hours to set the office right. As they worked, they heard the sawing and hammering of the men making the coffin for Livermore. By the time Little Joe's crew was done, the office was much as it had been except for the odor of coal oil in the front room and the bloodstains in the back room.

As they carried the crates of records from the office back to the bunkhouse, they glanced toward the number three bunkhouse, where men still milled about, each holding a weapon in his hand. At the bunkhouse, the men searched everywhere for Little Joe's revolver and carbine, though they did not expect to find them. Everyone knew that Greer's men had stolen them sometime during the day when the crews were out in the trees.

Well after midnight the hammering finally stopped on Livermore's coffin and most of the men retired to bed, weary of the day and worried about tomorrow. They fell into bed, some starting to snore quickly, others remaining awake and restless.

Little Joe stayed up awhile with Jack Chaney. They talked in whispers so as not to disturb the men or be overheard by anyone who might be a mole for Greer.

"Are you thinking what I'm thinking?" Little Joe asked Chaney.

The logger smiled. "I figure I am."

"We'll never know what's at the bottom of this until we see what's on the other side of the mountain, where the number three crew is working."

"That's it," Chaney replied.

"Tomorrow night, then, we'll slip away and find out."

CHAPTER 14

Morning at the logging camp came overcast and cool, but not nearly as cold as the atmosphere of suspicion that engulfed the men. On this morning, breakfast was ready at the usual time, but the men got up as they pleased and ambled in to eat.

The cook, at first, tried to enforce the no-talking rule, but the angry glare of the loggers cowed him until he retreated into the kitchen.

When Little Joe awoke, he found three men, their backs to him, standing at the foot of his bed. He stretched and rubbed his eyes, then glanced over at Chaney's empty bed. "Morning," Little Joe said as he crawled out of his bunk, which smelled of tobacco to keep the lice away.

Chaney, standing by the door, heard Little Joe's voice and sauntered over.

"What's going on?" Little Joe asked him as he pointed to the three men.

"Some of Greer's men have been up and about this morning, wandering around the camp. We thought these fellows ought to stay nearby and keep an eye out for you."

"Obliged," Little Joe said, getting up and putting on his caulked shoes.

"There's plenty of breakfast and plenty of conversation this morning," Chaney offered. "Also, I put men to work digging a grave for Livermore. He'll be buried beside the logger who died in an accident after he started asking questions about crew number three."

Little Joe grinned. "You know how to take care of things, Jack, just the trait I'd look for in choosing a new bull of the woods."

"You're not rid of the old one yet," Chaney answered with a grin.

Little Joe added, "But I don't think he'll be around much longer, especially after I see what's on the other side of the mountain."

Chaney scratched his chin and took a deep breath. "He may not be one you just up and fire. I figure he's got too much at stake in whatever he's doing."

Little Joe nodded as he started toward the dining hall, where he slid into a seat. Most of the loggers looked at him with respect.

Chaney sat down on the bench opposite Little Joe. "They know you don't know much about logging, Little Joe, but they respect you for your hard-headedness and your courage."

Stretching his aching shoulders and arms, Little Joe said, "That's a compliment, coming from these men. I never worked harder in my life than I did yesterday felling that tree."

"You're lucky you didn't get killed by that widow maker. That's something a logger learns to look for before attacking a tree. But one thing I want you to know, the two men that checked the tree out were impressed, you downing it in an afternoon and by yourself. Most fallers work in pairs. Word's spread around that you can do a man's work. The men respect that too."

"Not the men in crew number three, I figure."

"Yeah, but all the men in number one and two feel that way. Loggers can be hard men, 'cause it's a hard life, but we ain't mean to the core like those fellows are."

Little Joe took a platter of fried bacon and raked a half-dozen slices onto his plate, then spooned on some pan-fried potatoes. After breaking apart four biscuits, he covered them with cream gravy and began to eat, washing it down with coffee one of the cook's helpers brought him.

As he was lingering after breakfast, he heard a commotion up in the bunk room and footsteps running back to the dining hall.

"Cartwright," called a logger, "Roe Derus needs to see you."

Little Joe shoved himself away from the table and moved quickly out the front door, into the gray day. Waiting for him was Derus, who was leading Little Joe's pinto by a halter. Draped over the horse was the form of a man Little Joe thought he had seen among the number three crew.

Derus nodded. "Caught this fellow trying to

tamper with your horse this morning."

"He dead?" Little Joe asked.

Smiling broadly, Derus lifted his iron right fist. "He thinks he is. I gave him a solid right punch to the nose. He saw so many stars it's probably as close as he'll ever get to heaven."

"A couple of you pull him off and somebody get a bucket of water," Little Joe commanded.

Quickly, two men jerked him from the horse and let him slide to the ground. He groaned through a bloodied and swollen face.

Another man came up with a bucket of water and, at Little Joe's nod, dumped it on the logger's head. The man came to with a start, shaking his head and spitting water.

Little Joe glanced from the logger to the number three bunkhouse. Several of those loggers were walking down the hill, axes and peavey sticks in their hands.

"Men," Little Joe said, pointing in that direction, "you might want to get your weapons in case our friends want trouble."

Quickly, the men scattered, and just as quickly they returned, brandishing the sundry tools of their livelihood. Greer's men slowed when the loggers of the first two crews turned to face them.

Nat Greer, in the lead, motioned for his men to stop, then he proceeded cautiously. "I'm still bull of the woods," Greer called.

Little Joe gestured for him to approach closer. "Then come here. I want you to hear what happened to one of your men."

Greer swaggered closer, Little Joe's men parting so he could see his wet ally.

"Roe caught him tampering with my horse," Little Joe said. "Did you put him up to it?"

Greer shrugged in mock surprise. "I'm as shocked as you are, Cartwright. I don't want a man of such low character working in my camp. Gather your belongings and get out of here."

The man rubbed his chin and stood up, giving Greer a trace of a lopsided grin as he limped toward his bunkhouse, drawing the cheers of his bunkmates.

"I want honest men working for me," Greer said. His words dripped with mockery.

"Then ask them who killed Livermore so we can turn him over to the law."

Greer shook his head. "I figure it was one of your men, Cartwright. You just better hope Livermore's the only one that gets killed or hurt before this whole game is played out." Greer spun around and walked away.

"Roe," Little Joe said, "keep an eye on the bunkhouse up there and make sure that our wet friend leaves camp."

Little Joe looked beyond the ransacked camp office to a level plot of ground where two loggers were digging a new grave beside an older one. "We'll bury Livermore in an hour," he said, "and let's give him a good send-off with everybody there."

"Bring your axes," Chaney said.

The men dispersed, and Derus climbed atop Little Joe's pinto and rode around the camp to exercise the horse. Little Joe returned with Chaney to the camp office, where they looked through the papers that survived the ransacking to see if they could make any sense out of things.

For thirty minutes they sorted and scanned the records. But neither man was a natural with figures, and the records were too incomplete or scattered for the whole picture of Greer's fraud to emerge.

Both Little Joe and Chaney were scratching their heads when Roe Derus walked inside. "The one who was tampering with your horse, well, he's gone now. Odd thing, though."

"What do you mean?" asked Little Joe.

"Well, sir, instead of going down the road leading to Lake Tahoe and other logging camps, he took the trail that leads to the number three work site. Damnedest thing, now isn't it?"

Little Joe shook his head. "What's a logger usually do when he loses a job?"

"Simple," Chaney answered. "He finds another one."

Little Joe grinned, then glanced around the room to make sure no one could eavesdrop. "That's got to be it."

"Huh?" said Chaney.

"Come again," Derus responded, "because

I'm not following you."

"He's going to work for another logging out-fit, the same one that the number three crew works for," Little Joe whispered, rubbing his hands together, excited that he had figured it out.

Derus's eyes opened wide. "That would explain why we've never seen the number three crew bring in any logs."

"Exactly," Little Joe answered.

Chaney nodded. "There must be a logging camp, maybe four miles on the other side of the mountain. That would explain a lot of things."

Little Joe grinned widely as all the pieces fell into place. Nat Greer had been swindling Cartwright Enterprises out of considerable timber. Little Joe started to speak, but real-ized a logger had entered the room and was standing a few feet away, his hands crossed in front of his belt.

"Men," said the logger, "they're about to bury Livermore."

The smile darkened on Little Joe's face. He nodded, then stood up with Chaney and Derus. "We'll be right out."

The logger turned and departed.

"Do you think Livermore was in on this?" Little Joe asked.

Derus shrugged. "I didn't know him that well. He pretty much kept to himself."

Chaney looked down at the floor. "He had

to know, but that doesn't mean he was in on it. Greer could've threatened him to keep him quiet, and that would explain why he stayed to himself."

As he started for the door, Little Joe shook his head. "I just can't understand why he didn't tell me who attacked him when I asked. 'Books, two books,' those were his last words, and I can't make any sense out of them."

Just as the three reached the door, Derus pulled back. "I just had an idea. Tell me if it looks like the men from the number three crew are going to attend the burial."

Little Joe stopped at the door. "They seem to be heading that way, axes and all."

"Good," Derus said. "You two go on. See if you can lengthen the burial and try to keep them with their backs to their bunkhouse."

Chaney tossed Derus a puzzled glance. "What are you thinking?"

"Just playing a hunch from something in my prizefighting days," Derus responded. "Now just go on."

Little Joe shrugged. "Whatever you say, Roe." He led Chaney outside into the gray day, the clouds drooping low over the mountains and spitting occasional mist at the men.

As he stepped away from the bunkhouse, he saw more than a hundred men lined up behind a makeshift coffin near the office. Seeing Little Joe and Chaney, six of the big loggers stepped forward and lifted Livermore's box. Then the entire procession started forward, the grim-faced men carrying axes and peavey sticks in their callused hands.

Little Joe angled to intersect the procession, and with Chaney at his side, led the line of men toward the grave. Occasionally he glanced up the hill toward the number three bunkhouse, keeping an eye on Greer's men, who advanced with sneers and wisecracks, as if they were heading to a saloon instead of a funeral. Little Joe adjusted the procession's course so his men would approach the grave from the downhill side.

When Little Joe reached the dark grave, the six men carrying the coffin gently laid it down beside the hole. The other men fanned out behind Little Joe and Chaney, whispering to one another as they bounced their axes threateningly in their palms.

Nat Greer lifted his hand and his men halted behind him, forming another semicircle. He stared hard, as if his gaze could intimidate Little Joe. "Let's get on with it," Greer said, "my men have work to do."

"Yeah," sneered several.

Little Joe's men took a step closer toward Greer's favored crew, but Little Joe lifted his hand. "We came to bury a man, not to kill each other."

"Not right yet," Greer interjected. His men again laughed.

Little Joe lifted his hands for silence and waited a few moments. Up the hill he saw Roe Derus slipping toward the number three bunkhouse. Little Joe was still uncertain what Derus was up to, and knew only that he needed a little time. He hoped to keep the number three crew's attention. He glanced from Greer to Ben Tull and Ted Karnes, all staring at him with vindictive smiles.

Little Joe looked down at the coffin before him. "All good men are humble in the presence of death. Today we bury a humble man, a man murdered for reasons only his killer knows." Lifting his head, he looked up the hill again, surprised to see Roe Derus not at the bunkhouse but at the bath shanty, kicking through ashes of the fire that had been used to boil water for Greer's bath last night, and, Little Joe believed, to destroy Greer's bloody clothes after Livermore's murder.

"There's a judgment hanging over this camp by a power greater than all of us, and someone will be held accountable for the death of C. C. Livermore," Little Joe continued, staring at Greer.

The bull of the woods wore a proud smirk, as if announcing he was above the laws of man and God.

Little Joe paused just long enough to glance up the hill and see Derus squatting over something. Then he continued. "We bury the earthly remains of C. C. Livermore, but we can never bury his soul, which is now unchained from the deceit and fear that is strangling the life out of this camp."

Little Joe lifted his eyes to the hill again and saw Derus arising with something blackened tucked under his arm. Derus scurried away from the bath shanty toward the number two bunkhouse.

"Now a prayer," Little Joe said. He knew that no one would bow his head as men on both sides of the grave cast challenging glares at each other. He spoke reverently. "We give to Your care the remains and soul of C. C. Livermore. However he was as a man on earth, he did nothing to deserve this death. May he live eternally among men who are honorable. Amen!"

Behind Little Joe several men said "Amen" as well. The six men who had carried the coffin to the grave now slipped ropes beneath the wooden box, lifted it over the grave and let it slide down into the earth. As they pulled the ropes free, other loggers grabbed shovels embedded in the adjacent mound of fresh dirt and began to cover the coffin.

Little Joe stared at Greer. "The funeral's over. After your men eat lunch, get them back to work. I'm naming Jack Chaney as bull of the woods for the first two crews."

Behind Little Joe the men cheered.

Greer spat toward the grave. "He don't know enough to be bull of the woods."

"His honesty will make up for that," Little Joe shot back.

Greer shrugged. "We'll just see how long he lasts." He laughed and spun around. "Come on, boys," he called to his allies. "We've lunch to eat and work to do."

Greer's crew backed away for thirty or more feet before showing their backs and heading up the hill to the bunkhouse.

Little Joe held his men at the grave to give Greer's crew time to return to their quarters. The camp was as volatile as a powder keg, and though he wanted to get at the bottom of the swindle, he didn't care to lose any more men.

When the Greer gang reached the number three bunkhouse, Little Joe turned to his men. "Okay, men, grab a bit of lunch, then let's get out in the woods and cut timber."

The men started for their bunkhouses, and Little Joe fought the urge to race to his quarters and find out what Roe Derus had uncovered under the ashes at the bathing shanty. Instead, he walked calmly, taking extra time to give his encouragement to the loyal loggers. "We'll get to the bottom of this and make this a camp you can work in without fear."

As the men scattered, Little Joe found himself beside Jack Chaney, who spoke softly. "Roe found something, didn't he?"

"I hope it's the answer we've been needing," Little Joe said as they reached the bunkhouse.

Inside, Roe Derus stood in the corner, a sly smile on his face. In his hand, he lifted the charred remains of what looked like some kind of book. "Found what I was looking for."

"What is it?" Little Joe asked.

Derus shook his head. "Let's go to the office and look at it. Less chance of anyone seeing or hearing the wrong thing."

"Lead the way," Little Joe replied.

The three men strode from the bunkhouse and were quickly at the office. In the dimness, Jack Chaney lit a lamp as Derus plopped the charred and blackened book on the counter.

"In the days when I fought," Derus started, "some promoters kept double sets of books. A rigged set and an honest set. They'd show the crooked set to the boxer so they could take more of his money."

Little Joe's eyes widened. "So that's what 'books, two books' meant."

"Yes, sir. I figure Livermore wanted to get that off his conscience even more than he wanted to identify his killer with his last breath."

Jack Chaney shook his head. "To me, that says Livermore was an honest man until Greer got ahold of him, probably threatening him all the time."

"That's my fix on it," answered Derus.

Little Joe opened the ledger book and began to turn the pages, several crumbling in his hands into black flakes. "That's it," he said, pointing to the daily wages being paid to a logger in the number two crew. "A dollar a day, not a dollar fifty like the other ledger." Little Joe kept turning pages, then whistled. "Look at this."

Both Derus and Chaney leaned over his shoulder. "Members of the number three crew were getting two dollars a day."

"What?" Chaney gasped.

"Two dollars a day," Little Joe repeated, drawing his finger down the roster of the number three crew.

"So they were getting twice as much as the rest of us?"

Derus nodded. "Cutting timber for someone else while on this payroll."

Little Joe shook his head. "So the crooked books showed everybody getting a dollar fifty. Greer is a clever one."

"And a dangerous one," Chaney answered.

"The only thing we've got to do now is see what's on the other side of the mountain," Little Joe said.

"It's not the only thing, Little Joe," Derus said. "We've got to get you out of here alive."

Chaney nodded gravely. "They'll be watching the trail out of here and waiting for the chance to kill you."

Derus affirmed Chaney's observation. "You're a bigger threat to them than any of the rest of us."

CHAPTER 15

Two days out from Virginia City, Ben Cartwright trailed Roy Coffee under the flume that ran from the Cartwright logging camp to Lake Tahoe. Ben stared in the camp's direction, wishing he could go check on Little Joe. He had an uneasy feeling about his son's safety. Even though he knew Little Joe needed to grow up, it was still hard for a father not to want to step in.

Behind Ben rode Hoss, the packhorse trailing him. By nightfall the three men would be within five miles of Timberline Pass. Ben Cartwright had come to despise Timberline Pass, one of the early routes across the Sierras and one long out of favor with most travelers. It had been a rugged route back in '49, when the rush to California was on, but other less difficult routes had ultimately opened up and Timberline Pass was gradually forgotten except by old-timers like Ben and ruffians like Old Man Wharton, looking to avoid the law.

As Ben rode, he realized he hadn't been back to Timberline Pass since that day more than a dozen years ago when he and Roy had killed Clifford Wharton there for robbing a stage. It had been a brutal stage robbery, a

238

lone gunman killing the driver and a passenger, then wounding a pregnant woman, who saved herself by feigning death. The woman, though, had recognized Clifford Wharton, who was well-known around Virginia City for his laziness and the meanness of his three sons.

When word had reached Roy Coffee, he took up Wharton's trail and followed him across Truckee Meadows and into the Sierras. Wharton had been a shrewd one, and had doubled back to ambush the sheriff. Wharton had knocked off Coffee's hat and grazed his arm with a rifle shot, but the sheriff was not one to be deterred. He kept chasing and Wharton kept running, across the Ponderosa. Coffee had stopped at the Ponderosa ranch house to exchange his jaded horse for a fresh one. After checking Roy's wound, Ben tried to turn the sheriff back until he could get medical attention for himself, but Coffee wouldn't give up.

"It's just a scratch," Coffee had said with grit in his voice.

"Why's this one become an obsession with you?" Ben remembered asking. In light of subsequent events, Ben would never forget Roy's answer.

"That pregnant girl he shot," Roy had said, "could've been carrying my granddaughter a few years ago, Ben. I just can't let a man that would do that to a pregnant woman get away with it."

Ben had nodded. "I'm going with you, Roy.

If I can't stop you, then I don't want it on my conscience that you rode away wounded."

"Suit yourself, Ben, just hurry and help me change horses," Coffee had said.

The two of them had ridden away from the ranch house, south around Lake Tahoe, then headed west. Wharton's trail led them to Timberline Pass. Long out of use even then, the trail over the pass was rutted and eroded, the melting winter snows and the strong winds having gouged away at the mountain, making the trail even more dangerous than it had been during the rush era. Near the summit, Wharton's horse stumbled, its foreleg snapping in a rocky crevice. The horse had thrown Wharton to the hard ground and knocked him temporarily unconscious. The helpless mount kicked and thrashed at its broken leg, squealing in terror.

As Ben and Roy neared the summit, they had seen the flailing animal. Unaware that Coffee and Cartwright had ridden within carbine range, Wharton had made it to his feet, then staggered dazed around the injured animal.

"Give up, Wharton," Roy had commanded.

Wharton tossed Coffee a bewildered look, then dove behind his terrified horse to jerk his carbine free. The horse, though, kicked and thrashed at him, preventing him from getting his carbine. Desperate, Wharton jumped up with a pistol in his hand. He shot wildly, and was no match for Coffee's and Ben's carbines. They cut him down instantly, each firing two shots. Wharton had been hit three times, any one of which would have killed him, but neither Coffee nor Ben pondered who had made the death shot. It wasn't something they were proud of, just one of the things a man had to do in rough territory and rougher times.

"That pregnant girl he shot," Roy had said, "could've been carrying my granddaughter." Those words still haunted Ben, and he knew how Timberline Pass must surely haunt Roy.

Roy and Ben had taken Wharton's body back to Virginia City, and the old man's three sons, all in their late teens or early twenties, had vowed revenge. The three had always had a mean streak, and Roy was prepared to meet their threat head on. But the animosity in the Wharton brothers burned a vicious brand on their meanness. They didn't just attack Roy, they attacked his home, his family. His son, his only child, the father of his granddaughter, had died. His daughter-in-law, the mother of his grandchild, had fallen trying to protect her husband. Roy's wife had died weeks later of a problem the doctor couldn't describe, but Roy could — a broken heart.

That had left Roy and little Sara Ann.

Now there would be just Roy, unless they rescued Sara Ann. Ben knew that. Hoss knew that. And most of all, Roy knew that, though none of them said anything aloud about it. In fact, there hadn't been much talk on this trip, just grim determination, especially by Hoss, who still blamed himself for Sara Ann's predicament.

Of his three sons, Ben knew Hoss was the one who undersold himself, seldom giving himself proper credit for his strengths, not just physical, but mental as well. Of his sons, Hoss had the best sense of the land, the best sense of its wonderment and its fragility. He noticed things that the other two sons never stopped to consider. Maybe they were little things, but Hoss could tell you that the sugar pine's blue-green needles were grouped in fives and grew two to four inches long. The ponderosa pine's needles were grouped in twos and threes, growing from five to eleven inches long. He could identify birds by the call or the colored flash of their markings in flight, or deer and elk by their tracks. By looking at the droppings of a bear, he could tell what it had eaten the day before. These were talents that Hoss discounted, but skills that many learned professors in colleges back East made their intellectual reputations on. No matter what Little Joe and Adam ultimately did, Ben knew that in Hoss he had a son who would look after the Ponderosa as carefully as he would want. Next to his sons, the Ponderosa was the legacy Ben wanted to leave to the world.

The sky was overcast and the air moist and cool when darkness began to set in. The sun was little more than a faint glow behind the gray clouds to the west when Roy pointed to a gap in the mountains up ahead. "Timberline Pass," he said. His words were hard as granite.

Ben nodded. "What do you think, Roy, you want to go farther or make camp?"

"We've five miles to go. Hard terrain, Ben. My heart wants to go on, but my brain says to stop. We'll see better come morning."

"So will they," Hoss interrupted, offering the first words he had said for miles.

Coffee nodded. "The boy's right, Ben. Let's go until it's too dark to see, put us a little closer to them tonight. A cold camp tonight, no sense in them seeing our fire."

"It'll be a cold camp, then," Ben said, shivering as the trail darkened.

They rode a half hour farther, then stopped and bedded down for the night. They ate pieces of jerky and drank cool water from their canteens. It was a spartan meal for men who had more than food on their minds.

Tomorrow they must save Sara Ann Coffee. That night, with the cold and the worry, they slept fitfully.

Sara Ann had regretted seeing the man get robbed outside of Virginia City. Now, though, she was regrettably thankful for his misfortune. His money had bought supplies and extra blankets for the trip. The blankets kept her warm and the supplies kept food in her stomach.

But with the money, the Whartons had also bought ammunition. Lots of it. That ammunition was intended for her grandfather and Ben Cartwright and Hoss, if he was all right and accompanying them. Hoss would make the biggest target of all. Sara Ann knew she had to do something to even the odds, but she didn't know what.

At first she had resented their demand that she cook for them and do the camp chores, but what choice did she have?

"That's what women are for," Lem Wharton had told her.

"That and you know what else," Willis had said with a leer.

Vern scratched the front of his pants and grimaced. "I don't know about that. Whatever I picked up back in Fran's sure is making me wonder if I want to bed down another woman for a while. You fellows still burning down there like me?"

Lem nodded. "It's not as bad since we quit hard riding."

"But it's still bad," Willis said, casting Sara Ann a crooked smile and winking at her with his crossed eye.

With a skillet and a coffeepot to work with, Sara Ann had fixed meals of fried salt pork and coffee. The Whartons had set up camp halfway up the incline that topped out at Timberline Pass. Here the mountain leveled off for a bit, then dropped precipitously three hundred feet straight down. With the cliff behind her and the Whartons in front of her, Sara Ann had no route for escape. But what worked as a disadvantage to her worked to the advantage of her rescuers. She had a place to discard the ammunition where the Whartons could never get it.

The more she worked and cooked meals for them, the more relaxed the Whartons had grown around her. She liked the idea of keeping a fire going for them because it was as good as telegraphing the Whartons' location to her grandfather.

"You want me to go gather some wood?" she would ask.

Vern or Willis would just shake their heads. "What do you think we are, dumb or something?" they would answer, then one of them would rise and walk back down the trail to gather an armful of dead wood for her. Here the altitude was high and the trees petered out well before the summit.

The Whartons had grown so comfortable with Sara Ann doing their chores and not trying to escape that they untied her hands and gave her freedom around the campfire as long as she stayed inside the wall of rocks that was the perimeter of their natural stone fortress. They had been careful not to leave their guns around, but they weren't always so careful about their ammunition. Whenever she had a chance, while they were away or asleep or just plain inattentive, she slipped bullets from the loops in their gun belts or dug through their supplies for the cartridge boxes they had bought with the stolen money.

Then, to cover how she discarded the bullets, she took to throwing stones off the cliff. She would gather rocks from around the camp and pitch them over the cliff, ever careful not to get too close to the edge, for she did not like great heights.

"Why you do that so much?" Willis asked.

"Do what?" Sara Ann replied.

"Throw rocks off the mountain."

"What else is there to do?" she answered.

"Well, I got something you could do," he replied with his cross-eyed leer.

Sara Ann had bolted to Willis, shaking her finger in his face. "I'll cook for you, but I'll not do anything else for you. You're the ones that want to kill my grandfather."

"It ain't nothing against you, you're sorta purty," he said.

"You leave her alone, Willis," Lem commanded from his bedroll. "Treat her like a lady until I say otherwise."

Willis had seemed confused and embarrassed. He stalked away from camp and returned about an hour later, wearing a warped smile that paralleled his warped shoulders. "I got something for you," he said.

Sara Ann shook her head, suspicious of what he might be up to.

"Just for you," he said, advancing to her.

Sara Ann just backed away.

From his bedroll nearby, Lem shook his head. "Watch it, you're getting close."

Sara Ann had frozen with terror when she realized she was only a step away from the cliff's edge. Willis advanced another step. She had nowhere to retreat now. She glanced at Lem, who sat up on his blanket.

"Humor him, would you?" Lem yawned, then turned his gaze at Willis.

Tentatively, Sara Ann stepped away from the cliff and toward Willis. She caught her breath as she extended her open hand, palm up, to him.

He held his clenched fist over her open palm, then opened his fingers, releasing a handful of rocks.

Sara Ann flinched, and many of the rocks fell out of her hand and on to the ground at her feet.

Willis didn't understand her bewilderment.

"Rocks," he explained.

Still confused, Sara Ann looked from Willis to Lem, who shrugged.

"For you to throw over the cliff," Willis continued, a touch of exasperation in his voice. He offered what Sara Ann took for a shy smile, and stood before her as embarrassed as a young beau giving flowers to his first girl.

Sara Ann nodded and said "Thank you," out of habit rather than sincerity.

Willis's smile widened and he seemed pleased, especially when she turned around and began to toss the two dozen stones, one at a time, over the edge.

After that, every time Willis stood watch, he returned with a handful of stones for Sara Ann to pitch over the cliff. From then on, there had never been any question what she was tossing over the cliff when one of the Whartons would look her way. Gradually she had emptied the men's gun belts, and tossed six boxes of bullets away as well. When her grandfather arrived, the Whartons would have only the bullets in their guns to use against him.

Sara Ann was pleased with the deception because it might save her rescuers' lives tomorrow. Her grandfather was likely just a day behind her, and tomorrow he would arrive. As she prepared to crawl under her two blankets, she looked at the overcast sky overhead, the clouds spitting bits of mist at her. She hoped that somewhere not too far back down the trail her grandfather and Ben and, hopefully, Hoss would be here to rescue her. The air was cold and two blankets were not enough, but it was all she had and it would have to do. She pulled some firewood under the blanket with her to keep dry so she could build a breakfast fire in the morning as a beacon to her grandfather.

The high mountain air was cold, and Sara Ann heard her teeth chatter and felt her body shiver, but her discomfort turned to fear when she heard Willis clamber out of his blankets and crawl toward her. Her very blood turned to ice. She took a deep breath to scream, but hesitated a moment before crying out. There was something odd about Willis's touch. It was soft, not threatening. He was dragging something over her. It was a blanket! He was giving up one of his own blankets for her to use. Sara Ann was as bewildered as she was thankful for the blanket and his motives.

With the extra blanket, she slept better, though not entirely comfortable, not knowing what would happen after daybreak.

Come morning, she felt a boot nudging her in the side.

"You making breakfast or not?" Lem Wharton asked.

Shivering against the frigid early morning air, she tossed back her blankets and uncovered the wood.

Lem toed at the wood with his boot.

"I covered it up to cook your breakfast," she explained.

Lem laughed. "Wet wood makes more smoke."

Sara Ann didn't understand. "What do you mean?"

"You may be fooling my brothers, but you don't fool me. You've wanted to cook so you could lead your grandpa right to us. That's just what I want. So build a big fire, one that'll send smoke a mile into the air. All it'll do is bring them straight to us so we can send them straight to hell. That's what I want."

Sara Ann's lip trembled. Maybe Lem was smarter than she had thought. She wondered if he had checked the loops in his gun belt or searched for the boxes of ammunition.

Lem twisted his lips and pointed at her. "When the shooting starts, you better stay out of the way or you'll be the first one I shoot."

Sara Ann bent over the wood and pulled it toward the ashes of previous fires.

"If you stay out of the way, maybe we won't kill you when we finish our other business. Hell, Willis or Vern may want something from you." His words rang cold as the morning air and the ice in his eyes.

As she nursed a fire to life, Sara Ann tried to tell herself the trembling of her fingers was from the cold and not from fear. She knew she was lying to herself.

Lem walked to Vern's snoring form and nudged him with his boot. Vern snorted and rose, his eyes as wild as his disheveled hair. Then Lem turned to Willis, giving him a hard kick to the shoulder. Willis cursed and rolled over.

"You're getting soft, Willis, giving your blanket to the girl."

"Huh?" Willis said, rubbing his eyes.

"Dammit, Willis, I heard you slipping over to her and saw you cover her with your blanket."

Willis grimaced and shrugged. "Figured she might need it against the cold."

Lem spat at his brother's feet. "Don't go soft on me now, Willis. We've waited twelve years for this. Don't forget that Coffee and Cartwright killed our pa here."

With those words, Sara Ann bolted up from her knees by the fire and turned to Lem. She could take it no more. She pointed her finger at Willis, then moved it to Lem and Vern. "And you," she screamed, "killed my mother and father." She began to sob.

Willis frowned. "It weren't nothing against you," he said. "We'd been drinking. We were just out to get your grandpa."

"Oh, you got him all right," Sara Ann shot back, the rage building. "You'd've been more merciful had you killed him, then and there. He's lived a dozen years without the only child he ever had, blaming it all on himself."

"Shut up," Lem yelled, drawing back his arm and slapping her across the face.

Sara Ann fell sobbing to the ground so close to the growing fire that it singed the tips of her auburn hair.

"Fix breakfast and be quick about it," Lem said.

Vern stood watching, scratching at his crotch. "Dammit, am I ever going get over this itching?" He ambled away for a minute.

"Check the horses after you tend your business," Lem called after him.

At the mention of horses, Sara Ann stood up, dabbing at her red-rimmed eyes. The men moved the horses each day to ensure that they got a little of the scarce grass for grazing. She watched Vern's hike to the horses as she poured water from a half-empty canteen into the blackened coffeepot and then threw in a handful of store-ground coffee. She pulled a slab of salt pork from the canvas bag that held their victuals and tugged off a corner of the burlap wrapping. Kneeling by the fire, she heard a rip as she placed the slab of bacon on a flat rock. Looking at her red gingham dress, she saw a tear where the skirt had snagged on a piece of firewood. Her eyes moistened at how this new dress, the one she had worn for Hoss, was little more than a rag now. She thought of the dress back home, the one she had planned to wear to the Masonic lodge when she went dancing with Hoss. She wondered if she would ever again have a chance to wear that dress. She hated these men! Impatiently, she tapped her fingers on the slab of salt pork. "Are you lending me your knife," she scowled at Lem, "or am I to slice this with my teeth?"

Lem slid his knife from the scabbard he wore behind his back and flung it at the salt pork. Sara Ann screamed and jerked her hand away just as the knife stuck the spot where her fingers had rested. Lem laughed.

Sara Ann tugged the knife free. She held the blade up before her eyes, considering how satisfying it would feel to plunge the shiny blade into Lem's hard heart. She debated whether to lunge for Lem, but his hard gaze seemed to penetrate her skull and her thoughts. Lem's hand fell easily to his pistol. Sara Ann swallowed hard, then began to carve thick slices, pieces with lots of fat, fat that would become grease when cooked, grease that could be thrown in a man's face if she had to. Done, she shoved the knife in the rocky ground, put the skillet on the fire, then began to throw the thick pieces of pork onto it. The bacon sizzled and popped. Out of frustration, she spat in the skillet, the grease splattering into the fire, giving off an unhealthy aroma.

Out of the corner of her eye she saw Vern leading the horses across the rutted, jagged trail.

Lem noticed too and yelled at his brother. "Take them up over the top and stake them down on the other side so Coffee and Cartwright won't see them." Lem looked from Vern to Sara Ann on her knees frying the bacon. "All they'll see is the smoke from Red's fire."

He laughed. "It'll bring them right up here to us." Lem pushed himself up from his bedroll and moved to the slab of salt pork. After pulling his knife from the ground, he wiped the blade on his pants leg, then waved the sharp metal in front of Sara Ann's nose. "Don't you be poking my knife in the ground again or I'll dirty it on your innards."

Sara Ann gritted her teeth and fought the temptation to lift the skillet and throw the scalding grease in his face. She must be patient. Her rescuers were surely nearing.

Lem spun around and strode away from Sara Ann. Nearing Willis, still wrapped in his bedroll, he paused and kicked him hard in the shoulder. "Dammit, get up like I told you. We waited twelve years for this day. This'll make up for Pa and all those days, weeks, months, and years in prison," he screamed, his words as bitter as rock salt.

Willis threw his blanket back and shoved himself up, casting a scowl at Lem. Willis stalked away to hide behind a boulder for a few minutes, then returned, heading straight for Sara Ann, who was fishing pork out of the grease and placing the strips of meat on the flat rock since they had no plates.

When Sara Ann looked up, Willis offered her his closed hand. She shook her head because she didn't want anything to do with him or his brothers, the very men who had killed her parents and deprived her of a great part of her life. Willis, though, bent over and took her hand, pried her fingers apart, and dropped another handful of rocks in her palm. Without looking, Sara Ann tossed them over her shoulder to the precipice not ten feet from the campfire.

Willis looked from her to the cliff, then clambered around the fire and jerked his blanket from atop hers and threw it back on his own bedding. He sulked until Vern returned from moving the horses. Then the three brothers squatted by the flat rock where Sara Ann had placed the fried strips of bacon. They grabbed pieces of meat and ate silently. Sara Ann filled a single tin cup with coffee and they passed it around among themselves.

When they finished, Lem issued the orders. He and Vern would man the lookouts and Willis would watch Sara Ann.

"We might need to show her to bring Coffee and Cartwright in closer, before we open fire," Lem instructed Willis. "After the shooting begins, you can kill her or do whatever you want with her."

Willis looked troubled. His face clouded with doubt as if he wasn't sure what the best thing was to do with Sara Ann.

Sara Ann gritted her teeth. She would jump over the cliff before she let one of the Wharton brothers have her. Soon, Lem and Vern took up positions in the rocks to watch the trail. Willis sat eyeing her, a frown on his face, uncertainty in his eyes. Sara Ann kept the fire going and the skillet of grease nearby so she could heat it up when necessary.

Now, all there was to do was wait and pray and ponder. To pass time, she tried to think of pleasant things, and the one thing that kept coming to mind was the dance she had tricked Hoss into agreeing to attend with her. If she hadn't lost count of the days, the dance was tonight. She wondered if she would ever dance again.

She forgot about the dance the instant Lem called up the slope, "Here they come. There's three of them."

CHAPTER 16

Well after midnight, Little Joe slipped out of bed. Jack Chaney arose with him. Both men grabbed their boots and coats and eased outside, where one of the loggers stood guard. The lookout glanced over his shoulder at the pair emerging from the bunkhouse, then continued his watch on bunkhouse number three.

Little Joe and Chaney slid onto the wooden bench abutting the bunkhouse wall. The frigid air nipped at their faces and bare hands as they pulled on and laced their caulked boots. "Seen anything suspicious?" Chaney asked.

The guard shook his head. "Ain't seen a thing that worries me. It's the things that I ain't seen that's concerning me."

Chaney nodded. "I know the feeling."

As they stood up, both pulled on their coats and rubbed their hands for warmth. "We're going to do a little looking around," Little Joe whispered. "Don't let anybody know you saw us leave."

The guard nodded.

Little Joe and Chaney eased away from the guard, angling for the office, then made a wide swath around the number three bunkhouse, crossing under the flume a quarter mile from the dam. They swung wide of the flume and made a half circle to approach the stables from the opposite side in case someone might be watching in the pale glow of moonlight diffused by low clouds. At the stables, they knew Roe Derus would be waiting.

The high mountain air was cold, made even more so by the mist that seeped from pinpricks in the low clouds. Pulling his coat tighter, Little Joe knew he was headed into danger, and he felt naked without his revolver or his carbine. Chaney had taken some butcher knives when the cook wasn't looking, but they had no other weapons.

At the stables, the men slipped inside and were engulfed by the smell of dry hay and fresh manure. "Is that you, boys?" came the voice of Roe Derus from somewhere in the darkness.

"Yeah," answered Chaney. "You got mounts saddled?"

"Sure do," Derus answered, appearing as a giant shadow in front of them. "Now, Cartwright, I saddled you one of ours instead of your pinto. It would cause a stir if one of Greer's men discovered your horse was missing. If you're lucky, you can make it out there and back without them ever knowing you were gone. If you're unlucky, then your pinto will be fresh and saddled if you need to make a run for it."

"Good thinking, Roe," Little Joe replied.

"Another thing," Derus continued, "I've fed your pinto and the two you'll be riding. The other horses, at least the ones they're likely to give chase with, I haven't fed and watered for a day. It goes against my constitution to treat an animal that way, but sometimes that's what you have to do."

"Obliged, Roe. Sounds like you've thought of everything," Chaney told him.

"Just one other thing," Roe said. "You sure you don't want me to go along? No telling what you'll run into up the trail."

"No," said Little Joe. "We need someone that knows the full story, in case we have trouble. You hid the ledger, didn't you?"

"It's safe," Derus answered as he disappeared into the recesses of the stable.

Little Joe heard the movement of horses, and in a moment the vague shape of Derus reappeared out of the darkness. He led two horses.

"Mount up in here, boys, and I'll lead your horses outside and open the gate. Don't say a word once we get out of the barn." Derus stopped between them and gave each the reins to a horse. "These aren't fine animals like you're accustomed to on the Ponderosa, Cartwright, but they do for logging work. And they're not animals to spook easily."

Little Joe shoved his boot for the stirrup, but it didn't slide easily in place like it should have. Then he remembered the caulked boots he was wearing. He should have worn his regular boots, but it was too late now to change. He climbed awkwardly into the saddle and finally managed to slide his other caulked boot far enough into the stirrup to ride.

Derus led the horses and riders out into the night and opened the gate. Little Joe and Chaney aimed their horses for the hillside and were quickly in the trees. Circling wide of the flume and dam, they hit the number three wagon trail beyond sight of the camp. The trail was well-rutted and close to the trees which towered overhead and rustled in the slight breeze.

"Too narrow a road for them to pull any logs through," whispered Chaney, "and why wouldn't they cut some of this timber, closer to camp? It don't make sense."

Little Joe shrugged. "It will before the night's over."

"I just hope we're alive to tell someone," Chaney answered.

They rode a mile and a half along the wagon trail that curved around the massive peak screening the work site of the number three crew from the Cartwright logging camp. Gradually the trees thinned out, leaving the stumps of occasional fallen trees to stand like great tombstones along the way. In the soft glow of a moon hidden behind luminescent clouds, Little Joe could see through the thinned trees to a valley that looked eerily like a battlefield graveyard, littered with stumps and downed trees.

Chaney whistled softly as they approached the last stand of timber before emerging into the denuded valley. From the edge of the trees as far as the eye could see in the sky's soft glow, the land was stubbled with tree stumps, as if a giant scythe had been swept across the valley.

Little Joe started to say something, then bit his lip when a voice called out to them from the behind one of the trees. "Who is it?"

They had been spotted!

Little Joe and Chaney drew up their mounts. They couldn't see the sentinel.

"Who is it, dammit? Let me know or I'm shooting."

Little Joe took a deep breath and lowered his voice as best he could. "It's Nat Greer," he imitated.

"Oh, Mr. Greer," answered a man who stepped from behind a pine at the edge of the tree line. "What you doing out this time of night?"

The guard's answer confirmed what Little Joe had suspected — Greer was indeed involved. Little Joe stood in his stirrups and held his arms apart to make his coat seem bigger, so that his silhouette in the soft moon glow might look more like Greer's. He nudged his horse forward. Chaney fell in line behind him.

The guard moved incautiously out of the trees and toward the trail. "Ain't seen a thing, Mr. Greer, nobody snooping around or anything like that. It's just me and the cold."

Little Joe could just make out the shape of a carbine cradled in his arms. "He's got a gun," Little Joe whispered under his breath. Chaney slipped his butcher knife out as Little Joe tried to maintain his deception.

"How long before things are back to normal?" the guard asked, then stopped in the middle of the trail just thirty feet ahead. "Hey, you ain't Greer," he called.

Little Joe kicked his mount's flank and screamed, and the horse charged forward.

Little Joe ducked and saw a flash of light as the carbine belched fire. A bullet whizzed overhead.

Jack Chaney screamed.

Just ten feet in front of Little Joe, the guard took aim again. Little Joe, bending over the side of his mount, aimed his horse for the sentinel.

The carbine exploded, just missing him. Before the guard could fire again, the horse barreled over him. Screaming, the guard tumbled out of the way.

Little Joe jerked up on his reins and spun his mount around as Chaney's horse galloped past him. "Jack," Little Joe called. Then he realized the horse was riderless.

Little Joe jumped off his saddle, wrapping

the reins around his wrist, and with his other hand pulled the butcher knife from his belt. He led the horse back up the trail, looking for the guard and, more importantly, the guard's carbine. He must find them before he searched for Chaney.

In a moment he spotted a clump beside the trail and made out the shape of the sentinel. Lifting the knife to his shoulder, he advanced cautiously and found the man unconscious. By his size, Little Joe pegged him as a logger. Little Joe nudged the man's head with his boot, but the guard never groaned or moved. He would be out for a while, Little Joe thought as he slipped his knife back in his belt. Desperately, Little Joe began to search for the carbine, his eyes scanning the area, his boots toeing at the ground. He cursed himself for not finding the carbine and for not being able to check on Chaney sooner.

"Jack," he called softly.

He heard a moan back up the trail. Little Joe started toward the noise, but stumbled over something, then fell to the ground. The horse tossed his head against the tight reins and tried to bolt away, but Little Joe jumped to his feet, jerking the reins and tugging the nervous horse into submission. Once the animal settled down, Little Joe tapped the ground around him with his boot until the spikes clicked against metal. He cut loose a deep breath. He had found what he was after

— the carbine. He snatched the weapon from the ground, knowing by its feel and look that it was a Winchester. Then he started back toward the low groan that was Jack Chaney.

"Jack," he called. "You hurt?"

Jack moaned. "Bullet hit my right shoulder." He gritted his teeth. "If it didn't break my arm, then the fall did. I can't move it." He spoke in gasps. "Damn, it hurts."

"You be okay while I fetch your horse? Then we'll head back to camp."

"I'm a logger, I'm used to pain."

Little Joe laughed. "I'll return." He mounted the skittish horse and cradled the carbine in his arms. A Winchester carbine held twelve rounds in its magazine, Little Joe remembered. The guard had fired twice, so he knew he had ten bullets, maybe eleven if the sentinel had inserted an extra bullet in the magazine after levering a round into the chamber. Of course, he might have fewer shots than that if the sentinel didn't keep his weapon fully loaded.

Little Joe, though, had little time to check the load. He had to fetch Chaney's horse and then get the logger back to camp. He nudged his horse down the trail, past the last of the trees, then entered the broad, denuded valley. In the distance he could just make out Chaney's horse trotting around a broad hill in the middle of the wide valley. Little Joe turned his mount in that direction and urged him into a trot, then a gallop. He rode quickly across the valley, anxious to retrieve Chaney's horse and return so they could get to camp before daybreak and before Greer's men started back. He wondered if there were other men around, but he saw no signs of life.

None of this made sense until he rounded the broad, squat hill. There before him was a small camp, a half-dozen buildings, with men scurrying everywhere, carrying torches. Little Joe reined up his horse and heard the shouts of men, the sounds of alarm that he had not been able to hear over the noise of his galloping mount.

Chaney's horse had stopped near a corral where oxen bellowed and men ran for horses. Little Joe sat there a moment in disbelief, uncertain what he was seeing. Then a man, his face ablaze beneath the burning torch he held, pointed at Little Joe. "There's one," the torch carrier called, and instantly Little Joe recognized him by his voice. It was Ben Tull.

Little Joe jerked the horse around and retreated as fast as the animal could go. This wasn't a speedy horse like his pinto, but he just hoped he had stamina, because the animal would have to carry two men back to the Cartwright camp. Little Joe pushed his mount ahead. Near the line of trees, he glanced over his shoulder. A dozen or more men, many with torches, were starting into the valley, their horses at a gallop, their excited yells just audible over the pounding hoofs.

"Jack, they're coming after us," Little Joe yelled. "Ben Tull's leading them. Jack, be on your feet if you can. We don't have time to waste, we're riding double."

Little Joe tugged on the reins as he entered the tree cover. He saw one form on the ground and realized it was the guard. He rode on, fearing he might have missed Chaney.

"Up here," Chaney called, and Little Joe could make out a lopsided figure in the middle of the trail.

He reined up the horse beside Chaney. "We don't have much time."

Chaney lifted his good arm and took hold of Little Joe, then tried to throw his leg over the horse's rump. His dead weight almost pulled Little Joe out of the saddle. Little Joe struggled to get his caulked boot out of the stirrup, finally succeeding.

"Use the stirrup," he yelled.

Chaney stumbled against the horse. "Go on without me, Little Joe, they're gaining."

"No," Little Joe shouted, "try again."

Chaney stabbed his spiked boot at the stirrup, and this time got enough of a grip that he could pull himself behind Little Joe. "Let's go," Chaney yelled, and Little Joe slapped the reins against the horse's neck.

The horse staggered under the weight, and Little Joe cursed its stumble-footedness, but the animal caught itself without falling, then plunged forward up the trail. Little Joe battled to stay in the saddle, Chaney's spiked boot being caught in the stirrup, and his own leg flapping against the side of the horse. He tried to manage the reins and the carbine, but Chaney was making it difficult with only one good arm. With his broken right arm useless, Chaney had to hang on with his left.

Without looking over his shoulder, Little Joe knew the men were gaining, but there was nothing he could do about it.

Occasionally he heard a shot, but his and Chaney's lead was good enough that the bullets were spent by the time they reached them. That would change in a matter of minutes, though, as the gang galloped closer.

"We can't make it, Jack," Little Joe said, "not with both of us on this horse."

"I'll jump off," Chaney yelled. "I'm dead weight."

"No," Little Joe said, "we'll screen ourselves long enough to spook the horse and get off into the woods, both of us."

Little Joe shouted and struck the horse, driving it ahead, getting every last ounce of exertion it had. For maybe a quarter of a mile the horse was up to the challenge, but after that he winded. Around a bend on the flank of the mountain that overlooked the Cartwright camp and safety, Little Joe reined up hard and the horse slid to a stop. "Jump off," he yelled.

Chaney slid off the horse on one side, then Little Joe jumped off on the other, swatting the animal with his hat. Chaney screamed as the horse took a step. "No, my boot's stuck."

Little Joe cursed and pulled on the reins as he ran around to Chaney's side of the horse. The spikes in Chaney's boot had snagged in the stirrup.

Behind him Little Joe could hear the gang nearing, shouting, shooting in the darkness.

Throwing his hat aside, he shoved the carbine under his arm and held onto his reins with his left hand. "Get the boot off," Little Joe yelled.

"I can't, dammit, not with one hand."

Out of desperation, Little Joe jerked the butcher knife out of his belt and sliced through the leather laces. Only then did Chaney manage to pull his foot free of the boot still stuck in the stirrup.

"Hiya!" Little Joe shouted, swatting the horse with his hand.

The animal bolted forward, running in terror as the boot bounced against its side with each step.

"Hurry," Little Joe said. "Find cover."

Both men clambered up into the timber as fast as they could in the soft soil.

The thunder of pounding hooves grew louder and a light approached from down the trail.

Little Joe grabbed Chaney and pulled him

to the ground behind a broad sugar pine. Chaney cried out in pain just as the riders reached the bend in the road. Little Joe didn't look around the tree for fear of being spotted. He held his breath. The riders charged ahead after the mount.

"It worked," Little Joe said.

"For now," Chaney answered.

"Yeah, at least we've got a carbine."

Chaney shook his head. "There's not enough ammunition in it to take care of all of them."

"But it'll take care of a few of them. Think you can make it back to camp?"

"It's either that or a grave. Even if we get back to camp, it may still be a grave for the both of us."

Little Joe shrugged. "Getting back's our only chance."

"And it's slim."

"Even slimmer the longer we stay here and debate."

They got up and headed for camp. Little Joe estimated it was two hours at least until dawn. Their chances were better if they could make it back before sunrise. They circled wide of the wagon trail for a bit until Joe realized this would bring them to camp near the flume and the number three bunkhouse.

"We need to cross the trial," he said, "so we can come in below the stables, get Roe Derus to help us. He's the only ally we've got now."

"We better wait," Chaney said, the pain

evident in his voice. "The trail's too soft here, our tracks'll be easy to find. There's some rocky spots closer to camp."

"Longer we wait and the closer we get back to camp," Little Joe countered, "the more chances of them coming back and spotting us."

"I don't like it," Chaney replied.

"I don't either."

They worked their way down the slope, across the trail, leaving their footprints behind them.

"Maybe they won't notice," Little Joe said.

"And maybe Nat Greer'll want to kiss and make up."

After crossing the trail they made a wide loop down the slope, occasionally hearing the sounds of riders in the distance shouting to each other, trying to pick up their tracks. Chaney stumbled in pain behind Little Joe, and that slowed their progress. They made pitiful time. Dawn stripped away the cover of darkness before they reached the camp clearing. They came up on the campsite about 150 yards below the stables.

Hiding behind a big tree, Little Joe studied the layout, noting a large number of armed men, men he recognized as part of the number three crew. A couple stood atop the dam, and others stood on the roofs of the bunkhouses. Much of their attention seemed to focus on the trail, as a dozen men were headed in that direction, evidently to begin a sweep of the mountainside.

Little Joe looked to Jack Chaney. He was pale and breathing heavily, his right shoulder drooping. His coat was moist with blood at the shoulder and caked with mud and dirt all over. "Think you can make it?"

Chaney grimaced. "Got no choice."

"Let's get a little closer to the stables, then make our move."

Chaney gritted his teeth and followed Little Joe, who carried the Winchester in his hand. Moving from tree to tree, they made it within twenty-five yards of the stables. The rest of the way was over open ground.

"Maybe you better go on, Little Joe. I don't know if I can make it."

"We've come this far together, Chaney, and I'm not leaving you behind. Once they find our trail, it'll be easy to follow in the soft ground."

There was a commotion up the trail as a rider came waving a hat. Little Joe had a sinking feeling when he recognized the hat was his. "We've found their tracks," Ben Tull yelled. "We've got men on horseback following them, it won't be long till we corner them."

Nat Greer rode up beside Tull and dismounted. "Whoever finds them is to bring them to me."

Little Joe took a deep breath. With Tull's announcement, they had a momentary distraction. Now was the time to run for the stables. "Let's go, Chaney, this is our chance."

Crouching, they darted for the stables, made it quickly, crawled through the fence, and then slipped inside the building.

Roe Derus, in a back stall rubbing down an ox, yelled, "Get out, you sons of bitches."

Little Joe sighed. "It's us, Roe."

The bull whacker looked up and grinned. "I figured you was already buzzard meat, the way Greer's boys have been looking for you."

"There's still that possibility," Chaney managed grimly.

"Good possibility," Derus said. "All of Greer's men are armed. Our boys have been told to stay in their bunkhouses. Without guns, they can't counter them."

"Just saddle my pinto and I'll make a run for it," Little Joe said.

"No soap, Little Joe. They've got armed guards on the road, figuring you'll try that." Derus finished rubbing some salve in the sore of the bull ox's back, then emerged from the stall. "What did you boys find down the road?"

Little Joe shook his head. "The road leads to another logging camp a couple miles beyond the mountain. That camp's cleared an entire valley of trees."

Derus nodded. "Sounds to me like Greer's set up his own operation and he's cutting timber illegally on government land. He must haul it down by oxen to another logging outfit and sell it to them. He profits taking logs that ain't his and paying his crews with Cartwright money."

"The son of a bitch," growled Little Joe.

"That he is, Cartwright, that he is, but I wouldn't worry none about him right now," Derus added. "If something happens to you, ain't much gonna happen to him. He'll just say it was Cartwright orders that he was following. It never did make sense him locating a camp this close to the edge of a lease."

"He hasn't got me yet," Little Joe answered, stripping his coat off and tossing it into the vee-shaped feed trough nearby. He turned to Chaney, whose face was pale and slick from sweat. "You need help?"

Chaney grimaced. "Water. I'm burning up in this coat."

Little Joe tucked the carbine under his arm as he helped Chaney dispense with his coat, its shoulder moist with blood. Derus disappeared to the back of the stable and returned a moment later with a bucket of water. "It's from the trough, but I don't figure you mind right now."

Chaney shook his head and dipped his left hand into the bucket, cupping water to his mouth until he sated his thirst. Next, Little Joe took the bucket and drank his fill. Then he tossed it aside.

"What do we do now?" he said to Derus.

The bull whacker studied Chaney's arm.

"We need to get him to a doctor."

Chaney just shook his head and gave a sarcastic laugh. "If you think Greer's men are just going to let me leave here wounded, much less alive, you're all wet."

Derus twisted his head from Chaney to Little Joe. He grinned. "That's it, Jack, that's it."

"What's it?" Little Joe asked.

"The way we get the two of you out of here," Derus said, shaking his head.

"How?" Little Joe asked.

Derus smiled broadly. "The flume."

CHAPTER 17

They were up before dawn and soon riding over a trail so rugged as to have been scratched out of the mountain by the devil's fingernails. The trail slowed the horses and angered Hoss, who prayed Sara Ann was safe atop Timberline Pass. The trail went up and down, gradually climbing and then descending the stair steps of lesser rises that pointed toward Timberline Pass. The three men didn't push the horses, agreeing it best to give the animals easy rein for the hard work in flinty soil and thin air. Even so, the slow pace, a mile an hour at best, was hard on the men's nerves.

Hoss had been the first to spot it. "Pa," he said, pointing toward Timberline Pass.

Ben nodded at the plume of smoke rising in the thin air.

"Think it's them?" Hoss asked.

"No one else would be up here," Ben said, twisting around in his saddle and frowning at the trail. It had deteriorated badly since the rush. At one time hundreds of men and animals had climbed this trail. It was never the best trail nor the easiest, but it had been the straightest to the goldfields. This trail wasn't paved with gold, but the dreams of the men who used it during the rush were. And now it seemed only a hair shy of impassible. Or maybe the trail was no worse today than then, he thought, but back then he was a young man, an optimistic man who dreamed better than he observed.

Roy Coffee stopped his gelding atop a rise and surveyed Timberline Pass. "They'll likely spot us before long," he said, studying the final rise that the trail crossed before it reached the the base of the last incline up to Timberline Pass. Coffee pointed to the rise. "Once we get there, we'll be visible until we reach the bottom of the mountain. What do you think, Ben?"

Ben pursed his lips. "At the foot of the mountain, I'm thinking we hobble the horses and go up afoot. It'd be quieter that way and less chance of ruining a horse. It'll be good rest for the horses in case we need them to round up the Whartons."

Coffee scratched his chin. "I'm thinking we'll want to split up. I figure us old men should hide at the foot of the mountain and give Hoss a chance to make a wide circle away from the trail and see if he can come in near the peak or at least above the smoke. If he can get there without being seen, we'll have an advantage they won't know about. That okay with you, Hoss, the climbing and all?"

"Roy," answered Hoss, "I just want to keep

moving. As long as I'm moving, I'm getting closer to Sara Ann. I don't want to be waiting at the bottom of the trail for you or Pa."

Hoss pulled off his coat and strapped it to his bedroll. He twisted around in his saddle, checking to see that the supplies hadn't shifted on the packhorse. "I'm ready," he said.

Roy Coffee nudged his animal forward and the trio began the final leg of their trip. It took another hour and a half to get over the last rise and approach the foot of the final incline. Because the switchback trail zigzagged back and forth up the mountain, they had plenty of places to hide their horses under the steep slopes that led to the top.

Wordlessly, they dismounted, and each man checked the load in his revolver and his carbine. Ben spun the cylinder in his .45-caliber Colt single-action Army Model revolver. For a carbine, he carried a Sharps .45–90, not as fancy as any of the newer repeaters, but he liked its range and its accuracy. Hoss nodded with satisfaction that his Smith & Wesson .44-caliber Russian Model revolver, a big gun for his big hand, was ready. He jerked the Henry .44-caliber carbine from its saddle boot and held it under his arm as he fished a carton of .44 cartridges from his saddlebag.

He pointed up the mountain in the direction he planned to take. "Give me forty-five minutes," he said. "If I'm not in position by then, I'll do the best I can."

"Be careful, Hoss," Ben said, patting his son on the shoulder.

"Good luck," Roy added.

Hoss nodded. "Our luck'll be good as long as Sara Ann is okay." With that, he turned and started to scale the mountain. The way was steep and dangerous, his slick-soled boots slipping several times on the flinty talus that gathered in the pitted mountainside. The trees at this altitude had thinned out, and occasionally Hoss had to crawl in plain view of the peak. The climb was laborious and Hoss panted and drew deep on the thin air, having to take more rest than he thought appropriate. Still, he climbed and slid and cursed and climbed again, quickly losing track of time.

He figured it had been forty-five minutes, maybe longer, when he reached the position he had been hoping for, a stone den that could look down upon the smoking fire. He crawled between two boulders and smiled at the most beautiful sight he had seen in three days — Sara Ann. She was alive, sitting on a rock by the fire, tossing stones off the cliff's edge.

Across from her sat one of the Whartons, the one with the lopsided shoulders and the crossed eyes. Hoss recognized him from the encounter at Coffee's house. Hoss drew a bead on the man and held it. He wouldn't fire until Ben and Roy came up the trail.

Hoss looked down the slope and thought he saw Ben and Roy beginning their ascent. He looked for the other two Whartons, but they were too well hidden for him to spot.

Now it was a waiting game. Hoss alternated between checking Sara Ann and looking down the trail.

Before he saw the other two Whartons, he heard them.

"Vern," called one.

"Yeah, Lem," the other replied.

"I got a glimpse of them, not a good glimpse, but I only seen two of them," Lem said.

"We saw three on the trail," Vern answered.

"The sheriff and Cartwright are coming, but not her big husband," Lem called.

"There was three of them that came over the trail," Vern answered, a bit of panic in his voice.

"I know, dammit," Lem said. "These two are afoot."

"Maybe the other one's keeping the horses," Vern called back.

"Don't think so," Lem answered. "We've just got to watch out, make sure the third one doesn't double around on us."

By following the sound of their voices, Hoss finally saw a second Wharton, crouched behind two rocks with a view straight down the trail his father and Roy would be climbing.

Finally, after what seemed an eternity, Hoss spotted his father and Roy, inching up the trail. From his height, Hoss could see both men, though they were still screened — except for occasional glimpses — from the Whartons. Roy and Ben held their carbines at the ready.

Hoss watched Roy lift his carbine to the air and squeeze off a shot that echoed through the air. "You Whartons," Roy cried, "this is Sheriff Roy Coffee."

"This is California," Lem yelled back. "You ain't sheriff of nothing over here."

"Give us the girl," Roy yelled, "then we'll settle up."

From a vantage point still hidden from Hoss's view came Lem Wharton's voice. "We'll settle up first, then see what happens to the girl." There was a pause, then a sinister laugh. "You see them, Vern?"

"Not good enough to shoot," Vern answered.

"Willis," Lem called, and Hoss saw the one with Sara Ann stand up and glance down the trail.

"Yeah, Lem," Willis yelled, moving quickly beside Sara Ann and drawing his pistol.

"Don't let Red get away. Kill her if you have to," Lem commanded.

"Okay," Willis said, but his voice lacked enthusiasm. Hoss took aim at Willis. He let his finger tighten on the trigger, then released it when Willis grabbed Sara Ann and momentarily held her as a shield. Hoss swung the gun barrel away from Willis. Willis took Sara Ann by the shoulder and forced her to the ground, then dropped atop her, as if he were screening Sara Ann from danger.

"Sara Ann," Roy called with a touch of tremor in his voice. "Sara Ann, are you okay? Answer me!"

"Scared," she cried.

"It'll be over in a minute," Coffee assured her.

"Don't be so certain of that," Lem shouted.

Hoss saw Ben and Roy inching up the trail in a crouch. Finally Lem got a clear view of the two men on the trail. "There's only two of them," he cried, the warning echoing through the thin air. "The third one's got to be around here somewhere. Watch out for him, Vern."

Then gunfire erupted. Hoss looked first to Sara Ann, but her captor seemed to be more concerned with protecting than harming her.

Hoss glanced back down the trail. Ben and Roy were firing wildly, uncertain where their attackers were shooting from. By the puffs of smoke, Hoss knew the general location of each, but had a tough time spotting Lem, who was apparently farther down the trail than the one he had spotted. Hoss saw a flash of color as the one nearest him changed positions and drew a bead on Ben.

Hurriedly, Hoss squeezed off a shot, which missed, but pinged off the rock near the man's head.

"The other one's behind us," Vern yelled, twisting around for cover.

Hoss anticipated the move as he levered a fresh round into his Henry and took aim at

281

the man's back. When the outlaw spun around, Hoss squeezed the trigger, catching him full in the chest. The man screamed and fell back on the rock. "I'm hit!" he cried out in terror. "I'm hit!"

Lem screamed, "Where did it come from? Where is he?"

"In the rocks up the slope," Vern gasped.

Hoss slid back behind the boulders and waited, glancing around the rock to check on Sara Ann.

A barrage of bullets pinged off the rocks around Hoss, but he knew Lem was shooting wildly, out of desperation.

Then came a stillness, followed by loud curses. "Dammit, dammit," shouted Lem, "I'm out of ammunition."

That, thought Hoss, wasn't a wise thing to announce. He rolled over, tossing his hat aside so Lem wouldn't see it when he rose up to aim. Then Hoss peeked around the rock, down the slope. He saw Lem running to change positions, jumping the ragged trail and sliding among the rocks for cover as Roy and Ben kicked up dust with their fire all around him.

"Vern," he called, "how you doing? Where are you?"

"Not good. Water, I need water."

Lem jumped between rocks, working his way toward Vern, but drew fire from Ben and Coffee, their bullets spitting bits of rock when they hit. Hoss saw a patch of shirt among the rocks and took a bead on it. Lem darted for another location just as Hoss squeezed the trigger and sent the bullet cracking off the rock.

Spotting the smoke of Hoss's carbine, Lem lifted his pistol and snapped it at Hoss, forgetting that he was out of ammunition, then threw the empty weapon aside. Hoss ducked behind the rock. He would have been winged or worse had the pistol been loaded. He glanced down at Sara Ann and her captor, who had crawled off of her and now waved a carbine toward the trail. Sara Ann reached for a skillet and put it on the coals of the fire.

Hoss shook his head, confused. She could have hit him over the head with the skillet, but why was she trying to cook at a time like this? He just stared for a moment, and in that instant Sara Ann glanced up toward the rocks and her hands flew to her lips to cover a smile. She had seen him.

On hands and knees Hoss worked himself to a different location to observe Sara Ann. He took a new position and peeked toward the trail in time to see Lem weaving among the rocks toward the campsite. Cursing, he threw his useless pistol down.

From down the trail Ben and Roy squeezed off a half-dozen shots, but none of them struck flesh.

Lem drove in behind Vern just as Hoss

fired, his bullet clipping the heel off of Lem's right boot.

"Your pistol, your carbine, your cartridges," Lem screamed.

"Water, Lem, water, please," Vern coughed. "I'm dying."

Desperate, Lem grabbed his brother and rolled him over, pulling Vern's pistol from his belt and dragging the carbine from under him.

Vern screamed. "You're hurting me, Lem."

"Shut up," Lem shouted back, his voice high with panic. "You're dying anyway. Give me your gun belt."

Lem lifted Vern's pistol and squeezed off a shot in Hoss's direction, then another down the trail at Roy and Ben. Then he bent over his brother and unbuckled the belt, quickly pulling it free. "Dammit, what happened to our ammunition?" he raged, then fell against a boulder as Hoss fired another round.

Missed again. Hoss slapped the barrel of his Henry. "Come on," he shouted.

Lem lifted his head and fired the pistol at Hoss until it was empty. "Dammit," Lem screamed. "What happened to all our —." He stopped. "The girl, Willis, the girl. You got her?"

"Yeah, Lem."

"Throw her over the cliff, Willis, throw her over the cliff."

"No!" Roy Coffee cried. "Let her go. I'll trade myself for her, just let her go."

Hoss's blood turned cold as a glacier. He had never heard such terror in Coffee's voice. Hoss rolled over to a rock that gave him the best view of Sara Ann, even though he may have exposed himself to Lem. He didn't care. He had to save Sara Ann. He took aim at Willis, but the convict hesitated.

"She ain't done nothing, Lem."

"She's killed you, Willis, that's what she's done."

Willis scratched his head. "What d'ya mean?"

"Check your gun belt, Willis. You ain't got no ammunition more than what's in your pistol and your carbine. It ain't just rocks she's been throwing over that cliff."

Hoss grinned at Sara Ann's spunk.

Willis seemed further confused as his hand felt the loops on his gun belt. They were empty. "What else she throw off the cliff?" Willis yelled.

"Your bullets, you bastard," Lem cried.

Hoss took aim and fired just as Willis whirled around toward Sara Ann. Hoss's bullet grazed him on the arm. He screamed like a wounded mountain lion and charged Sara Ann. Hoss squeezed off another shot, but the bullet missed.

"I brought you rocks," Willis bellowed.

Sara Ann circled the smoking fire, keeping it between her and Willis.

Hoss kept a loose finger on the trigger,

fearful he might squeeze off a shot and hit Sara Ann by accident.

"Sara Ann," Roy Coffee yelled, "are you okay?"

Sara Ann didn't have time to answer, not with Willis stalking her. As Willis circled around the fire, Sara Ann moved backward, always keeping her eyes on him.

"Throw her off the cliff, dammit," Lem yelled.

Willis stopped.

Hoss held his breath. His finger tightened against the trigger. Just as he started to pull the trigger, a bullet splattered the boulder above his head, spraying bits of rock across his face. He flinched and fired, his aim so awkward that he hoped he hadn't hit Sara Ann.

His face stung from the rock fragments and his eyes blurred because of the threads of blood trickling into them. Hoss threw down his carbine and swiped at his eyes, then lifted his head to check on Sara Ann and make sure he hadn't hit her.

His heart stopped for a moment.

Sara Ann was still on her feet, but doubled up over the fire, like she had taken a gut wound. She seemed to be reaching into the fire.

"Sara Ann," Hoss screamed, "did I —"

Before he could finish the sentence, Sara Ann grabbed the hot handle of the skillet and flung its contents at Willis.

Scalding grease caught Willis in the chest and face. He shrieked in agony, dropping his gun, and stumbled around the ledge, lunging wildly for her, grasping blindly at the air and clawing at his own face as if he could wipe away the burn. Sara Ann danced around him, careful to avoid his outstretched hands.

"I brought you rocks," he shrieked.

"You killed my parents," she shouted back.

Willis stumbled dangerously close to the edge of the precipice. Sara Ann jumped at him and shoved him in the chest.

Desperately, he tried to twist around and grab something, but there was nothing to hold. He stumbled over the cliff, his cry of terror echoing off the mountain, then ending in a thud in the rocks below.

"Sara Ann," Roy shouted, "are you all right?"

"Yes, sir," she answered.

Lem shot Vern's carbine a couple times at Roy's voice, drawing return fire from Ben. When the carbine clicked empty, Lem threw it at Vern, his brother screaming at the blow.

Suddenly, Lem made a dash over the rocks.

"Don't leave me to die alone," Vern cried in a doleful voice. "Don't let me die alone," he sobbed, then gasped, then went silent forever.

With only the ammunition in what had been Vern's pistols, Lem ran desperately back across the trail toward his only chance of salvation — Sara Ann.

"Run, Sara Ann, run," Hoss shouted down the slope. "He's backtracking." Hoss fired his Henry at Lem until it was empty. Ben's and Roy's shots were no more accurate.

Sara Ann jumped on a rock and slipped, then cried out in pain. She stood up and tried to run, but she could only limp. She could not escape. Lem jumped over a rock onto the wide ledge and grabbed her around the neck.

She screamed as he pointed the barrel of his pistol to her temple.

"Come out, you sons of bitches," Lem yelled, "or I'll blow her brains out. Now."

Hoss gritted his teeth, then caught his breath when Lem started backing Sara Ann toward the ledge.

"I ain't got all day," Lem called.

Hoss doubled his fist and hit it against the rock. "Pa," he called, "he's got Sara Ann. I'm giving up."

"Wharton," Ben called, "anything happens to that girl, you've got nothing to hide behind. It won't do any good to hurt her."

Lem spat at the fire, his movements jerky and nervous. "It'll do me good, knowing I took somebody else down with me."

"I'm going down, Pa," Hoss yelled.

"We're giving up too," Roy answered. "Come on, Ben. I don't want Sara Ann hurt."

"That's it, boys." Lem laughed. "Now, bring your guns with you, because I want them and your ammunition belts. This bitch threw our ammunition over the cliff like she did Willis." Lem cackled crazily. "I wonder if the landing uncrossed his eyes."

Hoss slipped down the rocks, holding his empty Henry above his head with one hand while the other hand helped him maintain his balance. From down the trail, Hoss saw Ben and Roy reluctantly approaching, their guns held high over their heads.

"Any sudden moves," Lem yelled, "and I'll blow her head off." Then he shouted maniacally, "I came up here to get revenge for Pa, and now I've got to get it for my brothers too. There's two of them and there's four of you. Looks like I come out ahead."

Roy Coffee flinched. "You've always been ahead after what you did to my family."

Hoss shook his head. Damn the Whartons, damn them for all the misery they had brought the Coffees.

The paths of the three men converged twenty feet from the ledge and Sara Ann. They walked the rest of the way together.

The closer they came, the louder Lem laughed.

"Hoss," Sara Ann called, "are you all right? What happened to your face?"

"Just scratches from flying rock," Hoss answered. "I'll be fine."

"You ain't gonna live long enough to be fine, big man," Lem taunted.

Hoss, Roy, and Ben stepped off the final

ring of rocks that surrounded the ledge and stood on the opposite side of the fire from Lem Wharton.

"That's far enough, all of you. Remember, if you don't do what I say, I'll kill her." Lem jerked Sara Ann's head by the chin and shoved the gun to her temple.

Hoss flinched.

"Now, you fellows first put your carbines and your pistols on the ground in front of your feet."

All three obliged.

"Unbuckle your gun belts and drop 'em." Lem smiled as all three followed his instructions. "Now, one at a time, kick them to me."

Hoss went first, then Roy, and finally Ben, each backing up against the rocks when they were done.

"That's good, real good." Lem laughed. "Now, who wants to die first? Who'll it be?"

Hoss nodded. "Shoot me, you coward, standing behind a woman. I'm the one that killed your brother."

"No, Hoss," Sara Ann interrupted, "I pushed his brother off the cliff."

Roy Coffee shook his head. "Let the girl and the others go, Wharton. I'm the one that killed your Pa."

Lem laughed. "I can't do that now, not after they admitted killing my brothers." He scowled at Hoss. "I ain't standing behind no woman."

He shoved Sara Ann aside and she staggered on her lame foot, then caught her balance before she stumbled alongside the cliff.

Lem laughed again as he took a step toward the three men facing him. "I'll even kill you with your own guns," he said, sneering as he bent down to pick up a pistol.

Suddenly Sara Ann's eyes went wide. She lunged for him, her hand flying to the back of his gun belt.

She jerked something free, then lifted it skyward.

Hoss saw a flash of metal as her hand started down.

"What?" Lem screamed.

The knife came down and plunged into Lem's back.

He gasped and cried out.

Sara Ann pulled the knife free and stabbed him, once, twice, three more times, so suddenly, so furiously, that Hoss had barely started for her before she had turned away, the bloody knife in her hand.

Though Lem straightened up, his gun hand drooped and the gun fell at his feet with the others. His face went blank as he turned about and lurched for Sara Ann, who stumbled out of his way. Lem lunged where Sara Ann had been, tripping over her legs and flying off the cliff.

Hoss dove for Sara Ann and wrapped his strong arms around her, holding her as Lem's scream ended at the bottom of the cliff. Sara Ann sobbed and looked at the bloody knife in her hand, then flung it over the cliff. Hoss helped her to her feet. She broke free and limped to her grandfather, throwing her arms around him.

Ben's lip quivered and he let out a great sigh that seemed to echo off the mountains. "Thank God, you're safe, Sara Ann, thank God."

Hoss walked to the pile of guns and picked up his pistol and gun belt. He strapped the belt around his waist, then slipped the Smith & Wesson in the holster. Suddenly his knees were weak and mushy from the thought of how close Sara Ann had come to falling over the cliff. To disguise his momentary weakness, he dropped to his knees and picked up his father's weapons, offering them to Ben. His father took the weapons and shook his head.

"A close one, Hoss, a close one," he said.

Nodding, Hoss picked up Roy's gun and turned toward the sheriff. Hoss thought he saw tears in Coffee's eyes, but he turned his gaze away, uncomfortable that he was prying into Roy's emotions.

Hoss, still on his knees, knew Sara Ann would want to be with her grandfather, and was surprised when she limped back to him and threw her arms around him. For once she was taller than him. He wasn't quite sure what to do, his hands holding Roy's guns and Sara Ann holding him. Roy, though, took his weapons, and Hoss turned to Sara Ann and stroked her auburn hair.

Then she looked at him and rubbed the cuts and trickles of blood from his cheeks. Her eyes brimmed with tears and she kept sobbing, "Thank you, Hoss, thank you."

Hoss smiled. "I'll do anything to get out of a dance."

She laughed and squeezed him tighter.

CHAPTER 18

The flume?" Little Joe stared incredulously at Roe Derus.

"You got a better idea?" Jack Chaney asked, grimacing as he grabbed his wounded shoulder.

Shrugging, Little Joe grinned. "It might work."

"It has to work," Derus said.

"What'll we do for a boat?" Little Joe asked. "Something that would fit a flume?"

Derus turned around and pointed to his feeding oxen and broke into a little jig. "Boys, I found your boat."

Little Joe scratched his head and frowned. "Who are we kidding? Even if we find a boat, how are we gonna get it and us to the head of the flume in broad daylight? We don't have all day. They picked our trail up in the woods and they'll be here in less than twenty minutes."

"No," Derus said, "it'll work."

"What'll work?" Little Joe asked.

Derus pointed to the vee-shaped feed troughs where the oxen were placidly eating hay.

"It ain't Noah's ark," Little Joe said.

"It's not much, Cartwright, but it's a chance," Derus answered. "And that's more than you got if you sit on your butt in here."

"But how'll we get it up the dam?"

"Leave that to Roe Derus."

The bull whacker attacked the feed trough, jerking it from under the noses of the oxen and quickly prying loose three sets of legs, then throwing them aside. The trough was twelve feet long and maybe two and a half feet wide at the top.

Little Joe kept shaking his head as he watched. If it worked, it would be a miracle, but what other chance did he have?

Next, Derus began to yoke a pair of oxen, then another pair, chaining them together and hooking a singletree behind them. He ran to the back and returned with two six-by-six tarps and four lengths of rope. "This is where it gets tricky," he said.

Chaney and Little Joe could only watch in amazement.

Derus ran a rope through the corner eyelets in each end of both tarps, then he folded the tarps in half and draped one between each set of oxen. Quickly, he tied a rope around the neck and the rump of each animal to form a sling between each pair.

He turned to Little Joe and Chaney. "Crawl in, Chaney in the back one since he has the bad arm. Cartwright, keep that carbine ready where you can start shooting if things don't work out. I'm gonna cover you with hay, then start up the hill, dragging your boat. I'll tell them I'm gonna clean the trough."

"What if they don't buy it?" Little Joe asked.

Derus laughed. "Then you'd better sprout wings."

Chaney and Little Joe slid into the slings and Derus ran to the nearest haystack and grabbed armloads of hay to throw over the two fugitives. After a dozen hurried trips, Derus announced his satisfaction. He hooked one end of a chain to the vee trough and the other to the singletree. "Okay, boys, let's see what happens."

Derus started the team out, the tarp slings carrying Little Joe and Chaney between the skittish oxen. Unaccustomed to the ropes fore and aft, the oxen fidgeted and tossed their heads against their yokes as they stepped out into the corral. "Gee, gee," Derus called, guiding the animals to the gate. He ran ahead and pushed the gate open. "Hiya," he yelled, and the team started through the gate, the tow chain dragging the trough. "Haw, haw, haw," he shouted. The oxen cleared the gate and turned toward the dam. He started the oxen up the earthen incline to the top of the dam, where Nat Greer stood, his arms folded across his chest, talking to Ted Karnes and Ben Tull, who had dismounted from his horse and still held Little Joe's hat, which he had found back down the trail.

"Haw, haw," called Derus as the oxen moved by rote up the incline.

"What the hell are you doing, Derus?" Greer spat out.

"My job, Greer. The damn trough needs washing out."

Greer laughed. "You sure yoked up a lot of beef to drag something up here a man of your heft could carry."

"Whoa," Derus called, and the four oxen halted. "I figured when I was through, I'd head out the skid road and pull a stump that keeps getting in my way."

"Wait a minute, Derus," Greer said, pointing at the tarp slings between the oxen. "You sure you ain't hiding something in there? What's that between them damn animals?"

"Dammit, Greer, it's Cartwright and Chaney," Derus shot back.

Tull and Karnes stepped forward.

"Check it out if you like," Derus bluffed. "All you'll find are chains and grubbing tools I'll need to pull up the stump."

Greer laughed. "Nobody else is working. Why are you?"

Derus shook his head. "I guess I like working better than waiting."

"Derus, you're a fool, you know that?" Greer told him.

"At least I'm my own fool, not somebody else's, like your two shadows there."

Tull and Karnes lifted rifles toward Derus.

Greer shoved the gun barrels toward the ground. "Hell, we can't kill everyone. Leave him be. Come on, Derus, wash your trough and get on down the road to your stump. I don't want you around when any trouble begins."

Derus yelled and the oxen topped the dam, then he turned toward the flume loading chute. Halfway to the chute, he saw something that made his heart flutter. Chaney's socked left foot was hanging out the end of the sling. There was no way he could cover it now. He would have to keep moving, every step under Tull's and Karnes's hateful eyes.

The bull whacker drove the oxen past Greer and his two henchmen. Karnes eyed him suspiciously. Derus returned the glare, and spat at Karnes to distract him from Chaney's visible foot. "Throw down the rifle, Karnes, and let's settle this with fists."

Karnes's eyes narrowed, but he said nothing.

Derus drove the oxen over the sturdy wooden bridge that crossed the chute where individual logs were floated before being released. One sixteen-foot-log was already in the chute, held back by the spring gate. Derus knew he couldn't release the log, but he couldn't push it back out in the reservoir either. He didn't have time. On the flume side of the wooden bridge he saw an axe. On the reservoir side he spotted a peavey stick that he could use to hold back the log when he released the gate. Otherwise, the log with its massive weight would overtake their boat and crush it.

Derus marched behind the oxen and unhooked the trough from the chain. With his muscled arms he picked up the vee-shaped trough and put it in the flume chute beside the log. As he did, a clamor arose from beyond the stables. Several men were shouting and whistling.

The loggers on horseback had traced the two fugitives' trail back to camp and were waving at Greer. "Over here," they shouted, "quick."

Greer and Tull started down the incline, but Karnes lingered just below the top of the dam.

"Now," Derus called. Instantly, Chaney and Little Joe flung hay off and fought their way out of the slings.

Derus grabbed the peavey stick and poked it at the log as Little Joe and Chaney scrambled from between the oxen, across the dam, over the wooden bridge, then down by the chute, and jumped into the trough.

"There they are, at the flume," yelled Karnes, who topped the dam and charged toward the loading chute.

Derus cussed.

Karnes came running along the dam, firing his rifle, once, twice, three times.

"Get down," Derus shouted to Little Joe and Chaney.

"Open the gate," Chaney responded.

Derus had to wedge the log in before he opened the gate or it would crush the trough and its two passengers. Suddenly Karnes stood over Derus, aiming his rifle at Little Joe. Derus swung the peavey stick at the rifle, which spat flame and fire skyward. Karnes screamed as Derus whirled the peavey stick at him again, knocking the rifle loose and into the reservoir behind Karnes.

Then Derus jumped to the chute, Karnes behind him. The bull whacker jabbed the log with the peavey stick and pushed all his weight against it.

"Open the gate," Chaney screamed, lying down at the front of the boat.

Karnes clambered behind Derus, grabbed an axe, and advanced toward the chute. Standing on the walkway over the chute, he lifted the shining axe blade over his head and swung at Little Joe, who was sitting in the trough.

Just then Derus kicked the foot lever and the spring gate opened. The trough started sliding free.

Little Joe fell back in the trough. Karnes's axe missed him by inches, but embedded in a corner of the trough as it slid down the flume.

The axe held the boat from falling free of the gate. Little Joe lifted his carbine and aimed, but Karnes ducked just as he fired, so the bullet whizzed overhead. But in dodging the bullet, Karnes lost his grip on the axe handle and the trough began to slide away. He leaped for Little Joe, who instinctively lifted his feet to divert the blow.

Karnes screamed as his chest landed full on Little Joe's caulked boots. He flailed his arms at the searing pain, and instinctively Little Joe fired at Karnes's chest. The logger fell limp and Little Joe kicked him over the side of the flume. Instantly, the boat lunged down the flume. From all across the camp Greer's men fired at it as it began its descent.

Derus lifted his foot from the gate lever, and the spring gate shut before the log could get through it. Other men were running up the dam. Derus had to buy Chaney and Cartwright time. He tried to push the log back out of the chute and into the reservoir, but Greer and Tull were nearing him. With all his might he drove the spiked head of the peavey stick into the log and fell to his knees trying to wedge the handle into something that would lodge the log in the wooden chute, but the log rolled back over into its natural position.

Greer and Tull were upon him. Derus looked down the flume and saw that Little Joe and Chaney had a two-hundred-yard lead. That wouldn't be enough if Greer let the log loose.

Derus stood up to fight them.

"You son of a bitch," Greer yelled, and swung his rifle at Derus. The gun caught the bull whacker across the side of the head. All of a sudden the world was murky. Derus felt his knees give way and he collapsed on the top of the dam, then began to slide down the face of the earthen wall. Derus saw Tull and Greer climb atop the log and another logger open the gate. The log slid free. Then someone kicked Derus and he rolled down the dam until his body stopped against the corpse of Ted Karnes.

"We made it!" Chaney yelled. "Roe was right."

The trough shot down the flume, and the armed loggers from the number three crew fired their weapons. The bullets peppered the thick wood, sending splinters flying overhead.

Little Joe held his breath. He knew that only a lucky shot could hurt them now, because the thick walls of the flume screened them. Then the trough hit the incline where the flume dropped off the high plateau and the makeshift boat hurtled headlong so fast that Little Joe screamed at the exhilaration.

When the trough leveled out again, Little Joe glanced at Chaney. "How you doing?" he asked, then cursed, scrambling to kneel where he could get a shot off with the Winchester.

"What is it?" Chaney yelled. He looked down

the flume and spotted the two armed men up ahead.

Little Joe remembered Derus saying Greer had posted riflemen down the trail, but he didn't realize that those men would take position atop the flume. The trough was hurtling toward two riflemen stationed a hundred yards apart. The nearest one started firing, and the bullets plunked into the flume. One hit the back of the trough near the axe Karnes had embedded in the wood as he attempted to decapitate Little Joe. Little Joe squeezed off a shot, then another, but the bouncing trough threw his aim off for both shots. But the same buoyancy that threw off his aim also made the boat a more difficult target. Suddenly, the first rifleman loomed just ahead. Instead of firing the carbine, Little Joe grabbed it by the barrel and swung it for the armed logger as the boat shot by. The carbine caught the logger square in the head, knocking his rifle loose and sending him tumbling off the flume, screaming until he hit the ground.

Little Joe collapsed in the boat, just as fire from the next rifleman began to thud into the flume around him. Despairing of ever hitting this sniper with a bullet, Little Joe handed the carbine to Chaney. "Hold onto it," he yelled.

Reaching to the back of the trough, Little Joe worked the axe from the wedge in the wood and pulled it into the trough, turning to challenge the next sniper as the trough came within fifty yards, then twenty-five yards of him. Little Joe braced his knees against the side of the makeshift boat and rose up, drawing the axe back over his shoulder.

The logger fired and the axe shuddered in Little Joe's hands from a direct hit. Ten yards separated Little Joe from the sniper, who fired again and somehow missed. Little Joe swung the axe. It landed solidly in the man's chest. In that fleeting moment, as Little Joe flew by, he saw the disbelief in the logger's eyes. The sniper's rifle fell from his hands, then he collapsed forward, over the side of the flume, his head beneath the water. Little Joe screamed with triumph, then looked down the flume. He saw no other men posted ahead, so he collapsed into the trough, his heart pounding from the excitement and fear.

As he lay back in the speeding boat, the world overhead seemed to rush by at unearthly speed. He had ridden fast horses and fast trains, but never anything like this. Then, when the flume hit its next dive, Little Joe gasped for breath.

"Whoa," he yelled, "I can't take many more of those."

"Others are steeper," Chaney called.

"How long is this thing?"

"Twenty miles, all the way into Lake Tahoe."

The trough bumped and thudded against the flume, but the structure seemed to vibrate even more as if something larger was beating against it. As Little Joe looked between his legs at the drop they had just navigated, he saw a huge log start down behind them. The whole flume seemed to tremble from the log's slide. Two foolhardy men lay on their bellies on the log which cast up a spray of water when it hit the bottom of the drop.

"Behind us," Little Joe shouted to Chaney as he recognized Nat Greer and Ben Tull atop the log.

"Dammit," yelled Chaney, "the log'll crush us when it catches us."

"We've got to find a place to jump off," Joe shouted back over the screech of the trough against the flume.

"I can't do it, Cartwright, not with this arm."

Little Joe turned over and looked down the flume. His mouth gaped at what he saw.

At the next curve was a wide gap in the side of the flume. They were going to go careening over the edge to their deaths!

"Chaney," he screamed, "there's a hole in the flume. We're done for."

Chaney twisted his head around. "It's just a throw gap."

Little Joe looked behind him. The log was gaining, little by little.

The trough sped toward the throw gap. Propped up on the opposite side of the flume was something that looked like a partial apple crate.

The trough zoomed toward the throw gap, and Little Joe gritted his teeth. The trough hit the curve, then flew safely past the gap.

Glancing behind him, Little Joe focused on the cratelike contraption on the edge of the flume. "What was that on the side?" he shouted over the rush of the water.

"An inclined slat wedge," Chaney answered. "When it's dropped in the water, it diverts the log out of the flume, through the gap and over the edge."

Little Joe looked back behind him until the throw gap disappeared behind the curve in the mountain. He hoped the huge log would shoot through the gap, but in a minute the log — with Greer and Tull still atop it — reappeared up the flume, still gaining on the trough.

"How far's the next throw gap?" Little Joe cried. "It may be our only chance."

"Three miles, maybe less."

"Can we outrun them there?"

"I don't know, there's a steep dive between here and there. They'll gain plenty on us at that point. We can't pull the slat wedge in without stopping, and I don't know that we can stop."

Little Joe looked between his legs at the ominous log gradually gaining. "They're a minute or less behind us. How are we gonna stop?"

"Your left boot, Cartwright, give me your left boot."

"Huh?"

"Just do it, dammit."

Cradling the carbine against his chest, Little Joe lifted his left leg, unlaced the boot, then pulled it off. "Now what?"

"Put it on my foot," Chaney yelled, "as best you can. This will be our brakes."

Little Joe looked back and saw Chaney's socked foot raised over his forehead. Quickly he shoved the boot on, and laced it as best he could for the injured logger.

"Two miles at most," Chaney yelled. "I've got to turn around and try to brake us with my boots against the side." His bad arm was an impediment, but Chaney struggled, screaming at the pain as he managed to roll over on his stomach, then get to his knees and scoot them up under him. He sat up, the boat wobbling with his effort, and leaned back onto Little Joe until he could drag his legs out from under him. That done, he scooted forward to the front of the trough.

"You've got to get turned around, Little Joe, quick, so your head's at the back of the boat. The big drop is coming up fast. They'll gain on us."

Little Joe rolled over on his stomach, dropping the Winchester in the water puddled in the bottom of the trough. With a hand on each side of the trough, he pushed himself up and slid his feet behind him. Just then the trough seemed to fall from beneath him. He fell into the bottom as the trough went into a deep dive hurtling down the big drop twenty, forty, sixty feet.

Little Joe and Chaney screamed from the terrifying exhilaration. Then the drop leveled off and the trough sent up a spray of water as it slowed down.

Chaney started counting aloud. "One — tell me Little Joe — two — when their log — three — hits the bottom — four — of the drop — five — six — seven — eight — nine — ten — eleven . . ."

"There they are," Little Joe yelled as he saw the log head into a dive, Nat Greer and Ben Tull holding on for life.

". . . twelve — thirteen — fourteen — fifteen — sixteen — seventeen — eighteen — nineteen — twenty — twenty-one."

"Now," Little Joe shouted.

Chaney grunted. "We've got a twenty-one second lead, and their momentum will halve that by the time we reach the throw gap."

Lying on his belly, Little Joe saw Nat Greer lift his rifle and fire. The bullet flew harmlessly overhead.

"Cartwright, I'll try to brake us a little heading to the throw gap. You grab hold of the gap edge and let it pull you out of the boat. Get to your feet, grab the slat wedge and pull it over in the water. You'll have ten seconds, but not much more."

Little Joe could see the log was gaining. He lifted the carbine and fired, just to answer Greer's shot.

"Forget the damn rifle," Chaney yelled. "The throw gap's a hundred yards ahead."

Little Joe dropped the carbine in the bottom of the trough and got to his hands and knees as best he could, holding the end piece on the trough.

"Fifty yards," Chaney yelled.

Little Joe looked back over his shoulder in time to see Chaney spread his legs and dig his spiked boots into the wall of the flume. Chaney screamed, but the boat slowed some. Little Joe glanced quickly up the flume. The log was gaining. He could make out Nat Greer's sinister grin.

"Twenty-five yards." Chaney grunted from exertion.

Little Joe looked back over his shoulder, bringing his knees up under him.

"Ten yards."

Little Joe knew he had ten seconds at most. He pushed at the trough with his feet.

"Now," Chaney shouted.

Little Joe lunged from the boat, his hands snagging hard the far edge of the throw gap, his mind silently counting off the time.

One.

The boat slid from under Little Joe, the cold water stunning his senses for an instant.

Two.

He pulled his feet under him and tried to stand, but the water fought him.

Three.

The log was bearing down upon him.

Four.

Little Joe managed to plant both feet on the trough, but the left foot without the shoe slipped and he lost his balance.

Five.

He lunged for the slat wedge propped up on the opposite side of the flume and caught the hard wood frame.

Six.

He dragged himself up and tried to jerk the wedge free.

Seven.

It was stuck.

Eight.

With all his might, he tried to jerk it free.

Nine.

The wedge gave way, then fell into the flume.

Ten.

Little Joe pushed himself against the end of the slat wedge to keep it in place.

Eleven.

The log hit the wedge.

Twelve.

Nat Greer's grin changed to a grimace of horror. The massive log came within two feet of Little Joe, then veered off to the side, through the throw gap.

Greer and Tull screamed and flailed their arms, grasping for a hold in the air. The log flew in a graceful arc, then crashed to the ground fifty feet below, the thunder of its landing drowning out the final cries of Nat Greer and Ben Tull.

Little Joe released the wedge and twisted around just as the water swept him off his feet and into the flow. Thirty yards down the flume he saw the trough had slowed, but not stopped, despite Chaney's caulked boots and ingenuity.

"Are you okay, Cartwright?" shouted Chaney, who could not look back over his shoulder without losing his grip on the side of the flume.

"Wet is all," Little Joe called as he floated down to the trough, grabbed hold long enough for Chaney to release his feet, then collapsed into the belly of the makeshift boat.

They rode for a time in silence, then Little Joe cut loose a shout of victory. "Surely that's the last of them," Little Joe yelled.

Chaney nodded. "Roe Derus is a damn genius. I had my doubts about his idea, but I was wrong. I just hope he's okay and things are right at the camp."

"If they aren't now, they will be by the time I get word back on what's going on. And I owe it to you and Roe."

"We were only trying to do what's right."

"The two of you saved my life."

"Just wish we could've saved Livermore too. I figure he was honest until Greer forced him to do his dirty work."

Little Joe nodded. "Well, I think we'll need an honest man to run the camp once we get it straightened out. I'm going to recommend that you become the next bull of the woods."

"Man with a lame arm'll be more like a steer of the woods."

"You don't worry," Little Joe said. "We'll get that fixed up and everything'll be all right."

Chaney shook his head. "We're not home free yet," he warned.

"Why not?"

Chaney sighed. "The flume ends in a thirty-foot drop over water that's fifty feet deep."

"Damn," Little Joe said.

"That's not the half of it," Chaney answered. "Even with two good arms, I can't swim."

"Damn fine time to tell me," Little Joe chided.

"Hell, I didn't figure I'd live long enough to have to worry about it."

Both men laughed, then lay back in the trough and watched the sky pass overhead as they pondered how they would manage the plunge into Lake Tahoe.

CHAPTER 19

For several minutes Little Joe just leaned back and watched the sky and treetops pass overhead as the feed trough glided down the flume toward Lake Tahoe. Though uncomfortable for passengers, the vee-shaped trough made an acceptable boat, sliding easily down the flume's wooden channel and kicking up a fine spray of water at each descent. Occasionally the boat would nudge the side of the flume, jarring Little Joe back to his senses. Still tired from his abbreviated night's sleep, Little Joe realized that the rocking motion of the trough as it flowed toward Tahoe made him drowsier yet. It would be easy to fall asleep, as he and the wounded Chaney lay supine and head to head in the trough. As quiet as Chaney was, Little Joe thought he might have dozed off already. His breathing was coming now in heavy puffs.

Little Joe turned awkwardly over on to his stomach and propped his elbows on the side of the trough. "How far are we from the lake?"

Chaney was slow in answering. He tried to lift his head and look around, but he was too weak. "Ten miles, maybe less."

"How steep is the final descent?"

"Steep, but not as bad as the ones higher in the mountains." Chaney grimaced, then rubbed his bad shoulder. He grunted at the pain.

"Think we can stop the trough like we did at the throw gap?" Little Joe asked.

With effort, Chaney nodded. "Either that or I drown," he managed.

The attempt to speak seemed to drain Chaney's dwindling energy, so Little Joe didn't question him further. He glanced over the edge of the flume periodically, trying to glimpse Lake Tahoe. Water puddled in the bottom of the trough. Little Joe tried to keep the Winchester from getting immersed, but once, when he lifted his head to look over the flume, the carbine slid from his hand and into the pooling water. He cursed.

The way Little Joe figured things, they would stop the trough as they had at the throw gap, braking with their caulked boots against the side of the flume. Then they could climb over the trough's walls and shimmy down the flume's wooden frame to the ground. He guessed they would have half a day to find help or a good hiding place in case Greer's men came looking for them. Only problem was, between himself and Chaney, they had but three boots.

Finally, as the flume rounded the mountain, Little Joe caught a brief glimpse of Lake Tahoe, maybe three miles away. It was time to set their plan in motion.

"Chaney, you feel up to stopping the flume, or do you want to give me your boot and let me try it?"

The logger said nothing.

"Which'll it be?"

Still Chaney said nothing.

"Chaney, you okay?" Little Joe leaned over Chaney's head to look at him.

The logger was unconscious.

"Dammit," Little Joe cursed. What options did he have? He could abandon Chaney and save himself, but not in good conscience, not after the logger had stuck by him against Greer and his thugs. He could try to stop the trough, but what good would that do if Chaney were still unconscious? Or he could take the plunge into Lake Tahoe and hope that he could keep Chaney from drowning.

Little Joe shook his companion's shoulder. "Chaney, Chaney, can you hear me?"

The logger lay motionless, except for the rising of his chest as he breathed.

Little Joe reached for one of Chaney's hands and lifted it over his chest. When he released the logger's hand, it fell limply to his red flannel shirt. Little Joe shook him brusquely. "Chaney, Chaney?" he yelled. His rough handling drew but a low moan from the logger.

Time was running out. The lake was maybe two miles away. If he could wake Chaney, they might have a chance of stopping the trough and slipping over the edge of the flume. Little Joe couldn't count on that, especially since Chaney might not have the energy to stop the boat or climb down from the flume.

Little Joe shuddered at the thought of a plunge into Lake Tahoe's cold waters. What other choice did he have to save Chaney? Maybe it was just as well that Chaney was unconscious. It might make him easier to manage in the water. As big and heavy as the logger was, he might panic in the water, latch onto him and drag them both to their deaths in Tahoe's deep blue waters.

As Little Joe tried to brace himself in the trough to get a better view, he realized the heavy boot on his foot would be dead weight in the water. And if the single boot was a hazard to him, two water-logged boots could be fatal to Chaney. Little Joe rolled on his side, dropping the Winchester into the pool of water beneath him. He cursed as he unlaced his boot and dropped it atop the carbine. He had to get Chaney's boots off too.

Twisting around on his hands and knees, Little Joe tried to crawl over Chaney toward the logger's feet. He inched past Chaney's head, then his shoulders and chest, but the trough hit a sudden incline and Little Joe lost his grip, collapsing on Chaney.

The logger groaned at the impact, then again when Little Joe lunged for his shoes. Little Joe caught hold of the laces and worked furiously to untie them. He got one off, then the other, just as the boat took a dip.

Little Joe looked ahead and was terrified at what he saw. The trough had hit the final incline, which dropped all the way to Lake Tahoe. Beyond the wooden frame, Little Joe could see nothing but blue waters.

The trough was sliding faster and faster down the incline. Time was running out.

Little Joe tossed one boot over the edge of the flume, then the other. They would need those boots once they swam ashore. They would need the other boot too, and the carbine. He pushed himself back from Chaney's feet.

Quickly, Little Joe was behind Chaney, flailing at the bottom of the trough for the boot. He caught the laces and flung it over the edge, then scrambled to jerk the rifle out of the trough, but his knee wedged it against the bottom. When he raised his leg, he almost lost his balance and fell out of the boat.

The end of the flume was less than a hundred feet away.

Scooting farther back in the vessel, Little Joe managed to wrap his fingers around the gun barrel and wrest it free. He tossed the gun away and it tumbled out of sight.

The flume's end, just seconds away, stood thirty feet above water.

Little Joe glanced a final time at the vast blue waters below him, then fell prone in the trough, his teeth gritted, his eyes closed.

The trough cleared the end of the flume, and the sound of rushing water was left behind. The trough sailed beyond the flume and Little Joe felt the exhilaration of flight for a brief instant. Then the trough lost momentum and tipped forward, flinging him free.

For a moment he seemed to be climbing the clouds, and in the next instant his twirling body was falling, accelerating toward the depths of Lake Tahoe. Little Joe screamed from a mixture of fear and exhilaration. The fall seemed to take forever, but ended abruptly when he slammed into the water. The impact knocked the breath out of him, then the shock of the frigid waters made him gasp, sucking in a mouthful of water as he submerged. He thrashed his arms and kicked his feet against the water, and stretched his neck for the surface. His lungs burned for want of air. His body seemed to rise and rise and rise, yet never surface. Just when he felt he could no longer wait for air, he broke the surface, spitting water, coughing and gasping.

As spent as he was, he had to find Chaney quickly. He swam around frantically, lifting his head as far out of the water as he could. At first he saw nothing but water, then he circled back and glimpsed the flume and the shoreline a hundred and fifty feet away.

"Chaney," he yelled.

Only a slight echo answered.

Time was running out for Chaney.

Then he saw a patch of red flannel shirt not thirty feet away. He swam in that direction, only to find Chaney's body floating facedown in the water. He spun the unconscious form over and grabbed it from behind, hooking Chaney's chin in the crook of his elbow as he started inching him to shore. He jerked up on Chaney's chin, then slapped his chest to bring him to. As he swam on his back, Little Joe bumped his head against a floating piece of wood. He pushed it aside, then realized it was a plank from the feed trough that had broken apart in the fall. He wrapped his free arm over the plank and worked Chaney to it. Despite his exhaustion, Little Joe somehow managed to prop Chaney' head on the wide board and pull his body atop it.

Chaney lay motionless while Little Joe pounded on his chest once, twice, three times without success. In frustration, he knotted his fist and hit Chaney one final time. The logger coughed up water and mucus.

"No, no," he screamed, with panic in his voice. "The water!"

"It's okay, Chaney," Little Joe shouted. "You're floating on wood. We're not far from shore."

Little Joe moved to the end of the plank and aimed it toward shore. He paddled for land until his feet kicked bottom. Standing up, Little Joe shoved the plank the rest of the way to tree-lined shore, then helped Chaney to his feet. Together they staggered from the shoreline to a clearing bright with sunlight. The sun felt good on their wet bodies, and they collapsed to the ground.

Little Joe knew he had dozed off, but he had no idea how long he had slept. It must have been awhile, though, because the sun had dried his clothes. When he sat up, he felt cool but not chilled. Beside him, though, shivering so hard his teeth chattered, lay Chaney. Little Joe knew Chaney's problem was the festering bullet wound more than the plunge in the cold waters. He pushed himself to his feet, swaying, light-headed for a moment. When he caught his balance, he surveyed his surroundings. He was uncomfortable being so close to the trail, the trail that Greer's men could follow right to him. Glancing around the clearing, he spotted a clump of trees in a circle of rocks anchored near side-by-side boulders the size of draft horses.

Little Joe grabbed Chaney under the shoulders and helped him stand, then threw the logger's good arm around his shoulder. Together the two men, both barefoot, limped toward the hiding spot, the logger trembling with feverish chills. Even through Chaney's damp clothes, Little Joe could feel the heat of his fever. Little Joe knew he needed to build a fire, but he feared it might attract Greer's men. Chaney stumbled as they neared the rocks, but Little Joe somehow managed to keep him on his feet until they reached their hiding place.

Delirious by now, Chaney slumped to the ground, still shivering so much that his teeth chattered. Little Joe left him long enough to gather wood for a fire. Using dry grass, a shard of a stick, and a small stone, he started a fire using an Indian technique Hoss had taught him. He dragged Chaney close to the fire's warmth.

Little Joe slumped by the fire for a few minutes, trying to sort his thoughts. He was barefoot, exhausted, hungry, and most of all, scared, not so much for himself as for Chaney. Before anything else, though, Little Joe knew he must find the carbine and the boots he had thrown from the flume. His muscles screamed from exhaustion when he stood up, but he forced himself to retreat to the flume and begin his search. After a half hour he found the carbine. For another hour he searched without success for the boots. By the time he gave up, his feet were bruised, cut, and swollen, and he considered himself lucky to have found the Winchester, even though the stock was smashed and the ejection lever bent. At least he had a weapon.

On the way back toward Chaney and the smoky fire, Little Joe jumped a pair of cottontail rabbits. He killed them both with stones, preferring to save his bullets for Greer's men.

At camp he added wood to the fire, then skinned and cleaned the rabbits with a sharp stick before roasting them. He ate one rabbit and tore off bits of meat from the other to feed to Chaney. When Chaney begged for water, Little Joe went to the lake and returned with what water he could carry in his cupped hands. He made a dozen trips to quench Chaney's thirst.

As Little Joe let the water drip into Chaney's mouth, the logger grimaced, then screamed from the pain in his shoulder. Little Joe opened Chaney's shirt and pulled it back. He frowned at what he saw. The flesh was puckered and festering around the bullet hole. Chaney needed a doctor's care, but that was impossible for now. The wound, though, needed attention. Little Joe rose from Chaney's side and went to the carbine propped against one of the boulders screening the campfire from the trail. He worked the Winchester's bent lever, ejecting six bullets into his hand. He propped the carbine against the boulders and shook his head. Six bullets to fend off all threats. And he'd need to use one of the bullets to help Chaney.

Slipping five of the bullets in his pocket, Little Joe inserted the remaining one into the corner of his mouth, bit down on the lead slug and gradually loosened it from the hull. When the slug came free, he spit it aside and carried the hull over to Chaney. Kneeling beside the logger, Little Joe emptied the gunpowder over the wound, then tossed away the empty hull. He picked up a small twig and poked it into the fire until the end took to flame. Gritting his teeth, he touched the finger of fire to Chaney's shoulder. The powder flashed at the flame. Chaney screamed and lurched up, then sagged back down on the ground. Little Joe hoped his primitive treatment had killed the poisons that were swelling Chaney's shoulder.

Little Joe spent the rest of daylight adding wood to the fire and worrying whether it was best to leave Chaney and search for help or to stay with him. He couldn't abandon Chaney, not when the logger had stood beside him from the beginning of his stay at the camp. And yet, staying with Chaney might be sentencing the logger to death. But even if he walked away, Little Joe wondered how far he might get on bare feet. He pondered his dilemma into the night as he kept the fire going to warm Chaney.

Finally Little Joe trailed off into sleep, his shoulders propped against the boulder, the Winchester at his side. Gradually, as the fire died, the chill began to seep into his flesh, then into his bones. His sluggish mind was torn between the needs for warmth and for rest, but his body's overpowering need for sleep won out for a couple hours.

CHAPTER 20

Timberline Pass was miles behind them, both in distance and in thought, when they reached the flume of Cartwright Enterprises. Ben rode first beneath the spindly frame that sent water and logs plunging from the lumber camp to Lake Tahoe. He reined up on his yellow dun and let the gelding blow as Roy Coffee drew beside him. Twisting around in his saddle, Ben glanced at the three riderless mounts, stolen and ruined by abuse from the Wharton brothers. Behind the jaded horses and trailing packhorse rode Hoss and Sara Ann. Ben studied the girl and noted her sagging shoulders and her glazed eyes. She was exhausted. The euphoric surge of energy from her rescue had long since been depleted by the tedium and monotony of the return trip.

Ben settled gingerly back into the saddle. He was sore from the long ride and tired too, but his curiosity and worry about Little Joe kept him on edge. He stared up the trail toward the lumber camp and bit his lip. Little Joe was but three miles away. To come this far and not check on his son bothered him, but Ben could not impose on the others, especially Sara Ann, as weary as she was.

With a final glance up the trail, he pursed his lips and shook his reins, and the dun turned east toward Lake Tahoe.

"Wait, Ben." Roy Coffee cast him a knowing glance. "You want to check on your boy, don't you?"

"I can't deny that," Ben nodded as he reined up, "but we need to get Sara Ann back."

"She's young, Ben, and she'll have plenty of days to get over being tired, thanks to your and Hoss's help. A few extra hours is the least Sara Ann and I can do to repay you."

Ben turned the gelding around and studied the sheriff. As he considered Roy's suggestion, he slipped his fingers in to his vest pocket and they came to rest on a six-pointed piece of metal. He had forgotten about the badge Roy had taken from his own vest the night Sara Ann was abducted.

"I shouldn't delay the rest of you, Roy. Why don't you keep on going and I'll catch up with you after nightfall? This way, you won't lose any time."

Roy just grinned. "Ben, now that we've got Sara Ann back, I've got all the time in the world." Roy looked over his shoulder. "Looks to me like Sara Ann doesn't mind the extra time, as long as Hoss is around. From here on in the trail's easy on man and animal. We can't get much farther before nightfall anyway."

Finally, Ben nodded. "You've convinced me,

Roy, and I'm obliged. We could even stay the night, have us a hot meal at the camp. Only thing is, this is a hard crew up there. Nat Greer, the foreman, he's a mean one."

From behind Ben came Hoss's voice. "Did you say something about a hot meal tonight, Pa?"

Roy laughed. "Greer can't be any meaner than the Wharton brothers, and surely can't be as hungry as Hoss."

"You've a point," Ben answered, his fingers closing around the badge in his vest pocket. Slowly, he pulled the tin star out and held out his open hand to Roy. "Why don't you put this back on? You just don't look the same without the badge."

Roy took the badge from Ben and studied it. "The badge didn't mean anything over here in California, but even so I didn't feel right wearing it on this trip. Too many personal feelings involved. I didn't come up here in the name of the law."

"Maybe the law wasn't served, but justice was."

"I'm glad they're dead, but it doesn't bring my family back, and the lost years." Slowly, Roy hooked the badge back on his vest.

"You've still got Sara Ann."

"That I do, with your help," Roy replied, wiping a shine on the badge with his sleeve. "Now, let's go check on your boy and put your mind at ease."

"And get a hot meal," Hoss interjected from behind.

Ben led the caravan up the trail among the pines, moving ever deeper into the Sierras. The trail ran alongside the serpentine flume which stood on spindly wooden legs. Occasionally, when the train ran immediately beside the flume, Ben could hear the rush of water, but not once, oddly, did he hear the banging and splashing of logs in the flume. Perhaps there was a break somewhere down the line. He would ask Little Joe, he thought, when he reached the camp.

Eventually the trail rounded a bend and approached the final rise, where the mountainside leveled off into the plateau that cradled the logging camp. The light was still good when they topped the trail and saw the camp ahead. Ben smiled to see that the overturned sign had been reset and stood stolid and straight, like the Cartwright name. Maybe Little Joe had managed okay, he thought for a moment.

But if everything was okay, why were the loggers milling about and carrying axes and peavey sticks like weapons? Ben touched the flank of his dun with his boot and sent the gelding prancing forward. There had been trouble. His gaze swept the camp, and, noticing a plot of earth beyond the Cartwright Enterprises signpost, he reined his horse abruptly. His breath caught at the sight of two recent graves in line with an older one. The nearest grave was mounded with dirt so freshly dug that it had to have been spaded earlier in the day. The second grave looked only a couple of days older.

Ben's mind raced like his heart. Could it be Little Joe?

He kicked the flank of the gelding with his heel and the horse raced toward the camp, its pounding hooves sounding an assembly call as the loggers strode toward him. When Ben reined up, a hundred grim-faced loggers stood in a half circle facing him.

"Where's Little Joe? Is he okay?" Ben shouted.

Several loggers shrugged. "We don't know," one responded, as a couple broke away from the crowd and darted to the office.

"Maybe swimming in Lake Tahoe," answered another. His face was too grim for his response to be a joke.

Ben swallowed hard, then jerked his thumb over his shoulder and toward the graves. "Who's buried there?"

"C. C. Livermore's in one and Ted Karnes in the other," replied a logger.

"Livermore, the bookkeeper?" Ben spoke with disbelief.

"Murdered," responded another logger. "Karnes died trying to stop your son's escape."

Ben's mind was awhirl. "Escape? What?"

A logger started to speak, but another

nudged him in the side and pointed at the camp office.

Ben looked toward the building and saw a strapping man he recognized as Roe Derus moving gingerly toward him. His head wrapped in a bandage, Derus advanced slowly and nodded feebly at Ben. "Mr. Cartwright," he said, "we're glad to see you."

Just then Roy Coffee rode up and reined his gelding beside Ben's dun. "What's the matter, Ben?"

Several loggers pointed to the badge on Coffee's chest. "The law," one of them murmured.

"Where's Nat Greer?" Ben demanded.

"We're not sure," Derus answered.

"Then who's in charge here?"

A dozen loggers spoke at once. "Roe Derus."

"I guess I am," Derus said.

"Then I want an explanation," Ben demanded. He heard a noise behind him and saw Hoss and Sara Ann ride up.

"What's the matter, Pa? Is Little Joe okay?"

"There's been trouble, Mr. Cartwright," Derus said. "Little Joe found out Nat Greer was swindling Cartwright Enterprises. Greer was trying to kill him. One of Greer's men died trying to stop your son. I got banged up helping Little Joe escape down the flume, but Greer and one of his henchmen, Ben Tull, rode down after them. We don't know what happened to any of them. Last we saw, they were disappearing down the flume."

Hoss looked over his shoulder at the flume. He gulped. "Little Joe escaped down that contraption?"

Sara Ann shook her head in disbelief.

Ben leaned forward and crossed his arms over the saddle horn. "Go on, Roe, anything else?"

The bull whacker nodded. "The camp's been in turmoil the last few days. There've been a lot of bad apples working for Greer, but most of them got scared when Karnes died, and they left camp. Those that didn't leave before noon, left this afternoon. They were in on the swindle, getting two dollars a day for their work."

"A dollar fifty was what Cartwright Enterprises was supposed to pay," Ben shot back.

"Except for those Greer favored, the men got only a dollar a day. That goes for all of us here before you now."

Ben felt his jaw clench in anger. He twisted in his saddle to face Roy Coffee. "If any of you want to stay the night here, that's fine, but I intend to search for Little Joe."

"We're riding with you," Roy answered as Hoss and Sara Ann nodded their agreement.

Pursing his lips, Ben turned back to Roe. "I want you to run this camp until you get other instructions. I'll find my son."

Derus looked around. "You hear that, men?"

The loggers shouted their approval.

Derus took another step toward Ben's dun. "Jack Chaney was with your son, Mr. Cartwright. He's taken a bullet to the shoulder. If they made it to Tahoe, Chaney may be in bad shape now. He took the bullet early this morning. We'd've gone after them, but some of Greer's men drove off all the horses."

Ben nodded, then turned to Roy. "We ready to go?"

"Wait," Derus called. "You'll need something to eat in the saddle." He ordered a pair of loggers to run to one of the kitchens and bring back food. Derus sent another man to the camp office. "A couple of you fellows cut a half dozen or so limbs, wrap them with rags and fetch a couple cans of coal oil for torches. Darkness'll be fast upon you."

From the camp office came the sound of a slamming door as a logger came running back, holding a burlap bundle. He shoved the package to Derus, who offered it to Ben. "Little Joe can explain it, but these are records Greer tried to burn after your son figured out the swindle."

Ben took the burlap bundle and lifted a corner of the coarse cloth, studying the blackened ledger. Then he twisted around to undo his saddlebag and slip it inside.

"It's pretty fragile, but it'll prove Greer's mischief. He forced the bookkeeper to keep double books. Your son can explain, if he's still

. . ." Derus grimaced and didn't finish the sentence.

"I understand," Ben said.

Discomforted by his verbal slip, Derus glanced impatiently at the bunkhouses and then the toolshed as he awaited his men's return. "Whatever happens, Mr. Cartwright, I just want you to know the fellows respect your son. He's as decent as the Cartwright name, and not afraid of work or men like Greer."

Sighing, Ben nodded.

Two loggers emerged from the toolshed, carrying a half-dozen unlit torches and some cans of coal oil. They jogged over to the pack-horse and tied the torches and cans atop the animal. No sooner did they finish than two more men ran up with burlap sacks filled with food. The men gave one sack to Roy Coffee and tossed another to Hoss.

Ben circled his horse around toward Lake Tahoe.

"Good luck to you and to Little Joe," Derus said.

"Good luck," several of the loggers echoed.

Were it not for worrying about Little Joe's safety, Ben would have relished this moment for his youngest son. Little Joe had met responsibility and won the respect of honest men. But Little Joe had also faced danger in winning that respect, and Ben wondered if the price of responsibility had cost his son his life.

Ben gritted his teeth, then started down the trail toward Lake Tahoe.

The sky was growing dark, like Ben's thoughts.

This would be a long, tiring night.

At the knock on the door, Adam looked up from the table where he was reviewing reports on the ore tonnage removed from the Bristlecone during the last five days. "Yes," he called.

"A letter for you," replied one of the clerks from downstairs.

Adam jumped up from the table and strode to the door. This had to be the letter from Little Joe, the one that could help him figure out just what was going on at the Cartwright timber lease. The loggers that Cartwright Enterprises had hired to work the lease were either lazy or swindlers, by Adam's calculation.

He opened the door and snatched the extended letter from the clerk's fingers.

"We're closing up for the evening downstairs, Mr. Cartwright, unless there's something else you need us to do."

Adam shook his head. "I didn't realize it was that late."

The clerk nodded. "It's almost seven."

Adam was to meet Lucia Sinclair at the International Hotel for dinner. "You're right, it's closing time, and I'll be late to dinner if I don't leave now."

The clerk turned away and started for the stairs.

"Just a moment," Adam said, looking at the envelope. The flap had been unsealed by someone and tucked back inside the envelope. "Did someone downstairs open this?"

"No, sir," the clerk said emphatically. "That's how it was delivered to us."

"Thanks." Adam grabbed his hat and left behind the clerk. "Would you mind locking up so I won't be late?"

"Not at all," the clerk said, moving aside as Adam ran down the stairs.

At the bottom of the steps, Adam absently nodded to the mine employees calling it a day, then shot through the door. Outside, he tugged Little Joe's letter from the envelope and perused it quickly. "Damnation," he said in exasperation. Maybe it had been a mistake to send Little Joe up to the lumber camp. Adam had told Ben the specific information he needed, and Ben had instructed Little Joe. And now Little Joe had written gibberish about how the foreman was an odd duck. "Damnation," he repeated.

Maybe Little Joe couldn't handle responsibility. Maybe he would always be a kid in outlook. Maybe he didn't deserve to share in the Cartwright legacy that Ben Cartwright had bestowed upon him, a legacy of integrity and responsibility.

Adam wadded up the letter and shoved it

in his pocket. He strode briskly to the International Hotel, hoping to walk off his anger before he met Lucia Sinclair. He wasn't succeeding. Now he would have to make a trip into the mountains himself to check out the timber operation. That would take him away from the mine, where he needed to stay in day-to-day contact with the operations.

Running up the steps into the lobby, he saw Lucia sitting in one of the plush chairs, where she drew the admiring glances of a pair of portly mine speculators.

The smile on her face melted away as she arose elegantly from the chair. "A bad day?"

Adam sighed. "You send someone to do a job and he lets you down."

Lucia took Adam's hand and started toward the dining room. "I hope that person wasn't me."

"No, no," Adam said, shaking his head. "Little Joe!"

Lucia stopped and dug into her handbag. "This came for me today," she said, holding it before Adam's black eyes, "from Little Joe."

Adam snapped it from her hand.

"I don't understand," Lucia said, "just that he addressed it to me with a note atop the letter to deliver it to you."

Adam looked at the broken wax seal on the back. "Was it sealed when you got it?"

"Yes," Lucia said indignantly, "and it was addressed to me, so I opened it."

"No, no," said Adam, "I'm not suggesting you shouldn't have." There was only one explanation. Little Joe feared someone — likely Nat Greer — would read any correspondence he had with him. Since his letter had been unsealed, Adam realized Little Joe had been right. The letter to Lucia carried the real message. "Good going, Little Joe," Adam said as he scanned the letter. Finishing the missive, Adam bit his lips as he made mental calculations from the numbers Little Joe had provided.

"Bad news?" Lucia asked with concern.

"It's complicated," Adam said, taking Lucia's hand and dragging her toward the dining room, barely pausing for the headwaiter to seat them.

Adam slid into his seat without helping Lucia into hers, as he customarily did. Grabbing a pencil from his pocket, Adam turned the letter over and on the back began to work out calculations. A couple of times he flipped the letter over to check a number from Little Joe.

After a few minutes of permutations, he looked up at Lucia. "My suspicions were right," he announced triumphantly.

"Suspicions about what?"

"The timber operation. We're being swindled."

Lucia cocked her head, aghast. "You seem perversely happy about being swindled."

"Not about that, about Little Joe."

Lucia shrugged. "Now I'm really confused."

"We sent him up there to do a man's job, and he succeeded. Only thing is, he might not realize the trouble he's in, especially if Nat Greer realizes Little Joe's sent me such incriminating figures. Come morning, once I get my paperwork and payroll finished at the mine, I'll start toward the logging camp. It'll give me great pleasure to fire Nat Greer."

Leaving the logging camp, the search party had advanced at a canter until the creeping darkness of night forced them to slow down. From the burlap sacks, they had eaten cold potatoes, fresh bread, and cookies. Before the moon had risen to cast a pale glow over the trail, Ben soaked one of the torches in coal oil and lit it. They saw a ghostly shape that awaited them down the trail. Ben was the first to recognize the figure as a horse, and the horse as Little Joe's pinto.

Ben passed the torch to the sheriff, then caught the pinto and tied it to the string of saddle mounts.

"What do you reckon, Roy?"

The sheriff shook his head. "Since there aren't many others, that pinto may be the most recognizable horse in the Sierras. Whoever took him probably didn't want to be caught on a stolen horse, especially if Little Joe was killed." At his words, Coffee gritted his teeth. "Sorry, Ben, I didn't mean it to come out that way."

"We're all tired, Roy, we're all tired."

They rode on, Sara Ann Coffee riding asleep in her saddle, Hoss close behind her.

The moon was a dim light overhead when Roy Coffee spotted the broken bodies beneath a giant sixteen-foot log. In the glow of the torchlight, the skin of the two men was ghastly white, their faces frozen in the final contortions of terror as they had fallen to their death from the flume fifty feet above.

"Hoss," Ben called softly, "swing Sara Ann wide of this log so she won't have to see this."

"Sure, Pa," answered Hoss, who directed her mount away from the bodies.

Ben and Roy nudged their horses toward the bodies, but the animals turned skittish at the smell of death. Roy leaned over in his saddle and held the torch out toward the bodies. "Recognize either of them?"

"The near one's Nat Greer, so the other must be Ben Tull."

The sheriff nodded. "You don't think we might have missed Little Joe somewhere around here? Whatever threw this log out of the flume surely would've done the same thing to Little Joe."

Ben shrugged. "Maybe you're right, Roy," he said with dejection. "Let's look around." He lit a second torch as Hoss led Sara Ann farther down the trail, and searched in ever widening circles around the death log while Roy examined the bodies.

"They're pinned beneath the log, Ben. We can't bury them, so we might just as well ride on once we're certain Little Joe wasn't thrown out of the flume as well."

Shortly, Ben was headed toward Lake Tahoe with the others behind him. They rode until they lost track of time, approaching the lake well after midnight. Along the way, they had seen no sign of Little Joe except for his stolen pinto. They had extinguished all their torches save the one Ben carried, and it was burning as low as Ben's energy. His shoulder throbbed from holding the torch, his body ached from the extended trip in the saddle, and his mind reeled with doubts. Had they missed Little Joe somewhere along the trail? Was Little Joe still alive? And what about Jack Chaney, the logger with the gunshot wound?

Ben glanced over his shoulder to see Sara Ann sagging in the saddle, Hoss riding close behind her. Ben had held out hope they might find Little Joe at the end of the flume, but he was disappointed to uncover no signs of him along the shore.

"We should call it quits until dawn," Ben announced. "I'm not sure we'd recognize signs of Little Joe even if we saw them."

Roy nodded. "We're all mighty tired."

Ben pointed to two boulders down the trail. "We can camp there."

CHAPTER 21

Something stirred and awoke Little Joe with a start. Danger! He listened. He heard voices and horses. He straightened quickly, grabbing the Winchester and peeking between the boulders. Down the trail he saw riders. The lead rider carried a torch that burned low.

"Dammit." Little Joe gritted his teeth, then nudged Chaney with his foot. "Riders approaching."

Chaney groaned.

Little Joe cursed. Chaney's noise might reveal their hiding place. Or the dying fire might give it away. Forgetting he was barefoot, Little Joe scrambled to the fire and attempted to kick dirt over the embers, but stubbed his toe instead. He growled, then slid between the rocks and lowered the Winchester, drawing a bead on the lead rider. His muddled mind failed to recognize the lead horseman's familiar set in the saddle.

The rider neared with others close behind him.

Little Joe's finger tightened around the trigger.

The rider was within range.

Little Joe aimed for his heart.

There was something familiar about the man, but all Little Joe could remember was the riders with torches from the renegade lumber camp chasing him yesterday morning.

Little Joe squeezed the trigger.

Then his mind made the connection. Too late! Had he killed his father?

The rifle clicked.

Little Joe sighed thankfully, remembering that he had forgotten to reload the rifle when he had counted the remaining cartridges. A chill coursed down his spine as he realized how close he had come to hurting his father. "Pa," he screamed, his mind suddenly sharp and focused, "is that you?"

"Little Joe," Ben called back, "you okay?"

Both father and son shouted their delight.

The sun was just setting over the mountain peaks across Lake Tahoe when the Ben Cartwright led the others to the front of the massive ranch house that was the biggest dwelling in western Nevada. Ben had sent the first Ponderosa hand he had seen after getting back on the ranch to Carson City to have the doctor waiting at the house. A buggy parked in front of the house indicated the hand had done his job.

As Ben was dismounting, the wide front door of the house opened and Adam came out with the doctor on his tail.

"Who's hurt?" Adam asked.

"Our new logging foreman," Ben said, pointing at Jack Chaney.

"What happened to Nat Greer?" Adam asked.

"He's dead," Ben said.

"Sounds like we've got a lot to talk about, Pa," Adam answered as he ran to help Jack Chaney off the travois that had transported him from the lake.

Adam and the doctor assisted Chaney toward the house. When he passed Little Joe, Adam nodded at his youngest brother. "Good job, Little Joe, good job."

Little Joe perked up in the saddle. "Did you hear that, Pa?"

Ben climbed wearily out of the saddle. "Yes, Joseph, I heard him."

"And Little Joe," Adam called back over his shoulder, "what happened to your boots?"

Little Joe sighed. "It's a long story."

"A story," said Ben, "that will wait for dinner."

No sooner had Ben finished speaking than the kitchen door flew open with a clatter. Hop Sing ran out. "Welcome back, Mr. Ben. Many people stay for dinner?"

"Yes, Hop Sing, I've invited everyone to stay."

"One hour, please, then supper ready."

Ben shook his head.

Hop Sing's mouth flew open and his mouth went wide. "One hour, must have."

"No, Hop Sing," Ben said, "take two hours. I believe everyone'll want to clean up before we eat."

Hop Sing's dark frown turned into a bright smile. "Very good, Mr. Ben. Two hours is time for feast."

Hoss dismounted and walked over to Sara Ann, who sat wearily in her saddle. "You don't look much like dancing, Sara Ann."

"I'm so tired," she answered, "it may take me a month to recover enough even to think about a dance."

Hoss lifted his hands and she slid off the saddle into his arms.

"I'm not too tired for that," she smiled, and Hoss blushed as he escorted her into the house.

"Well, Ben," Roy said, easing out of the saddle, "I guess we did okay for a couple old fellows, though I feel my age in every joint in my body."

Ben laughed. "I don't remember being this tired since my sailing days."

"That's our problem, we don't remember anymore."

Both laughed.

Roy grabbed the reins of his horse and turned toward the barn. "Ben, I'll help you unsaddle all these horses."

"Roy," Ben replied, "I may not remember much, but I do recall having some hired help that can tend the horses for us tonight. Tie your animal and come on in." Ben slapped Roy on the shoulder and they marched inside.

"Amen," Ben said, and every head lifted around the table. Everybody was scrubbed clean and in fresh clothes, Roy Coffee having borrowed shirt and pants from Ben. Sara Ann wore a simple dress that had once belonged to Little Joe's mother.

"We've got a lot to be thankful for," Roy acknowledged. "Sara Ann's safe and Little Joe made it back okay."

"And," Little Joe piped in, "the doctor says Jack Chaney's gonna be okay."

Everyone around the table nodded at their good luck.

"And," Little Joe bragged, "I've got news for Adam on the logging operation."

"Not much that I don't already know, Little Joe," Adam answered, a cocky grin on his face.

"Joseph, Adam," Ben said, "this is no time to discuss business."

"Go ahead, Ben, let 'em talk a little business," Roy said. "I think the rest of us are too tired to speak. Ain't that right, Hoss?"

Hoss grimaced. "No, sir, I ain't that tired."

"Well, Hoss," his father said, "what is it you want to say?"

Hoss looked sheepishly around the table. "Pass the roast beef and the potatoes and the gravy."

Everyone laughed as the food started around the table.

"Now, little brother," Adam challenged, "what is it you're going to tell me I don't already know?"

Little Joe grinned like a cat approaching an open canary cage. "Bet you don't know what was happening at the logging camp."

Adam nodded. "We were being swindled."

Little Joe's grin receded a bit. "I bet you don't know how."

"Some of the men were cutting trees that didn't go into our flume," Adam answered confidently.

The grin narrowed a fraction more. "How did they cover it up?"

"Likely kept two sets of books."

Little Joe glanced at his father, his grin fading even more.

Ben shrugged. "I didn't show him the burnt ledger."

Little Joe turned back to Adam. "I bet you don't know how much we were losing. You think you're so smart."

"First, little brother, let me admit that I am impressed by you figuring all of this out. I thought this might be beyond your abilities, but I was wrong and I publicly acknowledge it. Now, as to your challenge. We were losing one log in every three."

Little Joe's smile dropped into a frown and he tapped the table in frustration with his fingers. "How'd you know all of this?"

"Your letter, Little Joe," Adam answered.

Little Joe looked exasperated. "I didn't put all that in my letter."

"That's right, Little Joe, but you gave me the figures on the average number of trees a day a team of loggers could cut. I knew how many we had on the payroll, and it was very easy to figure what they should be cutting. Greer was too tough a man to let his crews go lazy on him, so it became clear he wasn't giving us all our lumber and may even have been cutting timber outside the lease, which he could blame on us. I've already notified the federal timber office of the problem and they'll send inspectors out next week."

Little Joe shook his head in disbelief. "You got all of that just from the figures I sent you?"

"More or less, little brother," Adam answered. "You should know by now that you can't outsmart your older brother."

Little Joe clenched his jaw. Why was Adam always right? He just had to outsmart him at something, take him down a notch or two in front of the others. Through the remainder of dinner, he tried to come up with some way to outdo Adam.

After Hop Sing cleared the table, Ben called for a bottle of wine and glasses all around. "A toast to good friends and to our good luck the last few days."

Everyone stood and clinked glasses, then

346

downed the fine red wine.

Little Joe had an idea. "Pa," he said, "refill my glass." Turning to Hoss, he asked him to get his hat.

Hoss shook his head. "Is this what I think it is?"

Little Joe nodded.

"Dad-blame-it, Little Joe, this is what started all our troubles anyway," Hoss said as he retreated for his hat.

Ben passed the full glass of wine back to Little Joe, who turned confidently to Adam. "Oldest brother," he said, taking the glass and putting it in the middle of the table, then motioning for Hoss to cover it with his high-crowned hat, "I'll bet you ten dollars I can empty the wine in that glass without lifting the hat."

Adam shook his head in doubt. "Okay, Little Joe, you've got a bet."

Little Joe cast a confident grin at his brother and waved his hands. "Step back everyone." He moved a chair, then crawled under the table and began to make slurping noises.

As he did, Adam simply bent over the table, lifted the hat, and drank the wine, drawing giggles from everyone. Quickly, he dropped the hat back over the glass.

Little Joe stood up and wiped his lips on his sleeve. "Hmmmmm, good wine," he said, grinning confidently, especially when Adam reached for the hat.

Adam's hand stopped just shy of the brim. "Let me think about this for a minute," he said, withdrawing his hand. "You said you could empty this glass without your lifting the hat." Adam nodded knowingly at his youngest brother. "I guess that means you win if I lift the hat."

Little Joe's smile collapsed. "Well, heck," Little Joe admitted, "I should've known I couldn't fool you." He bent over the table, grabbed Hoss's hat and lifted it carefully to keep from spilling the wineglass. His hand froze when the hat cleared the top of the glass.

As he stared at the empty wineglass, his expression changed from disgust to disbelief. Then he glanced around the table and started to dance. "I did it, I did it," he called out. "I don't know how, but I did it."

Adam dug in his pocket and tossed him a ten-dollar gold piece. "It was worth ten dollars just to see the expression on your face, Little Joe."

Everyone laughed.